W9-AMT-846

"I love you so much," he murmured

Just for a second, Amanda's passion-clouded gaze cleared. Licking her swollen lips, she whispered distractedly, "It's been so long since you said you love me."

"You haven't exactly been bubbling over with heartfelt declarations yourself," Mark returned.

Amanda cried, "But you *know*—"

He shook his head. A hard flush painted his cheekbones as he said fiercely, "Don't talk, Amanda. Nowadays we always seem to get into trouble when we talk. So just feel. Feel my love. Let me feel yours...." The words were muffled between her breasts as he slid his arms around her and rolled onto his back, pulling her on top of him. When they met and fused, Amanda threw back her head, shaking with recognition, amazed that the sensations pulsing through her could feel so familiar yet always tantalizingly new....

ABOUT THE AUTHOR

After writing the very successful Welles Family
Trilogy, Lynda Ward took a well-deserved rest,
but with *Precious Things*, her latest
Superromance, Lynda once again stretches
the boundaries of category romance and
tackles important issues facing women today.
Lynda makes her home in Northern California.

Books by Lynda Ward

HARLEQUIN SUPERROMANCE

HARLEQUIN TEMPTATION

Precious Things

LYNDA WARD

Harlequin Books

TORONTO • NEW YORK • LONDON
AMSTERDAM • PARIS • SYDNEY • HAMBURG
STOCKHOLM • ATHENS • TOKYO • MILAN

Published May 1990

ISBN 0-373-70402-X

Printed in U.S.A.

For Anne Stuart Ohlrogge,
who cheers and encourages and inspires me—
and who has great taste in actors.

CHAPTER ONE

THE CRUISE SHIP PITCHED gently as its prow sliced across the black waves of the Caribbean, and a moonbeam streamed through the porthole, flowing over the naked bodies of the couple on the bed, transmuting their entwined limbs to silver and pearl. A moment later the ship righted itself, and the shaft of light angled away.

In the shadowy stateroom, Amanda Wexler sighed with contentment. Cradled in the crook of her husband's arm, she nuzzled his chest and listened to the slow, satisfied throb of his heart beneath her ear. She inhaled the mingled fragrance of their loving, as heady as brandy. Her lips tasted the copper-salt tang of his damp skin. "I've never been so happy in my life," she whispered.

Mark's fingers splayed across the small of Amanda's back to urge her closer, while with his free hand he stroked her hair. He brushed back the short, moist tendrils that curled at her temples. "I'm glad you're happy," he said. A rumble of laughter came from deep in his throat.

Amanda cushioned her small breasts against him. With a drowsy giggle she declared, "It should be a crime to feel this good."

"In some states it probably is," Mark drawled.

"But we're not in the United States right now," she reminded him solemnly. "This ship is sailing in international waters."

"That's a relief. Otherwise, can you imagine what our Wanted poster would look like?"

"Pictures like that are illegal...." When Amanda felt Mark's palm slide down along the sleek curve of her hip, she quivered with pleasure. Her hands commenced their own exploration of her husband's body, stroking his smooth chest, shaping the bones of the long frame that was lean almost to the point of gauntness. With the tip of a fingernail she inscribed circles around his navel while she resumed their bantering conversation. "Even if we're safe from the law out here on the high seas, what are we going to do in a couple of days when the cruise is over and we have to fly home to Oregon? Do we give up this forbidden ecstasy we've known together, or do we embark on a life of crime?"

The shoulder beneath her cheek lifted in an elaborate shrug. "I suppose we could wait until the next time we take a trip out of the country. You know, like for our twentieth anniversary...."

Amanda gasped and bolted upright. "You mean you expect me to wait another ten years?" With a squeal of mock outrage she batted at Mark with her fists. He pulled her down again and swatted her bottom. For the next several minutes they wrestled playfully, until at last they collapsed, winded and laughing, in a tangle of sheets.

Mark gazed at the invisible ceiling and groaned. "God, you wear me out. There's nothing I want to do more right now than make love to you again, but I know damn well it's going to be a while before I can rise to the occasion. I must be getting old."

Panting, Amanda reminded him, "We're both getting old—or, at least, middle-aged—although I'm not sure what you have to gripe about. I'm certainly not complaining."

"My performance has been that good, has it?"

"Considering how many times you've had your wicked way with me since we set sail from Puerto Rico, I think your performance has been downright impressive!" Amanda returned. "I don't remember you having so much energy on our honeymoon, when you were a mere lad of thirty-five."

Mark rubbed his knuckles against his chest as if polishing a medal. "Must be all the practice in the ten years since then. By now it's probably made me about perfect."

Amanda exhaled languorously. "I should hope so. If you get any more perfect, you're liable to kill me."

"Poor darling," Mark crooned, drawing her into his arms again. "I guess that's a chance we'll just have to take."

The teasing faded. They kissed, sipping and savoring, their embrace as comfortably familiar and nourishing as the taste of fresh bread. Then Mark said, "You know, I lied a minute ago."

"What?"

"I told you there was nothing I wanted more right now than to make love to you again. Well, I've just thought of something else I do want first."

"You mean . . . food?" Amanda guessed.

"Don't tell me your stomach is growling, too?"

"Not very romantic, is it? But we did skip dinner—"

"And go straight to the dessert," Mark finished for her. "I guess that proves our marriage isn't the grand passion we think it is. Otherwise, we ought to be able to live on love.''

''Maybe the very fact that we are so passionate is why we've worked up such an appetite,'' Amanda countered. Her hands slid lower, shaping and fondling. ''I think I have some mints in my handbag. Would they be enough to restore your flagging energy?''

''I doubt it.''

''Damn!'' Amanda declared with exaggerated frustration. ''In that case, I guess we don't have any choice except to get dressed and look for something to eat. The dining room will have closed hours ago, but we should be able to find some kind of snack in one of the lounges. I believe that bar near the pool is open all night.''

''I'm not surprised,'' Mark said. ''Who could sleep after listening to the piano player? He'd give anyone nightmares.''

Amanda giggled. ''Maybe if we tip him enough, he'll stay quiet until we've finished.'' She sat up, flipping the switch on the small lamp beside the bed, and their cabin was filled with light and color. Her dark brown eyes blinked against the brightness as she raised her arms over her head and stretched luxuriously. ''I need a quick shower before I pull on my clothes. Do you want to take one first?''

''Why don't we take one together?'' Mark suggested.

Amanda retorted, ''I thought you were hungry.'' She gazed down at him, studying his long face with its wide cheekbones and narrow jaw, high forehead and pointed chin. She was always amazed at how gawky a recital of Mark's individual features made him sound, when, taken together, the total effect was strong and strikingly attractive. She brushed aside the sandy-blond hair that had fallen into his light blue eyes and trailed her fingertip across the slight dip at the bridge of his long, narrow nose, the result of a boyhood fracture. "If we share a shower," she murmured, "we will never get out of this cabin, much less find anything to eat...."

All at once she swooped down and bussed his cheek noisily. Then she hopped out of bed and dashed to the bathroom, laughing. "Last one to the observation deck has to pick a song!"

AN HOUR LATER they left the near-empty lounge, where the bored pianist was playing requests—Mark had requested anything but "Feelings"—and they strolled away from the lights and the desultory music. They encountered only occasional passengers and uniformed crew members as they made their way toward the bow of the ship, where they leaned against the polished rail. The cool, damp air was like liquid silk on their faces. Amanda gazed with wonder at the star-spangled sky and the huge opalescent globe that burnished the endless water beneath. She declared, "What a glorious moon. I've never seen one like it."

"Yes, you have," Mark said. "It's the same moon that shines on Portland."

Amanda's lips twisted. "Except that in Portland the moon never shines in January. There's too much fog and drizzle."

"Well, my dear, that's why we're here right now and not in Oregon."

She nodded, inhaling the briny air. In the silence of the sleeping ship she could hear the low, almost musical hiss of the great hull moving through the water. Amanda stared toward the invisible horizon, her eyes barely able to discern a red beacon atop some distant island. She wondered if it was one they had passed before in their circuit of the Caribbean. There had been so many islands, exotic and beckoning, and the ship's itinerary had permitted no more than a tantalizing glimpse of most of them.

"I'm going to be sorry to go home," Amanda said, meaning it. "The past two weeks have been wonderful. I had no idea just how tired I really was—or how restful it could be to live like a Sybarite." Their stateroom had been comfortable, the service first-class, the food so rich it was downright decadent. Her one complaint was they they had never docked anywhere long enough. They'd cruised from Puerto Rico to Martinique, Barbados and Trinidad, and apart from the shopping districts in the immediate vicinity of the harbors, they'd seen very little of any of the islands. "If I have any gripe at all, I suppose it's that I wish there had been time to do a little more exploring."

"That's the problem with trying to cover so much territory in one trip," Mark pointed out. "Maybe we should plan to come back again and spend our entire vacation in one place."

"How about next winter? We could go back to Martinique and—" Amanda broke off, laughing at herself. "Lord, will you listen to me? Here I am already making plans for next year, and last fall when you first suggested this cruise, I wasn't all that crazy about the idea."

Mark frowned. "You never said anything."

"What was there to say? You obviously wanted to make the trip, and I knew you were right about us both needing to get as far away from the store as possible. It was just the idea of a sea voyage that I had trouble with."

Mark's tone reflected his expression. "I wish you'd spoken up. Even though I've always wanted to go on a Caribbean cruise, I don't like the idea that I coerced you into coming."

Amanda sighed, sorry she'd brought up the subject. She snuggled against him, her head on his shoulder, her hand resting familiarly on his hip. "You know perfectly well that I can't be coerced into doing anything I don't want to. If I'd had an alternate suggestion or some concrete reason not to take this trip, I'd have told you."

As a matter of fact, Amanda thought ruefully, she couldn't even remember why she had originally been reluctant. She supposed she must have been so keyed up from their annual buying junket to New York that the idea of still more travel had not sounded very appealing, or perhaps the prospect of spending two weeks confined to a ship could have made her feel claustrophobic. She ought to have guessed Mark would find perfectly delightful ways to relax her.... Striving to reassure him, she said teasingly, "If you want to know the honest-to-God truth, I guess the idea of going on a cruise made me feel old. I've always regarded sea voyages as something children send their parents on for golden wedding anniversaries."

Mark's tension eased. "Oh, well, you know how impatient I can be at times," he began. "I didn't see much point in waiting another forty—"

His comment was interrupted when suddenly a trio of youngsters, two preteen girls and a smaller boy in the lead, erupted from around a corner, whooping and skipping. The boy, who was glancing back over his shoulder as he ran, almost crashed into Amanda. She gasped and clutched at the rail, and quickly Mark wrapped his arms around her to steady her. The children raced on just as a flustered-looking woman appeared, trudging in their wake.

"Hey, you turkeys, watch where you're going!" she called after the three figures rapidly outdistancing her; then she grimaced apologetically at Mark and Amanda. "I'm sorry! Those crazy kids of mine should have been in bed hours ago, but I can't get them to settle down. They've been so hyper the last few days—"

"That's okay," Amanda said with a soothing smile. "They probably just need a chance to work off some of that excess energy. It must be hard for children that age to be cooped up on a boat for days on end."

"Not as hard as it is on me," the woman said, gasping and shaking her head in exasperation. "I *told* my husband we should have left them with their grandparents, but no, he insisted we let them share this 'once-in-a-lifetime adventure.' Now guess who's getting no sleep trying to keep up with the little hellions...." She waved tiredly and plodded on.

After the family disappeared from view, quiet returned to the deck. Mark did not release Amanda. He was enjoying her closeness, the warmth of her body in the almost-chilly air, the distracting softness of breast and thigh pressed into his side. He was also enjoying the silence. As the two of them stared out at the ocean, Mark realized he was grateful for the interruption that had prevented him from finishing his earlier remark. He did not want to talk about golden anniversaries or children when those topics would only remind Amanda that, even though it was feasible their marriage might survive five decades, there was unlikely to be anyone to plan a celebration for them.

He had seen the wistful yearning in his wife's face when she spoke to the young mother, a hint of envy that had not been in any way diminished by the children's rambunctious behavior or the woman's obvious fatigue. He suppressed a twinge of guilt. As much as he loved Amanda, as compatible as the two of them had always been, Mark knew that there was one issue in their outwardly perfect union on which they had always differed. She wanted a family, while he... It wasn't that he didn't want children, Mark reminded himself bracingly. A few months after their wedding, when Amanda had asked if he'd mind her abandoning her birth control pills, he had agreed willingly enough. Still, as the years had passed and she never conceived, Mark would have been less than honest with himself if he'd pretended he wasn't relieved.

He liked kids—that wasn't the problem, just as it wasn't a matter of resenting the inevitable disruptions parenthood would cause in his and Amanda's joint career and comfortable life-style. His reluctance wasn't even due to jealousy at the prospect of having to share his beloved wife with another person. Frankly, Mark had to admit that at some deep, atavistic level, there was a potently erotic charm to the idea of Amanda's body swelling with his child. But despite the joy he knew children could bring, Mark also knew that they were a risk, *such* a risk. The happiness he'd found with Amanda had always seemed a miracle, an unexpected blessing bestowed on a man who had been too scarred and cynical even to hope anymore. Oh, God, was he a coward not to want to risk that happiness?

He studied her profile in the moonlight. He wondered if the hunger he felt for her would ever pall. Somehow he doubted it. They had spent the past decade almost continually in each other's presence, living and working together twenty-four hours a day, yet the years of intimacy had not dulled her appeal. Even now he had only to look at her to want her.

He tried to imagine her old, old enough to celebrate that golden anniversary she'd mentioned, but the vision eluded him. Amanda was not really young anymore—hell, neither was he—but even as they both eased over the border into middle age, to him she appeared as fresh and ageless as she had the day they first met at the antique mart in Portland.

Amanda was a lovely woman, with the kind of bone-deep beauty that would endure all her life. Everything about her bespoke quality and breeding: the cameo-perfect lines of her pale, heart-shaped face and her small head with its shining cap of close-cropped hair, the rich, deep brown of burnished walnut untouched by gray. Not many women past forty could wear the boyish haircut, but the style suited Amanda, emphasizing her delicacy and sophistication. Mark liked the way he could brush her silky hair back and find perfect ears decorated with the ornate earrings she habitually wore. And he loved the sleek slope of her throat, the gentle swell of her bosom and the vulnerable curve of her nape, naked except for a few feathery tendrils. He was in heaven when he kissed the back of her neck. Sometimes in the privacy of their office, or at home when she was dressing, he would slip up behind her and wrap his arms around her, his hands cupping those delectable breasts that she thought were too small. Holding her against him, he would nuzzle her nape, and no matter how much she protested that she was too busy for such foolishness, as soon as the tip of his tongue dipped into the incredibly sensitive hollow at her hairline, her whole body would tremble and melt boneless in his arms....

Amanda was gazing blindly at the sky, and with a perception sharpened by a decade of intimacy, Mark knew her eyes were focused with longing on some poignant vision of what had never been. He sighed and conceded a truth that was useless to deny: he could not be happy if Amanda was not. Aloud he said, "I'm sorry. I should have suggested we adopt a baby years ago."

Amanda blinked. "I never know whether to be amazed or outraged by the ease with which you read my mind sometimes."

"It doesn't take ESP to know you've always wanted children."

"No, I suppose it doesn't," she agreed, turning to him with a candid smile, "any more than I need psychic power to realize that it never bothered you as much as it did me that we don't have a family—"

"Amanda," Mark interrupted hoarsely, but she shook her head.

"No, dear, don't apologize and don't pretend. I understand, truly I do. With your background, it's perfectly natural for you to have doubts—doubts about children, maybe even doubts about your ability to be a good parent. Personally, I think you're foolish to worry. You'd make a wonderful father. Still, I can see why, after having to raise yourself, you'd be less than eager to raise anyone else. That doesn't make it your fault."

She paused. "According to the doctors, it's not anybody's fault. We're both capable—it simply never happened. That's probably the main reason why I've never suggested adoption myself. I guess I'm selfish. As wonderful as it would be to have a baby, I want it to be your baby, *our* baby, and as long as there's the slightest chance..." Her lips twisted ironically. "I don't know.

Sometimes I wonder if there's not some cosmic reason we were never meant to be parents."

Mark persisted. "Amanda, don't go resigning yourself to fate when there are still steps we can take to remedy the situation." Framing her face gently in his hands, he searched her features. "Darling, are you absolutely certain you don't want to try to adopt? This is a subject much more important than choosing where to spend our vacation, so please don't say something just because you think it's what I want to hear. It's vital you be honest with me. All I want is your happiness, and if adopting a child will make you happy, then, fine, let's go for it. But we have to decide now. You're forty-two, and I'm forty-five. If we wait much longer, most agencies are going to tell us we're too old."

Amanda's lashes flew up. "You'd do that for me? If I say the word, you'll take on the care of a child now, even though we'll both be eligible for Social Security by the time he reaches college?"

"Yes," Mark said, swallowing the thickness in his throat. "If that's what you need."

She beamed. Laying her palms on his chest, she declared, "Thank you, Mark. Thank you for wanting to give me a child. Thank you for caring about me enough to put my needs before your own. But it's not necessary." Standing on tiptoe, she slid her arms around his neck and drew his face down to hers.

When the kiss broke off at last, she asked, "Have I told you lately how much you mean to me?"

"Oh, I think you may have mentioned it once or twice over the past ten years," Mark drawled.

"I hope so," Amanda said earnestly. "Sometimes we get so absorbed with the business and the busyness of living that I'm afraid I must seem to take you for granted—and I don't, you know. Not for one minute do I ever forget how important you are to me. You're everything I've ever wanted in a man, everything I used to dream about when I was a girl. There was a time when I thought I was incapable of the sensations you arouse in me, but now I can't imagine feeling any other way. I love you, Mark. All I ask out of life is to keep on loving you."

He could feel his body harden at her words. "That's a request easily granted, darling. I plan to keep loving you as long as there's an ounce of strength left in these decrepit old bones. I have every intention of becoming a very sexy senior citizen."

As he spoke, Mark was aware that his glib response was twisting Amanda's meaning slightly, that she had been referring not simply to physical passion but to that mystical emotion he had such trouble verbalizing. Even now, after all these years together, he tended to choke up when he tried to voice his sentiments, it was difficult for him to express his feelings any way except physically. "Hey, lady, wanna go back to bed?" he quipped, hoping she would find his invitation an adequate response to her heartfelt declaration.

Apparently it was. "I thought you'd never ask," Amanda said. Linking her arm through Mark's, she turned and they strode purposefully toward their stateroom.

"EXCUSE ME, Mr. Wexler...."

Mark glanced irritably at his clerk and muttered, "Just a moment, Sandra." He returned his attention to the elderly man with whom he'd been discussing antique timepieces. "As I was saying, a genuine Simon Willard clock would certainly be the jewel of your collection, but they're not easy to find, especially here on the West Coast, and you have to be wary of all the copies floating around. After Willard retired in—''

The girl poked Mark's shoulder. "Mr. Wexler, please!"

His eyes narrowed. Murmuring an apology to the other man, he quickly unfolded his rangy body from the Edwardian divan on which they'd been seated and stalked away, Sandra trailing after him. As soon as they were out of earshot, Mark turned and frowned at her. Sandra Pollard was a chunky eighteen-year-old with frizzy red hair; Amanda had hired her as soon as they'd returned from the Caribbean two months earlier. The girl was awkward but hardworking and willing to learn the business, and Mark's only real objection to their new trainee was her unfortunate predilection for a particularly penetrating jasmine perfume.

"Sandra, my wife and I have been willing to make allowances because we know this is your first real job, but surely you must realize that you cannot interrupt either of us when we're busy with a client!"

"But, sir, this is about Mrs. Wexler," Sandra insisted. "I think she needs you."

Mark scowled. Lately Amanda had been suffering from a stubborn case of the flu, but it was only today, after he'd insisted—*nagged* was probably more the accurate word—that she had finally agreed to stay away from work in order to see her doctor; after her appointment she was supposed to return home and rest. He demanded, "What on earth are you talking about? Did Amanda telephone?"

Sandra shook her head. "She's upstairs in your office now. She came in a few minutes ago. She told me she'd wait till you were finished with the gentleman, but she's ... she's—'' The girl gestured helplessly. "I'm sorry. I wouldn't have bothered you for the world, except that Mrs. Wexler is acting sort of strange—jittery, like she's worried about something, and I really think you ought to see what's wrong.''

Mark jerked his head to stare at the door on the far side of the shop. The showroom of Wexlers' Antiques and Collectibles was divided into display areas arranged to give customers an idea of how various furnishings and art objects might fit into their own homes—Amanda's idea, one of her best—and the entrance to the stairway leading to the second-floor office was through the "child's room," beside a nursery-size wardrobe filled with Victorian mechanical toys of cast iron. Mark's mouth tightened. While it was true he'd been so engrossed in his conversation with the customer, an enthusiastic and knowledgeable amateur collector, that he could easily have missed Amanda's unexpected arrival, it was unlike her to slip past without at least greeting him.

Something must have happened when she saw her doctor, Mark realized with alarm. Perhaps she was really ill—but Amanda was never ill. Ordinarily, her health was excellent, her energy boundless. During their cruise she'd been inexhaustible. Swimming, sightseeing, making love—she'd demonstrated the vigor and enthusiasm of a girl half her age.

Several weeks later, home in Oregon again, when fatigue and nausea had begun to trouble Amanda, it had been entirely in character for her to refuse to slow down. She had dismissed the symptoms as some bug she'd caught, probably a simple case of influenza that would soon abate. But her flu had not gone away; it had worsened. Just the evening before, when the two of them had stopped for supper during the drive back to Portland from an estate auction in Salem, Amanda had almost fainted in the restaurant. Only her promise to see a physician the very next morning had prevented Mark from carrying her directly to a hospital emergency room.

Now her appointment with the doctor was over, and instead of going home to rest, she had come to the shop and was acting strangely....

Rapidly retracing his steps to the divan, Mark told the other man, "Forgive me, but I'm afraid something has come up that I must deal with right away. If you don't mind waiting a few minutes, I'll have Sandra bring you some coffee, and we recently received some new auction catalogs from Sotheby's that you might enjoy browsing through...." As soon as the client was settled, Mark bounded up the stairs to his wife.

Considering his apprehension, the scene that greeted him in the office was almost anticlimactic. From Sandra's description, Mark had expected to find Amanda agitated, distraught. Instead, she was standing quietly at the window, next to the computer station, her gaze focused on the mall below, her mouth curved in a serene smile as she surveyed the pedestrians strolling along the brick sidewalks among the circular planters thick with spring flowers. When Mark closed the door behind him, she did not glance up right away.

Reassured by her composure, he paused for a moment, ordering his heart to slow down. She was wearing slacks and a silky shirt instead of one of the dresses she preferred for the store, but otherwise she looked as if she'd come to the office expecting to work. Thank God she appeared to be all right! He couldn't bear the thought of anything hurting her.

When Amanda remained silent, lost in her reverie, Mark crossed the office, bypassing their enormous partners' desk to stand behind her. He slipped his arms beneath hers and drew her back against the length of his body. Amanda stiffened slightly and her fingers flittered over his, as if uncertain whether to push him away. Then she relaxed. Her hands covered his, pressing them more firmly over her breasts as she snuggled against him.

"I love it when you touch me," she declared in a soft, dreamy whisper.

"I love it, too," Mark agreed with dry humor. "Every time I lay a finger on you, I find myself looking around for the nearest bed—which means it's probably a good thing we only have that little love seat here in the office, or otherwise we'd never get any of our chores done." He hesitated, and when he spoke again, the teasing note was absent from his voice. "Speaking of bed," he asked seriously, "why aren't you there right now? You promised you'd go straight home as soon as you finished at the doctor's."

Amanda shrugged. "I wanted to be here with you."

"I like being with you, too," Mark rejoined, his tone tolerant. "But even though I know how much you hate to miss work, you need to quit worrying about the store and think of yourself for once. Sandra may not be the world's greatest clerk yet, but she's learning and she tries hard. The two of us ought to be able to manage without you here for a couple of days. You're never going to shake this stupid flu of yours if you don't get some rest."

"It isn't flu," Amanda said.

Mark stilled. "What?"

"I don't have the flu," she repeated slowly. "That's not the reason I've been sick."

With great care Mark turned his wife in his arms. Catching her chin in his fingertips, he tilted her head until he could gaze directly into her face. The expression in her eyes was peculiar—shy, almost wary. He asked, "Amanda, what's wrong? When Sandra pestered me about you, I thought at first that she was overreacting—you know how the least little thing can fluster her—but now I realize she was right. Something *is* bothering you. What is it? Did the doctor upset you? Please tell me."

He watched her struggle for words. Gripping the lapels of his jacket, she licked her dry lips and tried to smile. "It's so silly," she ventured hoarsely. "Things like this don't happen to people like us, people our age...."

Mark looked confused. "What does our age have to do with anything?"

She swallowed. "You remember that cruise we took in January?"

"Of course I—" he began impatiently, only to break off in dismay. "You didn't pick up some weird tropical virus while we were in the islands, did you?"

She shook her head. "No. The doctor says I'm in perfect health." She paused, and the smile that had been flirting with the corners of her mouth suddenly burst forth, blinding in its joy. "Oh, sweetheart," she cried, "if I weren't forty-two years old, if I were thirty-two or twenty-two and I started throwing up every morning, what's the first thing you'd think of?"

Mark gaped at her. Beneath her hands she could feel his heart lurch. "Good God," he whispered. He closed his eyes, and she knew he must be counting backward, calculating the signs. "Are you sure? You've always been so irregular—"

"Yes, I'm very sure," Amanda answered, almost gurgling with happiness. "I didn't believe it at first, either, but the doctor performed the tests just to convince me. He said you have very definitely succeeded in knocking me up."

Too stunned to temper his tone, Mark demanded harshly, "Did he say why it should happen now, after all these years of trying?"

Amanda's smile faded slightly. "You know there's never been any particular reason why I couldn't become pregnant. The doctor told me that relaxing and forgetting about business for a couple of weeks was probably all we ever needed—and, of course, the way we spent most of those two weeks didn't hurt."

She gazed expectantly at her husband. He did not speak. He seemed frozen with shock. His long face was taut with tension; his eyes were oddly blank. Amanda felt a frisson of dread. Although she and Mark rarely talked about their innermost feelings, through years of propinquity the two of them had learned to communicate on a subliminal level. They were usually able to guess each other's moods, even thoughts, with surprising ease. Now she suspected he was deliberately shielding his mind from hers.

She swallowed dryly. "Please tell me what you're thinking," she said. When he continued to stare mutely at her, she cried, "For heaven's sake, Mark, tell me how you feel about this baby!"

The word shook him free of his silence. "'Baby,'" he echoed, testing the sound of it. "You—we—are going to have a baby?"

Amanda was slightly mollified by his use of the plural pronoun. "So it would appear."

Mark's peaked brows came together. "Did your doctor say whether it would be safe for you?" he asked urgently. "Darling, you're not a girl anymore."

"No, but I'm not exactly over the hill, either—lots of women my age have babies." She pleaded, "Oh, Mark, if you're worried about something happening to me, don't be. I'm in excellent health, and there's nothing in my medical or family history to suspect any problems with this pregnancy. Since my doctor is a general practitioner, he's referring me to an obstetrician, a Dr. Rhodes, who's supposed to be very good, and there are some special tests he'll probably want to administer in a couple of months, just as a precaution. But basically there is no reason to assume I won't be able to deliver a perfectly healthy baby in complete safety."

As she watched, the anxiety slowly faded from Mark's face. Then all at once his eyes brightened and his lips stretched into a grin of sheer jubilation. Shouting, "Amanda, you amazing woman!" he dragged her into his arms and began kissing her breathlessly.

Later, after the first spate of emotion passed, Mark returned to the showroom long enough to placate the customer he had abandoned. He apologized for the family emergency that had demanded his presence and promised to look for the antique timepiece the collector coveted. The instant the man exited the store, Mark left the baffled Sandra in charge while he loped back up the stairs to Amanda.

They lay quietly together on the love seat, Amanda curled on Mark's lap, her head on his chest. He inhaled the honey-and-herb fragrance of her freshly shampooed hair and fingered the cloisonné earrings dangling against her throat. When his hands slid down her body, he noticed that the waistband of her slacks felt as loose as ever, and her belly was still flat.

"I should have realized something was up the other day, when you insisted on eating that enormous Reuben sandwich from Rose's Deli," he teased her. "It's going to be fun watching you get fat. You've always been so slim, it'll be like sleeping with a different—" He broke off, grimacing. "We will be allowed to sleep together, won't we? There aren't any rules against it?"

Amanda reassured him. "The doctor says we can make love as long as I'm comfortable and you're still able to get your arms around me. He doesn't recommend sexual gymnastics—"

"Darn, just when I was thinking of buying a trampoline," Mark muttered.

"The trampoline will have to wait," Amanda said, chuckling, "but if you'll settle for a bed, we ought to be able to maintain a normal relationship for several months."

Mark groaned his relief. "Thank heavens! I wasn't looking forward to staying celibate till after—when is it—the middle of October?"

"That's the best guess, although it's hard to estimate accurately, given how unpredictable my system has always been. I figure the baby should arrive right about the same time as the fall buying shows in New York." Amanda looked rueful. "I guess we'll have to miss them this year."

Mark suggested doubtfully, "I suppose we could try to train Sandra enough to send her in our place."

"Don't you think it would be pushing things to ask for two miracles in one year?"

"Probably," Mark agreed. "But don't worry. I reckon we'll just have to adjust our schedules somehow—unless this obstetrician knows of some newfangled way to speed up the birthing process?"

"I'll make a point of asking him," Amanda said with a smile, "but I suspect we're going to be stuck with October. Personally, I don't mind. I love the fall. Besides, I think it would be rather nice if our baby was born on October 9."

Puzzled, Mark asked, "Why the ninth in particular?"

"Because that's my mother's birthday, silly. How could you forget? I was looking for her present the day you and I met!"

"Sorry," Mark said. "I was so dazzled by the sight of you poring over the jewelry display in my stall that day that everything else was wiped from my memory."

Amanda smiled indulgently. "Yeah, sure. Well, in case you really have forgotten, you helped me pick out a garnet necklace for her. Mother is almost impossible to shop for, but that was one of the most successful gifts I ever gave her. Still, I'll bet the birth of her first grandchild will top it!"

"No doubt."

Hearing her husband's altered tone, Amanda lifted her head. When she saw the anguish in his eyes, she realized he must be remembering his own parents: the father who had deserted his wife and young son, the despairing mother who had taken her own life when the boy was only fifteen. Even though Mark almost never referred to his childhood, Amanda knew his whole life had been colored by the tragedies of those early years.

She whispered contritely, "Oh, Mark, I'm sorry. I forgot. I wish...God, I can't tell you how much I wish that your parents—your mother—could be here, too, to share our joy."

"So do I," Mark said. "Mom adored babies."

He fell silent, his blue eyes clouded with memories. Amanda hugged him and waited for him to continue. After a moment he shrugged off his mood. "Forgive me, I didn't mean to get maudlin. Just for a second there I found myself trying to envision Mom as a grandmother, which isn't easy, considering she was only thirty-two when she died. In my mind she'll always be young, a thin, blond girl with a thick southern accent, who worked too hard and taped movie stars' pictures on the kitchen cabinets so nobody'd notice how bare the cupboards were. I can't imagine what she would have been like had she lived."

Amanda insisted, "But she does live. Your mother lives in you—she lives in this child I'm carrying. Our baby is her immortality."

"And ours, too," Mark reflected. "What a terrifyingly profound thought. I suppose I've never considered that particular aspect of having a family before."

"I have," Amanda said. She closed her eyes, and her mouth curved into a sad smile.

"What are you thinking?" Mark asked.

"Not much," Amanda replied with a gesture of dismissal. "I guess it's my turn to be maudlin. Actually, I was just remembering a silly little incident that occurred years ago—in fact, it was literally the day before our grand opening here. I never told you about it, because it seemed so trivial, but somehow it stuck with me."

"What happened?"

"You were away at the printer's, picking up our new business cards and flyers," Amanda reminisced, "and

I was alone in the showroom, unpacking stock and arranging displays—"

"That doesn't sound very gentlemanly of me, running off and leaving the most tedious, dusty jobs for you," Mark noted dryly.

Amanda made a face. "Now I'm sure I'd agree with you, but at the time, I was so happy I didn't care." She had been delighted to do the work, thrilled and exhilarated because at long last she was working for *them*. After three years of marriage they had finally realized their dream of being partners in their own shop. Amanda had resigned her job as manager of the furniture department at the store where she'd worked for years, and Mark was giving up his stall in the antique mart for a prestigious location fronting directly on the mall downtown. They were going to be their own bosses; they were going to have everything they'd ever wanted.

Mark nodded. "I remember the feeling. Those were very special days for us."

"Yes, they were. Everything that happened, even ordinary details like getting our telephones installed, seemed thrilling and new." Amanda's dark eyes narrowed. "While I was setting up children's furniture in the nursery area, the phone rang for the first time. I assumed the caller was a customer, and I was so excited that I dashed over to answer it without even bothering to put down the bisque doll I'd just unpacked. When I picked up the receiver, very proudly I chirped, 'Wexlers'.' I've never forgotten how wonderful it felt to give our own name."

She paused, swallowing. "But instead of a customer on the other end of the line, I heard this little girl's voice ask in confusion, 'Mommy?' The one word—dear

Lord, I can't begin to describe how desolate that one little word made me feel, how...barren. I found myself staring at the doll in my arms and the empty cradle where I'd been planning to put it, and suddenly all our hard work seemed pointless. As gently as I could I told the child, 'I'm afraid you have the wrong number, honey,' and I hung up. Then I burst into tears.''

Mark's arms tightened around Amanda. He held her against him as if trying to absorb her hurt. "Oh, darling,'' he croaked, "has it really been so painful for you?''

"Yes,'' she admitted frankly. "Sometimes when I started my period the disappointment would almost overwhelm me—not in the first years, while the doctors kept assuring us that we had a chance, but later, when I was thirty-five and then forty, and every month that passed meant I was one step closer to the time when there'd be no chance at all...''

Amanda paused to take a deep breath. When she spoke again, her mood had lightened. "But let's forget about frustration and depression. None of it matters anymore.''

She closed her eyes, and her face, transfigured by joy, glowed. Mark studied her rapturous expression with awe. To him she had always been a lovely, desirable woman, but now, as she sat in his lap weaving blissful fantasies, cradling her unborn child in her arms, suckling it at her breast, her beauty seemed almost preternatural—unreal.

She caught him by the wrist and pressed a kiss in the center of his palm. "Thank you for making my dream come true,'' she said.

"Amanda—'' Mark began.

She did not hear him. Shaping his hand over the curve of her bosom, she whispered, "Just think—in only seven more months I'm going to be nursing our baby. The miracle I've prayed for all my life has finally happened. Everything is different now."

Mark shivered. Her elation worried him. Although Amanda gave the impression of being a forthright, lighthearted woman, he knew that in many ways she was as reserved as he was, accustomed to hiding her deepest feelings behind witty words and a vivacious manner. In fact, through the years Mark had sometimes wondered whether the reason their relationship was so successful might not be because it was fundamentally shallow, based on mutual interests and strong sexual compatibility rather than profound emotions. He loved Amanda and he knew she loved him, yet to date nothing had occurred in their marriage to test the exact depth of that love. Suddenly seeing her so euphoric, so open—so vulnerable—he was apprehensive. Amanda was a strong woman, but how would she react if something spoiled her happiness?

And he would have been deluding himself if he refused to admit that he was frightened for his own sake, as well. From the moment they met, Amanda had been vital to his existence; he had been nourished and enriched by her as the desert was nourished by the rain. Could he survive without her life-giving presence? Not that he was afraid of her dying—nowadays women didn't *die* having babies—but what if motherhood altered her? What if her devotion to her long-awaited child proved so intense that she could no longer pretend even a superficial interest in Mark? Such things had happened before.

It wasn't jealousy; it was a change that worried him. The instant Amanda had made her stunning announcement, Mark was certain their relationship had changed in some essential way. After a decade of marriage a new dimension had been added without warning, and henceforth their business life, their social life— even their sex life—would be affected. In all innocence Amanda had admitted it herself, uttering the words like a benediction: *Everything is different now.* A truer, more threatening statement had rarely been spoken. Everything was different now—and that was exactly what Mark was afraid of.

CHAPTER TWO

THE MAÎTRE D' SCANNED the reservation list and said, "I'm sorry, Mr. Wexler, but the rest of your party hasn't arrived yet. We're still setting up the dining room for lunch, but if you'd care to go into the cocktail lounge..."

"We are running a few minutes early," Mark said agreeably. He glanced at Amanda. Despite the becoming coral pink of her dress, which contrasted vividly with her dark hair and eyes and cast a rosy bloom on her fair skin, Mark thought her cheeks looked a little pale. "Would you like to sit down while we wait for your parents?"

She nodded gratefully. "That sounds like a wonderful idea."

Mark slid his arm around his wife, squeezing her thickening waist through the loose folds of her dress as he guided her into the lounge. Although the changes in Amanda's body were only now becoming noticeable, she was determined to enjoy every moment of her pregnancy, and she had been wearing maternity clothes for almost two months. Mark settled her gently onto a banquette beneath a long window offering a spectacular panorama of both Mount Hood and Mount Saint Helens, and he sat close beside her. After the waitress departed with their drink orders, he regarded Amanda with concern. "What's the matter? Are you feeling queasy again?"

Amanda sighed and began to drum on the tabletop with her nails. "A little. I should have known better than to skip breakfast this morning. I very dutifully took all my vitamins, but I wasn't hungry."

"Not even for pastrami?" Mark asked lightly. He caught her fingers to still them. "You're worried about the medical tests this afternoon, aren't you?"

Amanda nodded jerkily. "I guess I'm just chicken."

"No, you're not," Mark said firmly. "You have every right to be apprehensive. No matter how important these tests are, they're still risky."

"Amniocentesis—the word even sounds scary," Amanda admitted with a shudder.

Mark's gaze bore into Amanda's as he lifted her hand to his lips. Her skin was damp with nervousness; he could taste the salt. "Please don't be afraid. I promise you everything's going to be fine. Your doctor is one of the best, and I'll be right there beside you the whole time."

"I know," Amanda whispered. She felt him shift nearer on the bench; their legs touched. The familiar warmth of his long, muscular thigh against hers was comforting and stimulating all at the same time. Curling her fingers to stroke the hard line of his jaw, Amanda said earnestly, "Sometimes when I think about what's ahead of me—and I don't mean just medical tests or even the birth itself, but the awesome responsibility of actually being a *mother*—I feel overwhelmed and inadequate and more than a little frightened by the prospect. Your being with me is the only thing that gives me courage."

Mark's blue eyes gleamed, and his voice was heavy with emotions as he began, "I promise I'll always be with—"

The waitress reappeared. Instantly Mark released Amanda's hand and pulled back, his expression hooded while he watched the young woman set his glass of red wine in front of him and splash mineral water from a pebbly green bottle into a tall tumbler of ice for Amanda. After the waitress departed, he glanced at his wife.

"You were saying..." Amanda noted dryly.

"Never mind," Mark muttered, relieved that she appeared to have forgotten her fear, at least temporarily. "My timing is invariably off whenever I try to make a heartfelt declaration." He lifted his wineglass in a wry salute, inhaling the fruity bouquet. "Cheers."

They drank in companionable silence until they were interrupted once more, this time by another couple passing through the lounge. "Jim, wait a minute," the woman called, catching her husband's arm. "Why, Amanda, Mark, how great to see you! It's been ages."

"Hi, Cheryl, Jim," Amanda exclaimed, beaming at her friends. James and Cheryl Bishop were members of the church Amanda's parents attended, and Amanda had known Cheryl, a perky blonde, since childhood, when they'd sung together in the Cherub Choir. The two girls had become intimate friends, and even though there had been periods through the years when they had not seen each other for months at a time, somehow they'd always managed to celebrate the major events in each other's lives. While Amanda was attending Bryn Mawr, she had flown home from Pennsylvania during spring break to attend Cheryl's marriage to a young law student with shoulder-length brown curls; Jim's hair had been short and definitely thinning by the time he and Cheryl gave Mark and Amanda Baccarat champagne glasses as a wedding present; and recently Amanda had found herself seated next to the senior partner of Smith, Bishop and McCall at the christening ceremony for her friends' first grandchild. Nowadays the two couples rarely bumped into each other, but whenever they did, Amanda was always delighted.

While Mark and Jim shook hands, Cheryl swooped down to hug Amanda. "We were talking about you two just the other day."

"Only good things, I hope," Amanda said, laughing.

Cheryl replied, "Actually, we were discussing the wonderful news your mother told us when we saw them at church on Easter Sunday. I can't tell you how thrilled I am for you." She surveyed Amanda with approval. "Pregnancy becomes you, you lucky thing. You have that special glow about you. With each of my kids, I went to pot the instant the rabbit died, but you—you're really blossoming.

Amanda said sheepishly, "If you're trying to tell me I'm finally developing a bustline at my advanced age, I've already noticed."

Casting a rueful glance at her own buxom figure, Cheryl insisted, "Unlike some of us, on you it looks good. In fact, everything about you looks good." She turned to Mark. "Don't you think this wife of yours is looking beautiful these days?"

"I always think Amanda is beautiful," Mark murmured.

The two couples chatted for several minutes, and then Jim glanced at his watch. "Hey, you guys, it's really great running into you, but we're going to have to rush if we expect to eat before we head out to the golf club. We're supposed to be teeing off at two-thirty. Amanda, the next time you see your folks, tell them we said hi."

"Actually, my parents are who we're waiting for right now."

"Oh, I didn't realize they'd returned from Japan yet," Cheryl commented. "In that case, perhaps we'll spot them ourselves. Well, so long, you two, and congratulations."

Mark and Amanda watched the Bishops disappear into the dining room. "Nice people," Mark observed, sinking back into his seat and laying his arm along the top of the banquette, behind Amanda's shoulders. "I've always like them."

"They are nice, aren't they? I ought to call and invite them over for dinner some night. Considering that Cheryl and I have known each other forever, it's a shame we don't meet more often."

Mark's expression darkened. "Yes, it is too bad. When you think of all the pressures that keep people apart these days—jobs, family, social obligations—a lifelong friend is rare and miraculous, something to be treasured."

Sipping the last of her mineral water, Amanda regarded her husband over the rim of her glass. Because she was attuned to his moods, she could hear the wistful undertone in his voice, the element of regret so repressed it was almost subliminal—regret because, unlike Amanda, Mark had no lifelong friends.

Mark was a man of such culture and polish that virtually nobody guessed he came from a background far different from Amanda's—that in some ways he had no background at all. Mark had no family, no acquaintances from childhood, no history that predated his early twenties. Even Mark's closest friends were ignorant of his life before then. If pressed, he claimed nothing of significance had ever happened to him until he was a young soldier stationed in Germany. Prowling through old shops in search of beer steins to sell to his buddies, he had discovered he possessed an eye for spotting objects of value and a knack for marketing them, and the direction of his future had been revealed to him.

Only Amanda knew differently. She was the one person aware of how completely Mark had raised himself, educated himself, essentially created himself. He had been determined to divorce himself from his poverty-stricken childhood, and he'd succeeded so completely—the persona he projected was so convincing—that at first even Amanda had been fooled. When they began dating, she had assumed that he, like her, had grown up in upper-middle-class comfort; it was not until he asked her to marry him that he'd revealed the truth....

They had been curled together on the couch in her apartment, drowsy in the afterglow of their loving, the night Mark related the bare details of his early life. The desolation in Mark's clipped words had been painful to hear—especially since only moments before his voice had throbbed with passion—yet Amanda had forced herself to listen. Intuitively she had realized that this moment of revelation was a truer indication of the depth of Mark's feelings for her than all his most ardent lovemaking. Besides, if the two of them were to seriously consider marriage, then it was imperative that they be open with each other. And so she had sat in silence while Mark talked.

He was born during World War II. Robert Wexler, his father, had been an eighteen-year-old soldier railroaded into marrying an even younger girl he met and impregnated while stationed in Mississippi. After the war the little family moved to Spokane, Mark's father's hometown, where Robert worked as a gardener—he always called himself a grounds keeper—for one of the tycoons of the Inland Empire. They had lived in quarters on the estate, and Bonnie, Mark's mother, had helped out whenever the housekeeper needed an extra pair of hands. The marriage was never a happy one. Robert abandoned his wife and son when the boy was ten, and Bonnie, who had loved movies and fantasized about life as depicted within the glossy pages of *Modern Screen* and *Photoplay*, committed suicide five years later. Stunned and grief stricken, Mark had moved his meager belongings into the back room of the grocery store where he'd been working after school. On the third night after the funeral, his employer's wife had found him crying and, pretending to offer comfort, had proceeded to seduce him. . . .

It had been when Amanda heard Mark struggling to make a joke of that sad, sordid little episode that she had finally checked him. The past did not matter, she had promised, silencing him with her kisses; henceforth the only history either of them need worry about would be that which the two of them created together. She had meant what she said, and Mark had taken her at her word. From then on, apart from the occasional glimmer—usually an inadvertent reference to his mother; Mark never mentioned his father—he did not speak again of his family. Sometimes Amanda wondered if his memories were so painful that he'd actually succeeded in expunging them from his own mind.

Amanda rattled the ice cubes in her empty glass, and Mark signaled the cocktail waitress for another bottle of mineral water. Grateful for the diversion, Amanda declared heartily, "I will invite Jim and Cheryl over for dinner some night soon. You're right—you and I devote too much energy to the store. Except for the cruise, it's been ages since we've done anything that wasn't job related. It's not good for us to be such workaholics, especially now."

Mark nodded. "Maybe I can make a golf date with Jim."

"And I'm sure Cheryl would be happy to advise me about setting up the nursery. Goodness knows she's had enough experience, with that brood of hers..." Amanda paused, smiling to herself.

"What's so funny?" Mark asked.

She shrugged. "Oh, I was thinking about Cheryl. She and I are almost exactly the same age, but now she has four children and a *grandchild*, for heaven's sake, while I'm only just getting started on my family."

Mark frowned. "Do you mind?"

"No, of course not," Amanda said, laying her palm protectively over her belly. "You know I want this baby too much to be self-conscious about my age. Still, it's odd the way things turn out. For half our lives Cheryl and I hit all the milestones together. We started kindergarten the same year, discovered boys the same year, graduated from college the same year—even if we did go to different schools—but somewhere along the line, I fell behind."

"You didn't fall behind, you just set your own pace," Mark corrected her. Leaning closer to Amanda, he covered her hand with his. The baby fluttered within her. Mark could not feel the movement, but he recognized the breathless glow on his wife's face. For a moment the two of them communed in tender silence with their unborn child.

Amanda turned her head. Mark was sitting so close that her hair grazed his cheek, and his sweet, wine-scented breath was warm on her skin. She gazed into his eyes, studying the sky-colored irises rimmed with black, the long, reddish-gold lashes. She whispered, "I hope our baby has eyes like yours."

Mark's lips twisted into an indulgent smile. "I hate to disappoint you, but from what Dr. Rhodes said when we went in for genetic counseling, I think it's much more likely the kid will inherit your coloring, which is fine with me. I've always been partial to brown, myself." Lightly he kissed the tip of Amanda's nose, only to have her pull away in embarrassment as her parents were escorted into the lounge.

"Hi, Mother, Father," Amanda called breathlessly, trying not to look flustered.

When he heard the catch in her voice, Mark suppressed a twinge of annoyance. It never failed to baffle him that a woman as secure and confident as Amanda could be intimidated by a couple like Alden and Joan Smollet, yet in their presence she tended to be uncharacteristically diffident and self-conscious. Personally Mark found his in-laws a little stuffy and more than a little insensitive where their only child was concerned, but hardly overwhelming. He got along reasonably well with them. He'd always known he was not the husband the Smollets had wanted for their daughter—they would have preferred someone like the mainline blue blood Amanda had been engaged to briefly during her college days in Philadelphia—but they had realized a woman in her thirties was unlikely to bow to parental pressure in the choice of a mate, and they had accepted the inevitable. Now, although both Alden and Joan professed delight at Amanda's pregnancy, Mark wondered exactly what kind of grandparents they'd prove to be.

Mark rose and shook hands with Alden, a spry man of seventy, whose grizzled hair had once been the same dark brown as Amanda's. Alden was a former real estate developer who, before his retirement, had played a significant role in the revitalization of downtown Portland. While no longer actively pursuing his profession, Alden was still considered one of the elder statesmen of the local business community, and he retained valuable contacts around the Pacific Rim. The trip to the Orient from which he and Joan had just returned had been made at the invitation of a Tokyo manufacturer who wanted Alden's advice about setting up a high-tech assembly plant in northern Oregon.

Joan Smollet was sixty-five, a stylish, slender woman with lighter coloring but the same elegant bone structure as her daughter. Mark knew that many people considered Joan better looking than Amanda, but he did not agree. When he had first been introduced to his future mother-in-law, he'd thought she might be one of the most attractive older women he'd ever known— might be, but wasn't. There was something lacking in Joan that made all the difference, some quality of warmth and vitality that Amanda possessed in abundance. Joan reminded Mark of the hybrid roses in the gardens of her gracious old home on Cumberland Road, overlooking the city. Like the flowers she cultivated with such enthusiasm—her one real passion— Mark found Joan beautiful, unblemished and cold.

"It's good to see you both. I'm looking forward to hearing all about your trip," Mark murmured as Joan pressed a ceremonial kiss on his cheek. He glanced at the maître d' hovering in the background. "I think our table is ready. Would you two care to have a drink here first, or shall we go on into the dining room?"

"I expect we'll settle for wine with our lunch," Joan said. She frowned at the melting ice in her daughter's glass. "And what have you been drinking, dear?"

Amanda sighed. "Mineral water, Mother. Nothing alcoholic, just gallons and gallons of mineral water. Doctor's orders."

She started to push herself up from her seat, but the unaccustomed weight she was carrying—and, Mark was certain, her mother's gimlet gaze—made her move awkwardly. He caught Amanda gently and eased her to her feet, the loose folds of her pink dress flowing around her.

Alden shook his head in wonder. "I still can't get over the sight of my little girl wearing a maternity dress. That's something I never thought I'd see."

Mark could feel Amanda stiffen. "Neither did I, Father," she said quietly.

Clearing his throat, Mark suggested, "Why don't we head on to our table? I don't know about the rest of you, but I'm more than ready to eat, and probably just about as soon as we've finished dessert, Amanda and I will have to take off for her doctor's appointment. But in the meantime, you can tell us about Japan."

During lunch Alden briefly discussed his overseas meetings and their implications for the Portland area, but most of the conversation was dominated by Joan. While Alden had devoted his time in Japan to business, Joan and their hostess had visited museums and attended a spring festival celebrating the cherry blossoms. "I can't tell you how impressed I was with everything I saw," she enthused. "Like all large cities, Tokyo has its share of problems, but basically Japan is a very beautiful, thoroughly fascinating country. I'm sorry we waited so long to visit it."

"I'm glad you had a good time," Amanda said. "Did you meet many people?"

"Well, Mrs. Shigeta and I became fairly well acquainted, and one evening she and her husband invited their whole family over to introduce them to us. They have two married sons and four adorable grandchildren, of whom they're very proud." Joan smiled. "I have to admit that it was nice for your father and me to be able to say that we have a grandchild of our own on the way."

Although Mark assumed his mother-in-law's comment had been a simple expression of pleasure, from the hurt on Amanda's face he could tell she was interpreting it as a reproach. Amanda had always been thin-skinned where her parents were concerned, but now, with her emotions heightened by her condition, she was liable to imagine slights where none were intended. Quickly he interposed, "Tell me, Joan, do you happen to know offhand if any of the Shigeta grandchildren are students? I've heard that the educational system in Japan is extremely competitive, and I'm curious to find out whether the rumors are true."

"As a matter of fact," Joan replied, "the subject did come up once. One day Mrs. Shigeta had to watch her youngest grandson while his mother went to class. When I asked what course she was taking, Mrs. Shigeta said her daughter-in-law was studying how to coach the boy so that he could pass his entrance exam for nursery school."

Mark grimaced. "You're kidding."

"No, she was quite serious about it. Apparently the Japanese seem to feel that if a child doesn't get on the right track at the very beginning of his education, his whole life can be affected."

"I know some people here in the States who'd agree with them," Amanda commented. She glanced up from the grilled salmon she'd been toying with, and Mark was relieved to see that she looked less upset. "Already we've had people advising us to start training the baby with flash cards from the day he's born. A woman I met at the dentist's office told me matter-of-factly that her eleven-month-old daughter can already identify the *Mona Lisa*."

Everyone laughed. "That's information no toddler should be without, obviously," Alden said, chuckling.

"I know," Amanda said. "It sounds so silly, but this woman was adamant. She insisted that being able to pick out a da Vinci painting would make it possible for her little girl to get into the right play group, and after that she'll probably be able to attend the right pre-school, and after that the right kindergarten and the right grammar school and so on, into prep school and college. When I asked whatever happened to letting children be children, she just stared at me."

Alden shook his head sadly. "I suppose some people feel that unstructured childhood is a luxury we can no longer afford, and I have to admit that they may have a point. Flash cards for infants seem a bit extreme, but still, it's a tough world and kids need every edge they can get." He paused. "I wasn't planning on telling you two this just yet—it was going to be a surprise—but

Joan and I have been talking to our lawyer about setting up a trust fund to pay for the baby's education."

Mark's mouth tightened. "That's very generous of you both, but it isn't necessary."

Joan looked chagrined. Flashing an apologetic smile, she said, "Oh, Mark, please don't think we're trying to meddle or that we're implying you won't be able to provide for your child. It's just, well, when you've waited for a grandchild as long as we have, you tend to build up a lot of dreams and aspirations, and we want to do something special."

Alden added quietly, "I don't know whether you two have thought about it, but it's extremely unlikely that I'll live to see this baby fully grown—"

Amanda jerked up her head. "Father!" she cried, stricken.

Hastily Alden continued, "No, no, my dear, don't worry. I'm not implying there's anything wrong with me. I'm just stating a fact. I'm in good health, but I'm seventy years old. I don't expect to make it to ninety. And having accepted that fact, it's only natural that I'd feel better knowing what my grandchild's future is going to be like. After all, everything I have will be his someday."

Moved by the uncharacteristic confession, Mark said, "I hope you live forever, Alden."

"From your lips to God's ears," the old man murmured. Then he frowned at his daughter. "Are you feeling all right, Amanda? You've barely touched your lunch."

Color returned to Amanda's cheeks as she pushed away her plate. "I guess I'm not very hungry. I'm a little nervous about my doctor's appointment this afternoon."

"Oh, really? Why?"

She took a deep breath and explained, "Actually, it's not a regular appointment at all. I'm going to the clinic to have amniocentesis. That's a test where the doctor draws a sample of the fluid in the sac surrounding the baby and then examines it for any genetic defects."

"But before your father and I left for the Orient, didn't you tell me that you and Mark had already had some kind of genetic test?" Joan asked, puzzled.

"We had genetic counseling," Amanda corrected her. "There were blood tests, and then we discussed our families' medical records in detail, to see if there was any history of disorders like dwarfism or Down's syndrome or cystic fibrosis." She paused and smiled at Mark. "The main conclusion the doctor drew was that both of us spring from good, healthy stock and are likely to produce equally healthy offspring."

"Then why must you have this other...whatever you called it?" Joan persisted.

"Because of my age," Amanda said frankly. "When the mother is over thirty-five, the odds of having a baby with genetic defects increases dramatically. By performing amniocentesis, the doctor can rule out numerous problems..." Suddenly her voice faltered.

A spasm of pain passed across Mark's face. He reached for Amanda's hand. "The baby's going to be fine, darling, I promise you," he whispered.

Joan said, "Mark's right, Amanda. It's perfectly natural to be concerned, but you mustn't let your imagination run away with you. Every expectant mother worries about whether her baby will be healthy. Just think how fortunate you are to live in a time when medicine is so advanced that those worries can be eased with a simple test."

Alden joined the chorus. Lifting his wineglass, he pledged, "A toast to Amanda's baby. May he—or she—be beautiful and bright and perfect, a credit to us all, and may we always be as proud of him as we are of his lovely mother."

THE ROOM WAS COLD, and Amanda shivered in the open-backed hospital gown. She perched on the edge of the examination table, her bare feet dangling as she glanced at the ominous-looking electronic equipment that lined the room, awesome and foreboding in the stark fluorescent light. Her eyes were round with apprehension. "You'd think I was expecting an android," she joked feebly.

Mark was standing beside her. His forehead crinkled as he followed her gaze. "'Gentlemen, we have the technology...'"

Recognizing the quote, Amanda bit her lip and said, "But I don't want to give birth to the Six Million Dollar Man. I just want a nice, healthy baby."

"That's why we're having these tests," Mark reminded her.

She arched one brow and peered sidelong at him. "*Who*'s having these tests?"

Mark heard the undertone in her voice. Relieved that her momentary panic had passed, he grinned. "Sorry, love. You know I'd do it for you if I could."

"I'll bet," she muttered. All at once she grimaced. Arching awkwardly, she tried to massage the small of her back with her knuckles. Quickly Mark slipped his hand through the opening of her gown and began to prod along her spine, his hard fingertips expertly locating all the sensitive spots beneath her bare skin. Amanda sighed deliciously. "God, that feels good. I always knew there was some reason I let you keep hanging around.''

"And I thought you just lusted after my body," Mark drawled, feeling her tense muscles relax. He continued to rub her back until the obstetrician, his nurse and a radiology technician entered the examination room.

Steven Rhodes was a genial man in his mid-thirties, with intelligent gray eyes and a receding hairline. When Amanda began consulting him, she had liked him at once and soon found herself referring to "Steven" so much that Mark had teased her about her involvement with a younger man. Amanda had retorted that she'd never become interested in anyone who couldn't remember Howdy Doody. In fact, despite his comparative youth, Dr. Rhodes was considered a brilliant obstetrician, and both Mark and Amanda were delighted he'd accepted her as a patient.

After Steven introduced the other women to the Wexlers, the nurse began arranging implements on a tray while the technologist busied herself with the ultrasound machine, flipping switches and entering instructions on a computer keyboard. The machine whined, and a small video screen with a gridwork of lines painted on it glowed.

"Well, Amanda, do you think you're about ready for all this?" Steven asked.

"No," she admitted faintly, "but I guess I'll go through with it, anyway."

"Good, that's the spirit." The doctor raised one end of the examination table slightly and adjusted the pillow. "Now, if we can get this husband of yours to help you lie down . . ."

As Mark gently eased Amanda into position, he could feel her fear return. Clasping her hand tightly, he stepped out of the way while the nurse draped Amanda's lower body and pulled up the gown to just beneath her breasts; then she began to slather a cold, colorless gel over Amanda's exposed abdomen. "Steven," Mark demanded, regarding the physician frankly, "is this going to hurt her?"

Dr. Rhodes answered with equal candor. "A little. There's no pain at all involved in a sonogram, but when I draw the amniotic fluid, there will be some cramping and discomfort. It won't last long, and I understand the sensation is more of pressure than pain. Someone described it as feeling like being poked with an elbow." He looked down at Amanda, who was clinging tightly to Mark's hand. "You're the patient—you tell me what you need to help you relax. Do you want a local anesthetic?"

Amanda smiled wanly. "That would just mean another shot, wouldn't it?" When Steven nodded, she exhaled windily and said, "Then, thanks, but no thanks. I hate shots. I think I'll settle for a bullet to bite on."

"Sorry, I'm fresh out of bullets, but I think we have something else that will keep your mind off the procedure." Steven dimmed the lights, and the room was filled with the blue-gray glow from the video screen. Then, at a nod from the doctor, the technologist pulled a long, flexible tube away from the wall. One end of the tube was attached to the ultrasound machine; at the free end was the transponder, a small probe that reminded Amanda of an electric curling iron, and when the woman pressed the device against Amanda's rounded belly, strange blurred images like radar blips appeared on the video screen. Above the whir of the machine a slow, slushy throbbing noise echoed eerily. "That's your heart, Amanda," the doctor explained. The technician moved the transponder, and the sound was drowned by another pulse, lighter, more rapid. Steven said softly, "Mr. and Mrs. Wexler, I'd like to introduce you to your baby."

Your baby. Filled with awe and reverence, Amanda watched as the sonogram took shape. Too fascinated by what she was seeing to be more than marginally aware of the doctor's breathing instructions, she stared unblinking as the blobs of light on the screen grew more focused with each sweep of the probe, coalescing into discrete, identifiable shapes. She was peering inside herself; she was overseeing the functioning of her own vital organs; she was actually observing her life force at work. But most of all, dear God, she was looking at *her baby*, the baby she had longed for so desperately, the baby that even now sometimes seemed too miraculous to be real.

Amanda had never told Mark, but more than once lately she had had nightmares. Several times she had awakened weeping, tormented by vaguely remembered dreams in which she endured long, agonizing labors only to be informed by a taunting world that there was no baby, no pregnancy, that there had never been anything but the hysterical fantasies of a barren, middle-aged woman.... But those troubled fantasies were wrong: there *was* a baby. She could see him. He lay curled inside her body, sleeping, growing, waiting for that moment when he would at long last emerge to lie cradled in her arms as he now lay nestled beneath her heart. My God, she could see his own heart beating! He was real, he was real, and he was *hers*.

"Darling, are you all right?" Mark's voice was hoarse with emotion as he wiped the wetness from Amanda's cheeks. He glared at the doctor. "Damn it, you said you weren't going to hurt her, and look at her now—she's sobbing!"

Steven smiled patiently. "I don't think those are tears of pain," he observed as he handed a filled syringe to his nurse and methodically sponged the gel from Amanda's belly. "If you don't believe me, ask her."

Mark turned to his wife again. Even in the unflattering light her face was radiant. "Amanda?" he murmured uncertainly, brushing her tumbled hair away from her temples.

"It's over already?" she whispered, sounding dazed. When Mark nodded, she relaxed with a reedy giggle. "Good heavens, after making all that fuss, I never even noticed. I was too busy looking at our baby." She turned her head so that her lips pressed into Mark's palm. "Did you see him, sweetheart?" she murmured, her breath warm on his skin. "Did you see his heart beating? Isn't he miraculous?"

"Yes, miraculous," Mark echoed. He bent to kiss her tenderly. "Just like you, my love—"

The obstetrician cleared his throat, reminding Mark that there were other people in the room. Mark stood tall and regarded him wryly. "Okay, what next?"

"Not a whole lot," Steven said, picking up Amanda's medical chart. "I'd suggest you take your wife home so that she can relax for the rest of the day, but after that she ought to be able to proceed with business as usual. We'll call with the test results as soon as we get them, which should be in a couple of weeks." He paused, glancing at the papers in his hand. "Did I ask whether you'll want to know the sex of the baby?"

Amanda raised herself on one elbow. "I can't remember if you asked us, but the answer is no. After waiting so long for this baby, I want to be able to savor every moment of my pregnancy, and that includes the anticipation and excitement of not knowing whether it's going to be a boy or a girl."

The doctor shrugged. "Whatever you want. Some people like to know in advance, to help in picking out baby clothes or decorating the nursery."

Mark said, "I'm afraid we haven't thought that far ahead. Actually, we're still trying to decide which room in our condo is going to *be* the nursery. Either the study or the guest bedroom will have to be sacrificed."

"There are a lot of adjustments when you start a family," Steven agreed, "but at least you have five more months to make that decision."

"And we're going to need every one of them," Amanda chimed in happily, her tone brighter now that the dreaded examination was finished. "It looks like it'll take us till October just to pick out names."

"I've had some patients who don't start thinking about names until it's time to fill out the birth certificate," the doctor commented.

Amanda declared, "At least we're not as bad as that! We both have names in mind, it's just a matter of getting the other one to agree. For example, Mark says no way will he let his son be called Junior, and I can't understand why he's so insistent that a daughter be Marilyn."

Steven looked interested. "Marilyn? That's a name I don't run into often these days. Most of the babies I deliver turn out to be Jennifers or Jasons. Is Marilyn a family name?"

Before Mark could reply, Amanda laughed. "It won't do you any good to ask him, Steven, because he won't tell. Frankly, I suspect that Marilyn was an old girlfriend, and Mark is too embarrassed to 'fess up."

"If you must know," Mark said, frowning slightly, "I happened to be thinking of Marilyn Monroe. I was thirteen when I saw *Some Like It Hot*, and the scene in the Pullman berth made a lasting impression on my malleable young mind.... But so what? Who cares why I like the name?"

Amanda patted Mark's hand indulgently. "That's all right, dear, your guilty secret is safe with me. If you want to name our daughter after an old movie star, I don't care, any more than I really care which room we decide on for the nursery or what sex the baby is. I mean, in the long run, boy or girl, what difference can it possibly make, so long as it's healthy?"

THE CALL CAME late one afternoon two weeks later. Mark and Amanda were in their office, seated on opposite sides of their antique partners' desk, going over the month's invoices, when the telephone rang. Mark answered. Moments later he set the receiver back in the cradle and stared numbly at his wife's bent head.

Amanda was squinting at a slip of yellow paper, her nose wrinkled. "I can't figure this one out," she muttered, comparing the paper to a computer printout, "and it doesn't seem to match any of the entries on the report. I think it's supposed to be the receipt for that spinning wheel we finally unloaded last week, but if it is, we're going to have to talk to Sandra again. She still doesn't know how to write up a consignment sale." Heaving a sigh of irritation, Amanda stretched across the desk to hand the receipt to Mark. "Here, will you please take a look at this and see if—'' She broke off, stunned by Mark's expression. His eyes were bleak, his face ashen and gaunt. The hand that still rested on the receiver trembled visibly. ''Mark?'' Amanda ventured, suddenly filled with dread. When he did not speak, she repeated his name. ''Mark, what's wrong? Who was that on the phone?''

His mouth moved, but no sound came out. He cleared his throat and tried again. ''That—that was your doctor,'' he croaked. ''He called to say he just got back the results of your amniocentesis.''

Amanda's heart faltered. She gulped and tasted acid. Hoarsely she pressed, ''And?''

''And he wants to talk to us. In his office. This afternoon. Now.''

Mark reached out and caught Amanda's hand. Gently he pried apart her paralyzed fingers, and the bill of sale fell to the desktop, wadded and illegible. Mark took a deep, stricken breath. ''Sweetheart,'' he said painfully, ''Steven wouldn't tell me over the phone just what the problem is, but he says the tests are absolutely conclusive. There's something wrong with the baby.''

CHAPTER THREE

STEVEN RHODES'S OFFICE STAFF had left for the day, and he was alone in the reception area when Mark and Amanda arrived. The instant they opened the door, the doctor stepped forward. He extended his hand formally to Mark, but his eyes focused on Amanda, who stood silently at her husband's side, her arm crooked lightly through his. Her pale face was expressionless. Steven's brow furrowed. "Thank you for coming so quickly," he murmured. His quiet voice echoed in the emptiness.

The two men shook hands gravely. "Thank you for waiting for us," Mark said, noting the direction of the doctor's worried gaze. He was worried for Amanda himself. She was . . . too still.

In their own office, when Mark had choked out the terse telephone message, he had expected Amanda to react with wails of anguish, perhaps even hysteria—not that he'd ever seen Amanda hysterical, of course. He knew she was a deeply passionate woman, yet in all the years they'd been together, she'd never let her emotions overwhelm her. She prided herself on her control—just as he himself did, Mark acknowledged with irony—but in truth, he realized suddenly, never in their decade of marriage had a situation arisen that would actually test their composure. Until now.

He looked at Amanda and wished that just this once she'd let go, vent her feelings. Surely it was better to cry, sob, rail at the heavens, than to suffer silently. Surely any kind of outburst was healthier than the mute misery with which she'd received the doctor's news. But no. As Mark had passed on Steven Rhodes's message, Amanda had withdrawn from him. All color had leached from her face, leaving only a chalky mask, and carefully she had arranged the papers she'd been sorting through into a neat pile on the blotter in front of her. Without a word she'd retrieved her handbag from the bottom drawer of the desk and tugged on her cardigan. She had not spoken when they locked the store, nor did she break the silence during the difficult drive out of the downtown area. While Mark bucked the rush-hour traffic heading toward the bridges that crossed the Willamette River, Amanda sat quietly beside him in the front seat of his Volvo station wagon, her eyes unblinking in the twilight, her small, cold hand resting limply on his thigh. Now, as Mark guided her into the doctor's office and settled her carefully into one of the chairs facing the desk, he wondered if she might be in shock.

A manila folder lay on the desk, and Mark could read the label bearing Amanda's name. Steven pulled a ballpoint pen from his pocket and started to open the folder. He hesitated. For a moment he chewed his lip in pensive silence. While he thought, he toyed with the pen, unscrewing the barrel, then tightening it again, over and over. As last he said tiredly, "Sometimes I hate my job. At moments like this I wish I'd dropped out of medical school and become a used-car salesman like my brother. I'd give anything not to be the one who has to tell you."

Mark, clutching his wife's hand, studied her drawn face with concern. Although she continued to display no visible reaction to the doctor's words, she looked almost old, he realized in amazement, wondering if his own expression was any less haggard. Maybe they were both old, he thought grimly. Maybe nobody was ever young and resilient enough to hear such news.

With difficulty he turned to Steven again and prompted, "You said there was something wrong."

The doctor took a deep breath. "I'm afraid the fetus Amanda is carrying has Down's syndrome."

The words beat at Mark's ears. *The fetus... has Down's syndrome.* Even as he struggled to absorb their meaning, Mark wondered at Steven's sudden use of medical terminology. The *fetus* had Down's syndrome. Two weeks earlier, during the sonogram, the life taking shape inside Amanda's body had been a baby.

"Down's syndrome," Mark echoed. "You mean it's a—a mongoloid?" He tried not to stumble over the words, but suddenly he found himself choking, sickened by visions of obese, clumsy children with vacant, slanted eyes and perpetually gaping mouths. From the deepest recesses of his mind welled up memories of taunting voices that jeered, *dummy, dummy....*

"'Mongoloid' is a term that's not used much anymore," Steven noted with a grimace, "but yes, we're talking about the same condition, the same genetic defect. Down's syndrome people are usually small, with certain distinctive facial characteristics, and they're usually developmentally delayed to some degree."

"And you think our baby—"

Steven interrupted him firmly. "I don't think, I know. I'm truly sorry, but the test results are incontrovertible. If you want me to, I'll show you the karyotype—the photographs of the chromosomes in the cells drawn during the amniocentesis. They give graphic proof that—''

"No," Amanda said.

The word was the first she'd spoken since entering the doctor's office, and the sound of her voice, sharp and clear, caught Mark by surprise. He turned to look at her. Color and animation had returned to her face, and Mark could see the obstinate tilt of her chin as she regarded the obstetrician.

"No, Steven," she repeated, her tone tolerant but determined, "you're wrong. Your test results are wrong. I don't care what you think your pictures, your kary-what's-its, show. Somebody's made a mistake." She tugged her hand from Marks' grasp and laid it in her lap. Her pursed lips softened to a beatific smile as her fingers fanned protectively over the curve of her belly. She murmured dreamily, "My baby's just fine."

Mark winced. "Oh, darling," he whispered, reaching for her again, "don't do this to yourself."

Amanda recoiled. Her dark eyes flashed. "I'm telling you, Mark, somebody has made a mistake," she repeated with asperity. "There is nothing wrong with my baby. If there was, believe me, I'd know."

"No, you wouldn't," Steven said with a quiet strength that commanded attention. "It's perfectly natural for you to want to deny news like this, Amanda, but the fact is, even though you are the one who's pregnant, there is no way you yourself can assess the health of the fetus. For that matter, neither can I, not without the right tests."

He flipped open the manila folder and pulled out a sheaf of papers, including odd, grainy black-and-white photographs of paired, lumpy-looking lines reminiscent of a preschooler's first clumsy attempt at printing. Spreading the pictures across the desk, he said, "Please, I want both of you to look carefully while I explain this. This is the karyotype from Amanda's amniocentesis."

Amanda squinted at the photographs, trying to understand. "You mean those—those squiggles are my genes?" she asked uneasily. There was something distasteful and distressing, a sense of violation, in knowing that her body had been probed clear down to the cellular level.

"Not yours," the doctor corrected. "This karyotype is a pictorial record of the genetic makeup of the fetus you're carrying. Even though it may look like a mass of squiggles to you, Amanda, it's amazing what a trained observer can learn by studying it." Steven drew a circle around one pair of lines. "Here, for example, are the chromosomes that determine the sex of the fetus. This bent line is the Y chromosome, and its presence indicates that the fetus is male." Lifting his head, Steven scowled. "I'm sorry. I just remembered that you two told me you didn't want to know the sex beforehand."

"We also told you the sex didn't matter as long as the baby was healthy," Mark reminded him roughly, waving aside the apology. "Please, Steven, just tell us what went wrong."

The doctor nodded and returned his attention to the karyotype. "You'll notice that the chromosomes come in pairs. That's how offspring combine the characteristics of their parents. Half of each pair is contributed by the father, the other half by the mother, twenty-three pairs in all for a total of forty-six chromosomes in the normal human cell. However—" He broke off.

"Something about these cells isn't normal," Mark finished drearily.

Steven took a deep breath. "No," he said, moving his pen farther down the photograph, "something about these cells isn't normal. If you'll look here on the twenty-first pair, you'll notice the difference. There's an extra chromosome. And as much as I hate to have to tell you, that extra chromosome is the signal for Down's syndrome."

Mark gulped. "But why?"

The doctor's expression was ironic. "How about asking me something easy, like how come things don't fall up? Don't you know that the one question science can never answer is *why*? We know how to recognize Down's syndrome, but we don't know why a third chromosome in that particular position triggers the condition, just as we don't know for certain why the offspring of older parents are more apt to be afflicted or why the severity of the condition varies so much from one patient to the next."

Amanda murmured, "But we must have done something wrong—"

"No!" Steven's usually mild voice was so sharp that Amanda jumped. A flush spread to the roots of his receding hairline as he insisted, "You didn't do anything wrong! If you're wondering whether either of you is somehow to blame for what's happened, that's a question I can answer, and the answer is no. You're both perfectly healthy, and Down's syndrome isn't an inherited defect in the sense that, for example, hemophilia is. It seems to be a genetic accident, one that can't be predicted or prevented. So, for heaven's sake, please don't compound this development with unnecessary guilt!"

For several seconds Amanda and Mark stared help-lessly at each other. Her hands had left her belly, and now, although the office was comfortably warm, she tugged her sweater tightly around her shoulders and clutched the lapels over her chest, as if warding off a chill. Mark remembered the day she had told him she was pregnant, how she had cradled an imaginary in-fant to her breast and whispered dreamily of nursing her baby. She closed her eyes now, and he could see her mouth quiver. He wondered if it was physically possi-ble for a heart to break.

Knowing he could not succumb to his own pain, knowing he must somehow remain strong for Aman-da's sake, Mark struggled to keep his voice steady as he addressed the doctor. "If there's no possibility of a mistake in the diagnosis and our baby really does have this syndrome, then—then just how bad is it?"

Steven sighed. "I'm afraid there's no way to tell. That extra chromosome is a signal, but it doesn't give any information about the severity of the condition. Down's syndrome can vary tremendously from one patient to the next. In some people the symptoms are mild enough that they are able to live virtually normal lives. In other very rare cases there are organic problems—with the heart, for example—so severe that survival is impossi-ble."

Amanda stirred in her seat. To Mark's amazement, when she spoke she still sounded hopeful. "So what happens now, Steven?" she asked, trusting. "How do I ensure our child is only mildly affected? You know I'll do absolutely anything you tell me to, even if it means staying in a hospital bed for the next four and a half months. Are there medicines I'm supposed to take? What about surgery? I've read about operations being performed on babies still in—in their mother's..." Her words trailed off as the doctor slowly shook his head.

"No, Amanda," Steven said gently. "There is nothing you can do to alter the fetus's condition. I told you before, Down's syndrome is a genetic mistake, something that's determined at the moment of conception, just as the fetus's sex is. It cannot be changed. Maybe someday medical science will find ways to ameliorate the symptoms, but for now there's no cure." He paused. "There is only a choice."

"'A choice'?" Amanda echoed uncertainly. "What choice?"

Steven glanced at Mark. For a long moment the men communicated without words while Amanda watched them in bewilderment. Digging her nails into the arms of her chair, she jerked her head back and forth as she grew increasingly agitated. Her long earrings tinkled, the bright musical sound jarring in the strained silence. "Why are you two looking at each other that way?" she demanded, her voice reedy with tension. "What's going on?"

Mark reached over and pried Amanda's clenched fingers loose from the upholstery and wrapped them reassuringly in his big, warm hand, while Steven rose from his chair and crossed around to the front of the desk. He squatted in front of Amanda so that his eyes were on a level with hers.

Amanda blinked hard. "I'm very confused," she whispered dreadfully. "You both seem to understand something that I don't. What's happening? What—what is this choice you mentioned?"

Steven took a deep breath. "I'm talking about the choice you're going to have to make, Amanda—a terrible choice but the only one you have in a situation like this. The choice between whether you want to deliver a handicapped baby in October, or whether you want to terminate the pregnancy now.''

THE APARTMENT WAS DARK. Sulfurous light spilling in through the picture window from a street lamp silhouetted the living room furniture in eerie detail, but the entryway was enveloped in shadow. While Mark closed the front door, Amanda automatically dropped her purse in its accustomed spot on the cherry secretary the two of them had rescued from a barn on Sauvie Island. When she reached for the switch on the wall above the desk, her hand froze. She wasn't ready to face brightness, the harsh glare of reality. Her eyes were burning; she needed darkness. She heard the dead bolt snap into place as Mark locked the door. Slowly she turned. Her husband loomed over her, a column of shade—the darkness she needed. Stifling a sob, Amanda fell into his arms.

They clung together in feverish silence, their suffering too intense for words. Amanda clutched frantically at Mark, nuzzled her face against him and tried to cry. Her eyes remained hot and itchy and dry. She blinked and rubbed her cheek against the lapels of his blazer. Through the soft fabric she could feel his heart beneath her ear, a sensation she had always found uniquely comforting, but its lurching arrhythmia was so unlike the slow, satisfied pulse she enjoyed listening to after lovemaking that it might have been a different organ beating inside his chest. She felt his tension increase. His grip tightened with suffocating force around her, and his rangy body began to shake. Above her she heard him utter a peculiar strangled sound, like a swallowed groan. Amanda lifted her head and squinted through the shadows. She tried to murmur his name, but before the sound could escape, his mouth was hard on hers. She could taste salt on his lips.

It was not an erotic kiss, but one of desperation, of two tortured souls meeting in the darkness, trying to absorb each other's strength. Mark held Amanda so tightly against him that she was certain the crest on his brass buttons must be imprinted on her breast. As they swayed and trembled, reeling against the anguish that buffeted them, his tears scalded her skin. She had never, ever known him to cry before. She envied him.

At last Mark lifted his head and framed Amanda's face with his hands, his thumbs tracing her cheekbones, his long fingers weaving into her short, silky hair. He sniffed and sighed deeply, raspily. "Darling, you're allowed to cry, too."

Shaking her head fiercely, Amanda wailed, "But I— I can't!" No matter how hard she squeezed her eyelids together, the release she craved refused to come. Her eyes remained dry. Her temples pounded. Every part of her ached, and every breath was edged with a strain so sharp she was afraid to inhale for fear of cutting herself. She wondered what would happen if she simply stopped breathing altogether.

But her breath did not stop, and her tears did not start. She held Mark and shook with frustration—the only time she could remember being unsatisfied in his embrace—until eventually sheer self-preservation forced her mind to retreat from the pain. She began to focus on more mundane matters. With a touch of mordant humor she registered the fact that as they fumbled around in the dark, paper was being crunched beneath their feet—undoubtedly the mail, which neither of them had bothered to pick up from the rug beneath the slot.

Amanda squirmed and cleared her throat. "I think we're tromping all over the bills," she said hoarsely.

Keeping one hand anchored at her waist, Mark reached past her to flip the wall switch. Light flooded the entryway, and Amanda winced at the brightness. When her eyes began to adjust, she peeped at her husband.

He looked...astonishingly normal, she decided, searching his features for signs of the emotions that had just racked him. A lock of sandy hair had fallen across his high forehead, but no shadows darkened his light eyes; no betraying moisture was beaded on his long lashes. Amanda felt almost annoyed that he could appear so cool.

And sound so composed, she added mentally when he glanced down at the magazines and envelopes lying crushed and soiled on the floor and joked, "Don't worry about the bills, darling. There are always plenty more where they—"

All at once Mark's composure evaporated. His face turned gray and he recoiled, jerking his hand from Amanda's waist as if she was burning him. Baffled, she gazed at him, waiting for an explanation, and then suddenly she gasped. She knew what had happened. He had felt the baby move.

Her eyes widened in dismay. Staggered by the implications of his rejection, she croaked, "For heaven's sake, Mark!"

She watched him visibly resume control of himself. He took a deep breath and squared his shoulders. His color returned to normal, but his voice sounded unnaturally low pitched. "I'm sorry. I didn't mean to cringe like that. It's just—it's just..." His words faltered and died.

Biting her lip, Amanda said, "We have to talk."

"I know." Mark laid his hands lightly on her shoulders. "Listen to me, love. I know we have to talk, I know there are things we have to work out as quickly as possible, but I also know you're in no shape right now to make any sort of plans."

She shrugged. "I'm all right."

Mark shook his head. "No, you're not. You're about ready to collapse. You're pale and shaky, and considering how late it is, you must be starving."

Amanda frowned petulantly. "I'm not starving. I may never eat again."

"Darling..." Mark chided her.

Amanda sighed. "Okay, okay, I realize I'm behaving childishly. I guess I just don't feel very... rational at the moment. They say shock does that to people—depletes the blood sugar or something. You're right. I'm sure I'll think a little more clearly once I've eaten—assuming I can figure out what to fix us that won't choke me."

"Why don't you let me worry about cooking dinner?" Mark suggested. "You need to rest. You sit down and put your feet up, while I see what sort of meal I can throw together for us."

"Are you certain?" Amanda asked, studying his face and suddenly realizing how tired and sallow Mark looked, his skin stretched like parchment over the strong bones. "I guess I'm being very selfish, aren't I?" she murmured contritely. "Here you are, so sweet and considerate of my needs, when all the time you must be hurting as badly as I am."

Mark's mouth twisted. "Don't worry about me. I'll survive," he muttered. "Right now your welfare is the most important consideration."

But what about the baby's welfare? Amanda pleaded silently, realizing as her mind shaped the words that she was not ready yet to speak them aloud. Suddenly she felt completely exhausted, the last reserves of her flagging strength drained. Her knees wobbled. "I think—I think maybe I do need to sit down, after all," she ventured in a thready whisper, swaying dizzily. Mark barked out her name and swept her up into his arms.

He carried her into the living room, striding across the lush Oriental rug to the long sofa beneath the picture window. After he settled her gently onto the cushions and helped her slip off her sweater and shoes, he started to turn on the table lamp beside her, but she shook her head. "Please leave it off. I'll rest better."

"Whatever you want," Mark said.

For a long moment he bent over her, his face sculpted by the stark streetlight, and Amanda had the feeling he was struggling for words. When he remained silent and stood to leave her, she clutched at his arm and blurted, "I love you so much, and I'm so scared for us!"

He caught her fingers in his. Pressing a soft kiss into the palm of her hand, he whispered, "I know, darling. I know." Then he turned and stalked out of the room.

Amanda shifted fitfully and tried to make herself comfortable, but the pillowy sofa felt hard and lumpy beneath her back, and the upholstery scratched. She could hear Mark moving around in the kitchen, rummaging through the cupboards. The noise disturbed her. She thought with compunction that she ought to be in there with him, assisting. She could at least set the table. The two of them always shared chores, and it seemed unnatural to leave all the work to him, no matter how much he wanted her to rest. But rest eluded her. She covered her eyes with her forearm, trying to block out the light streaming through the window. Finally she rose on her knees on the cushions, reaching over the back of the couch to tug the drapes closed. Instead she leaned her forehead against the cool glass and stared into the night.

Her eyes were drawn almost magnetically to the red beacon that hung in the sky above the twinkling lights of the city. The signal beamed from the peak of Mount Tabor, the volcanic cone that jutted abruptly from the flat expanse of eastern Portland. A thickly wooded recreation area covered the mountaintop. Amanda had not visited the park in years, but now she found herself reliving cherished memories of a day she'd spent there in the company of her father, when she was very little.

Alden had never been an indulgent parent, too preoccupied by the demands of his business and social life to pay much heed to the little girl who craved his attention, but for some never-explained reason, one sunny summer Saturday he had elected to spend the day with his daughter. He had driven her to Mount Tabor Park. The two of them had picnicked on the grass, hiked among the cedar and spruce, fed ducks in the pond, even played a clumsy but enthusiastic game of one-on-one on a small basketball court beside the road near the crest of the mountain. Alden had laughed more freely than Amanda could remember him ever doing, before or since, and her small heart had swelled with happiness as she basked in the glow of his undivided attention.

Then, without warning, the idyllic atmosphere of the day had changed, altered by her father's casual remark that the depression in which the court was located was actually the mouth of a volcano. Suddenly Amanda was petrified with fright. Alden's comment was meant to instruct and amuse her, but what he had not realized was that the only volcano Amanda had ever seen was on television, in an old movie where a Polynesian princess threw herself into a seething crater to appease angry gods. The image had terrified her. Certain the asphalt beneath her feet was about to crack open and spew forth lava, Amanda began to blubber.

When she saw the look of annoyance that crossed her father's face, an erupting volcano seemed far less ominous than the possibility of losing her father's approval, and quickly she stifled her fear. "I'm sorry, Daddy. I didn't mean to be silly and cry. I won't do it again. Please don't be mad at me," she had pleaded, scrubbing away the tears with her fists, and after a moment Alden's expression had softened.

To Amanda's amazement, he actually apologized. "I'm sorry, too, Mandy," he crooned, hugging her with uncharacteristic gentleness. "I didn't mean to scare you. I thought you understood." By tacit consent they abandoned their basketball game, and as the two of the strolled back toward their car, Alden tried to explain in simple terms how all the landscape of northern Oregon had been formed by volcanic activity. The momentary deviation from the day's mood was soon forgotten.

After the impromptu geology lesson, her father bore Amanda off to a pastry shop where he dazzled her by ordering a slice of a rich chocolate torte that Alden claimed the baker had prepared especially in Amanda's honor—one layer for every year of her age. By the time they reached home, she had been replete and limp with exhaustion. Amanda could remember Joan chiding Alden for permitting their daughter to become overtired. "You know how she gets. She won't sleep, she'll fret and fidget all night." But when Alden tucked her into bed, Amanda had dozed off at once, smiling in the afterglow of the most perfect day she'd ever known in all her short life.

That day with her father *had* been a perfect day, Amanda thought poignantly as she huddled on the couch and stared at the red beacon, the memory of which she still cherished some thirty-five years later. The day was all the more precious because it had been unique. Although Alden had promised that someday he'd take his daughter on another outing, afterward, whenever she pressed him, he always seemed to be too busy with work, or else he and Joan needed to dress for some social event. If Amanda wanted to play—somehow the pet name of Mandy was forgotten as easily as his promise—surely the maid could drive her over to visit one of her little school friends.... The day on Mount Tabor was never repeated. Eventually Amanda quit asking.

But she had continued to treasure the recollection of that summer afternoon, and ever since then she had looked forward eagerly to the time when she would be all grown-up, a mommy with children of her own, whom she would take to the park as often as they wished....

"Amanda, dinner's ready."

Mark's deep voice drifted through the apartment, interrupting her reverie. Amanda did not respond. She could smell chicken grilled with lemon pepper, but the usually appetizing aroma failed to stir her. All at once the ceiling fixtures flicked on, and her view of the city was marred by a dim reflection of the living room behind her, Mark standing beside the light switch. Amanda sighed and let the curtain slip through her fingers. As it fell into place across the window, she turned reluctantly to face her husband.

"Dinner's ready," Mark repeated quietly. His hair was tousled, and he'd finally discarded his blazer and tie. A smudged dish towel was secured around his narrow hips. He said, "I didn't fix much, just some spinach salad and chicken, but I figured quick was better than fancy."

"It smells wonderful," Amanda said politely. When she saw Mark's lips twist at her lack of enthusiasm, she levered herself off the sofa and padded across the rug in her stocking feet. Twining her arm through his, she walked with him into the dining room. They sat together at one end of the long, oval table, and Mark served her. When she saw the dark greens glistening with vinaigrette and the golden-brown chicken breast still sizzling from the broiler, she insisted, "I meant what I said a minute ago. The food looks and smells very good. It's just that I don't have much of an appetite right now."

Mark's brow creased slightly. "But you will eat, won't you?"

"Of course," Amanda said lightly, picking up her fork. "I promise I'll be a good, dutiful girl and clean my plate. After all, even if I'm not hungry, I still have to think about the—" She broke off abruptly and froze, her hand suspended in midair. The fork slipped through her fingers and fell with a clatter onto the tabletop. Amanda groaned.

"I can't do it," she whispered hoarsely, staring at her husband with wide, stricken eyes. "I tried—I really did—but I just can't sit here and eat and pretend everything is normal, when you and I both know nothing is ever going to be normal again."

Mark studied her ashen face and came to a decision. Expelling his breath in a huff, he said, "Okay, we'll talk now. I had thought that it might be better for us to postpone the discussion until we'd both had a chance to collect ourselves, but you're probably right. Waiting just makes it worse." He glanced at the two untouched plates of food. "Here, let me stick these in the refrigerator. We can always reheat the chicken later, if we still want it."

While Mark whisked their dinner back into the kitchen, Amanda returned to the living room. Her steps felt ponderous, plodding, weighted with the burden of her worries. She thought she could hear her heavy tread echo throughout the apartment. She curled onto one end of the couch and tucked her feet beneath her. As she waited for Mark to join her, she glanced around, observing her surroundings objectively, as if the condominium were simply another stop on the home tour conducted annually as a fund-raiser by one of Portland's civic groups.

The condo itself was nothing exceptional, as Amanda was the first to admit—the best thing about it was its location in the Council Crest district of the city—but she and Mark had decorated it with grace and imagination. They'd furnished the small, rather ordinary rooms with an eclectic mixture of antiques and contemporary pieces that reflected their excellent taste and transformed the flat into something of a showplace. Amanda loved the home she and Mark had made. It could not compare with the polished perfection of her parents' mansion on Cumberland Road, but she'd always been proud to show off the flat to visitors. She'd just never noticed before how quiet, how...hollow it seemed with only the two of them living there.

It was definitely a home for adults, Amanda conceded. Now that she thought about it, she realized their friends with families virtually never brought them along when they came to call. She wondered if people left their children behind because they knew the condo was filled with delicate treasures too tempting for clumsy, inquisitive hands. Or was it because the formal beauty of the place alarmed and intimidated little visitors? From personal experience Amanda was acutely aware of how difficult it could be for the average youngster to grow up inhibited by such surroundings. How much more constraining would such a life-style prove for a child already hampered by major disabilities?

Mark emerged from the kitchen carrying two glasses of white wine. "Here, maybe this will help you relax," he said, trying to hand her a wineglass. When she shook her head, he noted, "I know Steven told you to avoid alcohol, but I can't see how one glass of Chablis in four months is going to damage anything."

"Of course not," Amanda snapped waspishly. "The damage is already done." Watching Mark's mouth tighten, she accepted the glass. As she inhaled the bouquet, she grumbled contritely, "Oh, hell, I'm sorry. I didn't mean to sound like a bitch."

Mark sank onto the couch beside her, so close his thighs brushed her bent legs. He patted her knee, rubbing her nylon-clad skin in long strokes that mimicked the soothing cadence of his voice as he murmured, "I don't think you sound like a bitch. You just sound tired and heartsick."

"'Heartsick,'" Amanda echoed as she sipped her wine. "That's a good word for it. My heart is sick, weak and shaky. I don't think it will ever recover from the shock of hearing Steven Rhodes tell me to have an abortion.''

Mark's fingers stilled on her leg. ''You're not being fair, you know. Steven didn't tell you to do anything. He only pointed out your options.''

''Yes, and what wonderful options they are. Either I wait another four and a half months to see if I'm going to give birth to a baby who's severely handicapped, or else I go ahead and kill it now.''

For several moments her bitter words hung between them, ugly and full of pain, until finally Mark said with care, ''Maybe you'd be better off if you tried to be a little more objective. At first I couldn't understand why Steven suddenly quit talking about the 'baby' and started referring to it as the 'fetus.' Now I realize that was his way of distancing himself from the problem, putting it in perspective. Maybe you should do the same.''

Amanda's dark eyes grew round with despair. She set her wineglass on the arm of the couch and laid her hands on her belly, shaping the swelling mound through the thickness of her dress. ''Tell me, please,'' she asked, her voice low and desolate, ''exactly how am I supposed to put things in perspective when the problem you want me to distance myself from is growing inside my own body? Every time it moves, I feel it.''

Before Mark could stop her, she grabbed his wrist and deliberately forced him to fan his fingers across her stomach. From his strained expression and the tension in his arm, she knew he was struggling not to flinch. ''You feel it, too,'' she ordered. ''That's a baby in there, not an *it*.''

''Listen to me, Amanda—''

"No, damn it, you listen!" she cried. "This isn't a space movie, and my body hasn't been invaded by some alien creature. This is our child we're talking about—our son!"

As he gently freed himself from her grasp, Mark said, "But it doesn't have to be."

The quiet strength in his voice dampened Amanda's rising hysteria. She picked up her glass of Chablis again and gulped it to the dregs. Staring at Mark, she whispered dreadfully, "You—you think I ought to have an abortion, don't you?"

He massaged the bridge of his noise as if the old fracture ached, rubbing the slight dip with his fingertips until a blotch of red formed, clownish against his pallor. He sipped his own wine in silence. Then he said slowly, "I think, my darling, that you ought to do what's best for the most people—you and me, for example. We have a good life now, one we've worked long and hard to achieve. Consider what it would mean for us to start raising a handicapped baby at our age. God knows neither of us is all that young anymore. As you yourself pointed out once, we'll be eligible for Social Security by the time he's grown. Even under the best of circumstances, it's going to be difficult. Just imagine coping with a teenager when we're in our sixties! But at least with a normal child, there'd be an end to it eventually. With Down's syndrome, in all likelihood we'd be committing ourselves to taking care of him for literally the rest of our lives."

Mark paused for breath. "And if you think it's selfish of me to be so concerned about our personal welfare, if the prospect still doesn't faze you, then at least give a little thought to the child himself. What would his future be like, the quality of his life?"

"But we don't know what the quality of his life would be like," Amanda pointed out. "Steven said there's no way to tell from the test just how badly the baby is affected. He might be almost normal."

"Or he might not be." Mark emptied his wineglass and set it on the cocktail table. Leaning closer, he propped his arm along the back of the sofa so that his fingertips brushed his wife's neck. "Listen to me, Amanda," he urged, toying with her dangling earring. "Whether you believe it or not, I find all this as painful as you do. I feel as if we're the butt of some cruel, hateful joke, and it makes me want to hit something, someone. Only there's nobody to hit. You heard what the doctor said. It's not anyone's fault. What has happened is a random genetic mistake, and now it's up to you and me to correct that mistake."

"But does it have to be by aborting this baby?" Amanda asked tremulously.

"Unfortunately, that seems to be the only option available." Mark paused, frowning pensively. Then he ventured, "You know, there's something I don't understand. You've always been a staunch advocate of a woman's right to choose whether or not she'll terminate a pregnancy. Haven't you ever asked yourself what choice *you'd* make?"

She shook her head. "Considering how badly I've always wanted to have a baby, it never occurred to me there could be circumstances under which I might want to... not have one."

"But what about the amniocentesis?" Mark persisted. "I know that Steven and the genetic counselor tried to explain its purpose to you. Didn't you listen? Didn't you understand that the whole point of the test is to discover whether the fetus has any abnormalities?

It should enable you to make an informed decision as to whether you want to proceed with your pregnancy. If you know there were no circumstances under which you'd ever contemplate abortion, why did you put yourself through such a painful, dangerous procedure at all?''

Amanda's expression was ironic. ''I didn't think of it that way. I guess I was naive ... or maybe downright stupid. From the moment I found out I was pregnant, I've done whatever the doctors have told me to, from giving up alcohol to actually trying to eat liver now and then. To me the amnio was just one more thing I had to endure to make sure the baby was all right. I never let myself consider that it might not be.''

''And now that you have considered?'' Mark pressed.

Amanda bit her lip. ''Oh, God, I don't understand anything anymore,'' she declared despairingly. ''I feel like someone who's spent years of agony in a hospital and then on the day she's finally cured and released, on the way home she gets hit by a truck. What possible sense does it make to let me finally conceive after all these years and then snatch the baby away?''

''There could still be another baby, you know,'' Mark pointed out quietly.

Amanda snorted. ''When? When I'm fifty-two? You know how long we tried without success. Do you really think lightning is liable to strike us a second time in the same decade?''

Mark attempted to smile. ''We'll just have to work at it that much harder,'' he murmured, cupping her cheek. He trailed his fingers over the delicate line of her jaw and down her throat, until they dipped into the neckline of her blouse and settled on the lush curve of her breasts. His voice deepened to an insinuating growl as he added, "I know I'd be willing to make any extra effort required."

"But I wouldn't," Amanda said simply, laying her hand over his to still his downward progress. "Not the way you mean. I couldn't risk becoming pregnant and having to face these same decisions all over again. I couldn't bear it, emotionally or physically."

"I know it wouldn't be easy—"

"'Wouldn't be easy'?" she choked out. "My God, Mark, do you have any idea what a second-trimester abortion entails? Usually when a woman is as far along as I am, they give her a shot to induce labor, and she actually has to endure all the pain and trauma of delivery, but then the baby is . . . stillborn." Amanda shuddered, and her voice sounded wistful, distant. "I guess I should have known this was going to happen. I had nightmares, but I didn't understand what they really meant. I dreamed I gave birth, only—only there was no baby. . . ."

Studying her ghastly expression, Mark told her, "Then we'll adopt. One way or another you'll have your baby yet, Amanda—I promise you. The world is full of children who need someone to love them."

"Our own child will need love more than most," she reminded him softly.

Mark looked chagrined. "I know, darling, I know," he said, letting his hand fall away from her, taking care not to touch her belly as he shifted away from her on the couch. "I know the child you're carrying will require an extra measure of love just to survive in this world, much less thrive. But, God help me, what I don't know is whether I'm capable of giving him that love."

CHAPTER FOUR

To Amanda's surprise, no bad dreams disturbed her during the night, but her sleep was fitful and unsatisfying, and she awoke in the morning as tired as she'd felt the evening before. When she dragged herself to her feet, she noticed that Mark's pillow had been pounded into a shapeless mass and his sheets were tumbled. Usually they slept snuggled together in the center of the king-size bed, but during the night both of them had been so restless, tossing and twisting, that they had remained on their own sides of the wide mattress. Apart from a perfunctory good-night kiss, they had not touched.

She could hear Mark in the shower. She thought of other mornings when she'd awakened to the musical sound of water sluicing down the glass walls of the steamy cubicle. Invariably he invited her to join him there, and more often than not, she did. Today she was afraid that if she went into the bathroom, he might ignore her. She pulled on her robe and trudged off to the kitchen.

When they met a little later at the dining room table, conversation was desultory. Amanda had donned one of her favorite new maternity dresses, a high-waisted blue denim jumper with a ruffled hem, which she wore over a blouse of cool eyelet cotton with a deep V neck. Cameo earrings underscored the vague frontier style of the ensemble. More than once in the past Mark had complimented her on the outfit—he claimed he particularly appreciated the way the dress emphasized her burgeoning bustline—but today he seemed not to notice.

Amanda nibbled her toast without enthusiasm. Finally she announced, "I'm going to be a couple of hours late getting to work this morning."

Mark's offhand nod did not match his wary expression. "Stay home as long as you like. Sandra and I can cope. In fact, if you don't feel like coming to the store at all today—"

"I'll be there later this morning," Amanda said. "I want to drop by my parents' house first. I need to talk to them."

Mark refilled his coffee cup and stared at the curls of vapor wafting up from the surface of the black brew. "Do you want me to come with you?" he asked tonelessly.

Amanda shook her head. She was amazed at how unruffled she sounded, how civilized. "No, thanks. I'll manage." She started to take another bite of toast and discovered that she had crumbled the crisp bread between her fingers; buttered crumbs littered the tabletop. "Oh, damn," she muttered, reaching for her napkin.

Mark sighed and set down his coffee. His light blue eyes were compassionate. Touching her arm, his fingers strong and reassuring on her skin, he said quietly, "Amanda, please. This isn't some British play, and you don't have to keep a stiff upper lip while the world crashes in on you—" his voice roughened "—and you most certainly don't have to face your parents alone when you tell them about the baby. Considering how much they're looking forward to this grandchild, I know it's going to be difficult to explain what's happened—maybe impossible. For your sake, if not for theirs, I think I should be there with you when you try."

Amanda glanced at her husband's hand and thought of the bleak, lonely hours the two of them had just spent, when they'd both been so wrapped up in their own misery that neither had been able to reach across the cold percale sheets to offer comfort to the other. She wondered if the night had presaged a new phase in their relationship. Meeting Mark's gaze squarely, she insisted, "This is something I have to do on my own."

"But why?" he queried. "From the beginning, you and I have always done everything together. Why change now? I'm well aware that my relationship with Alden and Joan is problematic, even after all these years, but they are my in-laws. Apart from you they're the only family I have. Why are you suddenly so eager to cut me off from them?"

"Why are you so eager to cut yourself off from your own child?" Amanda demanded inexorably, tugging her arm loose, and for the first time Mark began to sense the deep, driving anger fueling her pain.

"That's not fair, Amanda. It's not the same thing at all."

"I think maybe it is." Pushing her chair back from the table, she methodically swept the fragments of toast onto her plate and carried it into the kitchen. When she returned to the dining room, her face was set, as austerely beautiful as an ivory mask. "I'm leaving now," she announced without preamble. "I should make it to the shop before noon. In the meantime, please tell Sandra it's time to polish the depression glass in the big hutch. Somebody's been fingering the Fostoria, and I noticed prints all over it. And while you're at it, why don't you ask her about that receipt for the spinning wheel? The girl's never going to be a success in the antique business if she doesn't learn how to write up a simple consignment sale."

Before Mark could respond, Amanda was gone.

"GOOD MORNING, MRS. WEXLER," the maid greeted her, holding the door wide for Amanda to step into the terrazzo-tiled entry. "Your father isn't here right now, but I believe Mrs. Smollet is working in her garden. Shall I tell her you're here?"

Amanda shook her head. "No, thanks, Inez. I'll go on out back and see her there. Heaven help anybody who tries to drag my mother away from her roses...."

"Especially now, so close to the festival," Inez said with a grin.

"Right. At all costs we must never forget the Rose Festival," Amanda concurred. As she traversed the long corridor, parlor and solarium until finally she emerged through the back door into her mother's formal garden, she thought about the spectacular celebration held each June. The Portland Rose Festival featured a huge floral parade, concerts, fireworks and sports ranging from regattas and hot-air balloon races to skiing atop Mount Hood, but in the Smollet household the one event of any real significance during the ten-day-long gala was the International Rose Show. For as long as Amanda could remember, her mother had been an active participant.

In Portland, the City of Roses, Joan Smollet's roses were renowned. Bed after impressive bed of beautifully groomed bushes thick with magnificent flowers marched in terraced steps down the hillside overlooking the city, and through the years both her gardens and individual blooms had won so many awards that finally, in fairness to other contestants, Joan had retired from competition and concentrated her efforts on judging. Once, while Amanda strolled through Lloyd Center viewing the blossoms that had been entered in the show, she had overheard a disgruntled rosarian gripe that it had been just his luck to be rated by Joan Smollet's team of judges, because nobody's flowers could possibly hope to meet her exacting standards. Amanda had considered interrupting the man's complaints to inform him that her mother's own roses met and surpassed those standards.

The morning sky was overcast but still bright. Shading her eyes, Amanda stood on the patio and scanned the garden, which extended to the property line far down the slope. The air on the hillside was so quiet that she could hear bees buzzing. The rose beds had been expanded over thirty years ago; before that there had been a big glass greenhouse where Joan's floribunda bushes now grew, and a tall evergreen hedge had separated the garden from a lawn equipped with a swing set and sandbox.

One long-ago spring, Amanda recalled, her mother had had a professional beekeeper install a couple of hives near the greenhouse, presumably to improve pollination. Amanda supposed the experiment must not have proved a success—at any rate, it was never repeated after that one year—but she still remembered how fascinating the humming white boxes had seemed to her, especially after her parents sternly ordered her to stay far away from them. Dutiful child that she was, Amanda had obeyed—until the day in the fall when the beekeeper returned to remove the hives.

Peeking around a corner of the greenhouse, Amanda had gawked in amazement as the man in the veiled hat fearlessly waved his smoker and subdued the angry insects swarming around him. He cracked open one of the hives and pulled out a thick slab of comb dripping with amber honey. Amanda's mouth had watered for a taste, but she had known her mother and father would never permit her to eat raw honey, which was probably full of dirt and heaven only knew what kind of germs. But the beekeeper, glancing surreptitiously over his shoulder, had broken off a small piece of the waxy stuff and held it out to Amanda in his big gloved palm. She gasped, stunned not just by his casual disregard for her parents' wishes but by the realization that she too had a mind of her own, that it was in fact possible for her to deliberately act in a manner contrary to their will. She had grinned conspiratorially and snatched the honeycomb from the man's hand. Huddled in her secret hideaway—a hollow space under the hedge—she had chewed thoughtfully on her illicit treasure, savoring the sweetness of disobedience for the first time, and the only thing that had dampened her delight in the forbidden treat was the realization that the honey sticking to her face and fingers smelled exactly like attar of roses, her mother's favorite perfume.

At last Amanda located Joan two levels down, crouched over a bed of hybrid teas. Although on occasion Joan hired a man to help her with heavy jobs like trenching and cultivating, she did all the rest of the gardening herself. Amanda watched with amusement as her mother stood up and dumped an armload of grass trimmings into a wheelbarrow filled with weeds, leaves and other garden rubbish. She wiped her hands on her overalls, leaving long streaks of damp, black earth on

the crisp poplin, and she straightened the ragged brim
of the shady straw hat that had been part of her gardening costume for almost as long as Amanda could
remember. Ordinarily Joan was the most fastidious
person in the world, the sort who'd faint before she'd
appear publicly in soiled or worn clothing, but when it
came to her rose bushes, no task was too dirty, sweaty
or smelly. Amanda wondered sometimes if her mother
would be half as casual with a grandchild.

Joan spotted Amanda and waved. When Amanda
started down the flagstone stairs, her mother called,
"Careful, dear. I've been watering and the steps are
slippery." They met beside a Tropicana rose, its coral-
orange blossoms vivid against the dark foliage. Joan
tucked her pruning shears into the pocket of her overalls and kissed Amanda's cheek. "What brings you here
this morning? Don't you have to work today?"

"I'll be going into the shop a little later," Amanda
said, "but first I need to talk to you and Father."

"Your father isn't here right now. He had a golf date
this morning. I believe Jim Bishop is one of the four-
some." Joan peered narrowly at Amanda. "Are you
feeling all right? You look a little peaked."

"I—I'm okay," Amanda murmured, hesitating under her mother's watchful gaze, suddenly doubtful she
had the courage to relay her news. "I do need to tell you
something, but I guess it—it can..." Her voice thick-
ened and failed.

"Amanda," Joan chided her, "it's not polite to leave
people dangling like that."

Clearing her throat, Amanda said glumly, "I know.
It's just that I think I'd better wait until Father is here,
too."

Joan looked affronted: "There's nothing you can say to your father that you can't say to me."

"Maybe not, but it would be easier for me if I didn't have to say it twice." Seeing her mother's hurt expression, Amanda sighed. "Please, I'm sorry if I've offended you. I certainly didn't mean to. Only, well, it occurs to me that I barged in here assuming you and Father would just drop whatever you're doing in order to listen to my problems. I never even asked whether the time was convenient for you, which clearly it isn't. I mean, Father's out at the country club, and you're obviously busy getting ready—"

"Young lady, you're babbling."

"Yes, Mother." Desperately Amanda tried to change the subject. Turning to the tall rose bush beside her, she cupped one of the brilliant blossoms in her hands and inhaled the rich, fruity fragrance. "I love Tropicanas—the color, the scent.... They're just about my favorite of all your flowers. I've never seen anybody else's that could touch them. I've always thought it was a shame you stopped competing."

Joan smiled. "Well, I figured it was time to let someone else have a chance," she murmured, pulling the shears from her pocket. "Here, let me give you one for your desk at work." Expertly she scanned the bush for a bloom opened to the right stage for cutting, and she snipped off the cane with deft fingers. As she trimmed off the thorns, she told her daughter, "We'll get some paper to wrap— Oh, no."

Startled by Joan's cry of dismay, Amanda demanded, "What's the matter?"

"Just look," Joan said with distaste, holding the rose gingerly for Amanda's inspection.

Amanda blinked at the fragrant orange bud, which to her seemed as wonderful as before. On close examination she noticed that a single petal appeared to be shaped a little oddly, but the distortion did not affect the beauty of the blossom. "I don't see anything wrong with it," she ventured, "except possibly that one petal—"

"It should be perfect," Joan said flatly. Before Amanda could stop her, her mother tossed the rose into the wheelbarrow full of garden waste. "Sorry about that, dear," she muttered, turning to stride up the steps. "It looks as if I won't be able to give you any of my Tropicanas, after all. Can't be too careful—it could be thrips, in which case the whole bed may be infested. Perhaps once I've sprayed... In the meantime, why don't we got back up to the patio? I've been working out here almost since sunup, and a break sounds very appealing to me right now."

After Inez set refreshments on the wrought-iron patio table, Joan dropped her hat on one of the extra chairs, and she and Amanda basked in the warm morning air and sipped coffee.

Amanda stirred cream into hers and observed, "You know, it never fails to amaze me how much you actually accomplish this time of year. It's all Mark and I can do to keep up with the tourists who come into the store during the festival, but you— Honestly, Mother, I get tired just thinking about your schedule! Not only do you have this huge garden to take care of, which is a full-time job in itself, but you always participate in a number of social events, and then with the judging—"

"I'm not going to be a judge this year," Joan said.

Amanda stared. "You're kidding."

"Oh, no, I'm quite serious," Joan insisted. "I've been judging rose shows for ten years now, and when you take into consideration the time I spent studying and testing and apprenticing before I earned my accreditation, I do believe I've done more than my share. I'll still be hosting my annual party, of course, but after that I intend to relax. As much as I love roses, I'm ready to concentrate on other things—such as becoming a grandmother."

Joan swallowed the last of her coffee and set down the cup. Lounging back in her chair, she crossed her legs and eyed her daughter levelly. "And now, Amanda Louise Smollet Wexler, I think you've hedged long enough. Quit trying to stall me with small talk and tell me what's wrong."

Praying for courage, Amanda said helplessly, "I don't know where to begin."

"The beginning is always a good place." Joan pursed her lips. "You know, dear, no matter how much a couple want children, starting a family invariably puts a lot of stress on a marriage. Are you and Mark having problems?"

Amanda toyed with the loose folds of her denim jumper. "Not . . . exactly the way you mean, Mother."

Joan's hazel eyes narrowed as she watched Amanda's nervous fingers. "Does it have something to do with the baby?" When Amanda failed to respond, Joan pressed, "Isn't about now when you should be getting back the results of that medical test you took a couple of weeks ago?"

Amanda nodded jerkily, a sour taste in her mouth. Gulping, she whispered, "The doctor called yesterday. He told us the baby is a boy—"

"A grandson? How wonderful!"

"And he told us our baby has Down's syndrome."

Joan blinked. "Oh, my God," she breathed, clenching the metal arms of her chair so tightly that her knuckles blanched and tendons stood out in her slim hands, making them look ropy and arthritic. "Oh, my God."

"Dr. Rhodes says there's no way to tell in advance how badly the baby will be affected," Amanda rushed on, trying to give her mother reassurance that she herself did not feel. "He might be almost normal."

Joan shook her head as if to clear it. Then she lifted her chin and squinted at Amanda. "What have you done?" she demanded harshly.

Recoiling from her mother's accusing glare, Amanda gasped. "What do you mean, what have I done? Are you trying to say it's my fault the baby's...damaged?"

"You must have done something wrong," Joan insisted in a rush. "Things like this don't just happen. You must have taken drugs—and no, I don't mean illegal drugs, but some medication with horrible side effects, like Thalidomide all those years ago—or else you strained yourself working in your store, pushing around furniture and crates that were too heavy for you, or—" she flushed "—or maybe you and Mark did something weird when you . . . you—"

Amanda fought back the urge to titter nervously. "For your information," she interrupted, hoarse with embarrassment, "there is no such thing as sex 'weird' enough to produce Down's syndrome. Drugs don't cause it, and neither does overexertion. Contrary to what you said a second ago, things like this *do* just happen. My obstetrician called Down's syndrome a 'genetic accident.'"

"But there's never been any history of genetic problems in our family," Joan said doggedly. "I can't recall ever hearing of birth defects on either your father's side or mine." She paused. "But, of course, that's only half the story, isn't it? What about Mark's family? He's never talked about them. Is he even familiar with their medical history? Damn it, I always knew that eventually you'd regret marrying a man with no background—"

"Mother!" Amanda exclaimed indignantly, half rising from her seat.

Joan had the grace to look abashed. She rubbed her aching eyes and exhaled raggedly. "Oh, Lord, Amanda, I'm sorry. That was snobbish and uncalled-for. Mark's a good man, and over the years he's proved a far better husband to you than your father and I ever imagined he could be. I didn't mean to put him down. Right now I feel so shocked and sickened that I scarcely know what I'm saying."

Hearing the weary regret in her mother's voice, Amanda subsided. "I suppose it's only natural to lash out at any convenient target," she conceded. "Mark said he'd like to punch somebody. I want to throw things. But Steven—Dr. Rhodes, my obstetrician—was adamant. He told us it's stupid to waste time looking for a scapegoat that isn't there. He said what we really need to do is accept the situation as a fact as quickly as possible, because only then can we decide how we're going to deal with it."

Joan nodded, collecting herself. "That sounds reasonable. This doctor of yours must have a lot of common sense. You ought to listen to his advice."

Amanda made a face. "I can't. Steven is so sensible that he refuses to give advice. He outlined our options, but he insists on remaining neutral. He says Mark and I have to make up our own minds what we're going to do.''

''And have you?''

''Made up our minds, you mean?'' Amanda queried, her tone heavy with irony. ''Mark has. It took him about thirty seconds to come to a decision. He thinks I ought to have an abortion.''

Joan winced. ''What an ugly word,'' she muttered. She studied her daughter thoughtfully. ''I gather you don't agree with Mark?''

''I don't know whether I do or not,'' Amanda admitted frankly. ''I'm discovering feelings I never knew I had. I want this baby so much, and the idea of terminating my pregnancy sickens and terrifies me—but so does the prospect of trying to raise a child with Down's syndrome.'' She lifted her shoulders in an exaggerated shrug. ''It's a hell of a choice.''

Instead of responding at once, Joan busied herself with the silver coffee service. She looked questioningly at Amanda's cup, but Amanda waved her back, saying, ''I've already taken in too much caffeine this morning. If I drink any more, I'm liable to have heartburn all day.''

''You wouldn't want this stuff anyway,'' Joan concurred, pouring the rest into her own cup and grimacing when she tasted it. ''It's cold and vile.'' She called for Inez, who appeared promptly and bustled back into the house with the pot to refill it; seconds later, it seemed, she returned with fresh coffee and rolls.

Watching the little domestic scene, Amanda was impressed by the woman's efficiency, but she suspected her mother was less interested in a hot beverage than she was in stalling for time while she thought.

Amanda's suspicions were confirmed when Joan poured herself a cup of coffee and then ignored it. She propped her elbows on the wrought-iron table, laced her fingers together and rested her chin on her hands. Staring past Amanda, her gaze directed out over the city spread in a panorama before her, Joan mused in a peculiar diffident voice, "You know, under most circumstances I don't really approve of abortion. I can't honestly say my reservations have any religious basis— I've never believed that God intended women to be forced to bear children they didn't want or couldn't raise—yet somehow the whole idea of abortion strikes me as terribly distasteful. I suppose that's partly because when I was of childbearing age, the operations were still clandestine and illegal and very dangerous. In fact, in college I was acquainted with a girl who—" Joan broke off abruptly. After a moment she took a deep breath and continued. "But things are different now, Amanda. For women of your generation, abortion is an option, one more way to cope with a difficult situation. And as much as it hurts me to say it, in a case like yours, when the only alternative is to give birth to a severely disabled child, I think your husband is probably right. I think it would be best for you and Mark, for everyone, if you end this pregnancy now."

As Amanda listened to her mother, it occurred to her that this was the first genuinely serious conversation the two of them had had in twenty years. The last time she could remember discussing anything significant with Joan had been when she'd flown home from Bryn Mawr to try to explain to her parents why she'd broken off her engagement to what's-his-name in Philadelphia—and that "discussion" had consisted mainly of Amanda shaking with barely suppressed rage while her mother pontificated on what a fool she was to throw away such a good catch. At that moment, Amanda had vowed never again to live in her parents' house. As soon as she'd finished school, she found a place of her own, where she was determined to meet life on her own terms. A decade later when she and Mark decided to marry, she had presented him to her parents not for their approval but as a fait accompli.

But now Amanda and Joan were communicating as equals, two mature individuals debating a vital issue, and the interaction felt good. In light of their newfound rapport, Amanda was truly sorry she couldn't agree with her mother's point of view.

Taking a deep breath, Amanda asked, "Has it occurred to you that if I lose this baby, you'll never have any grandchildren?"

Joan's tone was wistful but resigned. "A long time ago your father and I accepted that for one reason or another we'd probably never be grandparents. If we have to, we'll survive that disappointment again."

"But you don't have to," Amanda said.

The creases on Joan's forehead deepened, and two sharp lines bracketed her mouth. "Are you trying to get me to tell you I think any grandchild, even a retarded one, is better than none at all?" she demanded, her words edged with exasperation. "I'm sorry, but I can't say that because I don't believe it's true. I want to be able to take pride in my grandchild. I want to be able to look at him and know that after your father and I are gone, our lineage will continue, as strong and vigorous as before. If that's not possible, then I'd rather see us end abruptly, with you, instead of slowly petering out like some of those old royal families you hear about, so inbred that everybody's either a bleeder or a raving lunatic."

Amanda flinched, and her mother paused to frame her next words. "My dear," she resumed earnestly, "I understand that personal convenience is not the only thing at stake here. There are moral issues involved, and you must believe I'd never try to talk you into something that would violate your principles. But there's another point to consider. What about the baby? Isn't it selfish and a bit cruel to deliberately bring a handicapped child into the world just because you want to be a mother?"

"Mark asked me more or less the same thing last night," Amanda murmured, studying her hands, twisting her wedding ring. "I've been thinking about it ever since, and finally I've decided that's not a valid question. No one deliberately sets out to produce a handicapped child, but every pregnancy presents the possibility of birth defects. The risk has always been there. The only thing that makes it different now is that we know in advance. If it wasn't for the amniocentesis, we wouldn't be having this conversation. We wouldn't find out about the Down's syndrome until after our son was born, and then nobody would be trying to decide whether he should be... terminated."

"But there might be other equally painful decisions you'd have to make," Joan countered. "When I was a girl, a lady I knew, one of my mother's friends, lost a baby—or, at least, that's what I was told. It wasn't until years later that Mama let it slip that the child had been a mongoloid and its parents put it in an asylum rather than take it home. The poor thing eventually passed away in the institution—pneumonia, I believe—without ever learning to walk or talk. Mama said its death was a blessed release."

Amanda shuddered, as horrified by her mother's casual callousness as she was by the incident described. For the first time she wondered if she wasn't being foolishly optimistic to hope her parents could accept a grandchild who failed to meet their lofty standards. Huskily Amanda insisted, "People are a little more enlightened now than when you were a girl, Mother. They don't hide handicapped children in the attic anymore."

Something in Amanda's tone caused Joan to recognize her lack of tact. "Oh, no, no, of course not," she agreed quickly. "Times have changed, thank God—although probably not as much as you think. It's still not an easy world for the disabled."

Amanda pointed out, "It's not an easy world for anybody, yet somehow we manage."

"But could your child?" Joan pressed. "I will concede that I've heard Down's syndrome babies can be very sweet and loving, and, naturally, I've seen the occasional news report about the Special Olympics, which is very touching and inspirational, but what happens to these children when they're no longer so young or so cute? How do they cope as adults?"

"It's my understanding that with proper education and supervision, many are able to lead fairly normal lives," Amanda said.

"'Fairly normal,'" Joan repeated, shaking her head. "What a delightful prospect...." She hesitated a moment before continuing with care, "You know, Amanda, although it's obvious you've already made up your mind what you intend to do, there's another point you need to consider before you commit yourself to any particular course of action. I'm not sure how your father is going to react to this news—"

"He'll hate it."

"Of course, he'll hate it! Any sane person would hate it. That's not what I meant," Joan dismissed impatiently. "I'm talking about what Alden will do if you present him with a grandson who's mentally retarded."

Amanda murmured, "I hope that in time Father might learn to accept him."

"And he would, at least in a familial sense," Joan said. "Your father is not so narrow-minded or prejudiced that he'd disown his own flesh and blood. He wouldn't turn against an innocent child for being…less than sound. Neither would I, for that matter. But your baby's condition does have certain ramifications for the future. There are practical problems that will have to be resolved. For instance, I suppose that educational trust fund Alden just established will go to waste now—"

"Not necessarily," Amanda tried to interrupt, but her mother plowed on.

"And what about the rest of your father's estate? Even though he sold his company years ago, he still owns a lot of property and other assets that have to be managed. Of course, after we're dead, at first everything will be yours, but Alden is not going to be very happy to learn that eventually the fruits of all his years of hard work may be inherited by someone incapable of handling—"

"Mother!" Amanda cut in, almost shouting. Joan broke off and gaped at her, flabbergasted. "Mother," Amanda repeated in a more normal voice, but with bitter emphasis, "I don't care what you and Father do with the estate. It's yours, and you must dispose of it

however you think best. I don't want your money, for myself or for my child."

Joan grimaced skeptically. "It happens to be a great deal of money."

"I know that," Amanda snapped. "I also know Father worked very hard for every penny. Personally I wish the two of you would find some way to blow it all on yourselves while you still have the energy to enjoy it. You told me what a good time you had in Japan—maybe you could go back there again. If you want to tour all the Orient, or the whole world, that's fine with me. It's your money. Spend it on yourselves. You already invested a fortune on my upbringing and education. I don't need any more."

Amanda fell silent, her anger fading as she thought poignantly, *All I've ever needed more of from you and Father is love, and that's the one thing neither of you seems capable of giving me.*

Studying her daughter's mournful expression, Joan said quietly, "I know you're not a mercenary person, Amanda, and if I seemed to be advising you to consider the possibility of an abortion in terms of money, then I apologize. That would be a heinous thing to suggest. What I'm trying to do is remind you that life is a series of trade-offs. If you keep this child, then you may discover that you have to give up other things that are equally important to you. Just make sure you understand what they are before you throw them away."

She glanced at her wristwatch and exclaimed, "Oh, my, I had no idea it was so late. I should have cleaned up ages ago. Your father ought to be home from the golf club any time now, and as soon as he's showered and changed, the two of us are supposed to meet some people down at the marina." She peered narrowly at

Amanda. "Of course, I could always cancel, if you need me here...."

Waving aside her mother's suggestion, Amanda reached for the silver pot. "Please, you go ahead and get ready for your appointment. I'm going to drink one last cup of coffee, after all, and then I have to leave for work."

Joan looked speculative. "You're not going to wait for Alden?"

Amanda shook her head tiredly. "I don't think I have the guts to face Father right now."

"Does that mean you want me to tell him?"

"If you would."

Joan sighed. "Very well, dear. Whatever you want." Bracing her palms on the edge of the table, she pushed back her chair and levered herself clumsily to her feet. "In that case, I'll go on inside now," she said. Then she leaned over and kissed Amanda's forehead. "I'll pray for you," Joan whispered, patting her daughter's shoulder awkwardly. As she headed for the solarium door, her footsteps appeared labored, almost halting, like those of an old woman. It was the first time Amanda could recall seeing her mother act her age.

After Joan left her, Amanda turned away and stared out over the hillside. The haze was beginning to clear, and far beyond Portland she could see the sun glinting off the glaciers on Mount Hood. The mountain peak with its cap of eternal winter provided a surreal contrast to the ranks of bushes thick with summer-colored blossoms in the foreground. Amanda surveyed the garden one last time. Her gaze was attracted to the level where her mother had been working when she'd arrived. The wheelbarrow full of garden waste still stood in the path, and atop the trash heap Amanda spotted the Tropicana rose Joan had discarded as unfit. Even at this distance its vivid coral color was breathtaking. Amanda thought about the bloom, its fragrance and beauty unmarred—at least in her own opinion—by the fact that one of its petals was misshapen. She wondered if her mother had tossed the flower into the rubbish because she truly feared it was infested with microscopic pests, or because she had been offended that it failed to meet her exacting standards.

Amanda glanced over her shoulder to see if anyone in the house was watching her. When she was certain she was unobserved, she darted down the stone steps to the wheelbarrow and snatched the rose from the pile of grass clippings. Then, holding the blossom to her breast, she slipped out of the garden through the gate that opened onto the street where her Chrysler was parked, and she drove away.

CHAPTER FIVE

IT WAS ALMOST NOON when Amanda stepped into the shop. She didn't see Mark, but Sandra was near the front of the store, in the dining room display area, polishing the depression glass. The girl glanced up from the diamond-patterned cake stand she was wiping and waved. "Oh, hi, Mrs. Wexler," she greeted her boss, her frizzy red curls bobbing. "What a pretty rose."

Amanda fingered the thornless stem. "Thank you. It's one of my mother's."

"That's nice. My mom always says that taking care of my brother and me doesn't leave her time to grow anything but dandelions," Sandra said with a laugh. "By the way, have you heard the wonderful news yet? Isn't it exciting?"

Amanda's thoughts were so concentrated on her personal problems that for a fraction of a heartbeat she could only gape, shocked by the clerk's airy remark. Then, almost in the same second, as she watched Sandra inspect the heavy glass for fingerprints, Amanda realized the girl could not possibly be referring to the baby. "What on earth are you talking about?" Amanda asked.

Sandra did not reply at once. Her brows beetled when she spotted a smudge on the foot of the cake stand. She spritzed it with ammonia water and buffed vigorously until all the facets sparkled. Gingerly lifting the glass by the edges, she presented it for Amanda's approval. "How's this?"

Amanda blinked back the sharp, nose-tingling chemical fumes. "That's beautiful. If you make everything in the hutch so shiny, people are going to need blinders to look at it." Sandra beamed. Amanda asked, "So what's the wonderful news you mentioned a moment ago?"

The girl looked puzzled. "Haven't you heard yet? I didn't mean to spoil Mr. Wexler's surprise, but I figured as soon as he found out, he would have telephoned you at home—"

"I wasn't at home this morning," Amanda said. "I had to go out on personal business."

"Oh. When Mr. Wexler said you weren't feeling good, I assumed— Oops, saved by the bell!" Sandra broke off when two women strolled into the shop.

Amanda thought she recognized them as clerical workers from one of the nearby offices, and she realized they must be on their lunch break; the busiest portion of the day was commencing. "Customers," she muttered. "I'd better get my act together and start doing my job."

Sandra shook her head. "I can take care of them. Why don't you go on upstairs and talk to Mr. Wexler? I know he's dying to tell you what's happened. I'll buzz you if I need help." She wiped her hands on the polishing cloth and stepped forward to greet the women. "Good afternoon, ladies. Is there anything special I can show you today?"

Amanda climbed the steps to the office. When she opened the door, Mark was seated at the partners' desk. He was in shirtsleeves, his blond hair disarranged on one side, as if he'd absently run his fingers through it, and he was staring at a yellow writing pad covered with scrawled notes. As Amanda stepped inside, he jerked up his head, and his mouth stretched into a brilliant, toothy grin—the first genuine smile either of them had displayed in the past twenty-four hours, she thought in amazement.

"Great, you're here!" he exclaimed, in his excitement leaping to his feet so abruptly that he almost knocked over his chair. In a rush, he added, "I tried to reach you at your parents' house, but the maid told me you'd already left. I was afraid you might have decided to stop somewhere else before coming here. I'm glad you didn't."

"I drove straight over," Amanda said.

Mark laid his hands on her shoulders, shaping her fine bones with his fingers. As she gazed up at him, baffled and slightly alarmed, Amanda could feel him tremble. "Darling, what is it?" she asked.

Taking a deep breath, Mark explained shakily, "I—we—got a call this morning. The phone was ringing when I stepped into the office. The call was from Delaware, a woman named Susan Hendrix—Susan *Gunderson* Hendrix—"

"Gunderson!" Amanda gasped. "Good Lord, Mark, you don't mean—"

He nodded. "That's right, she's old Otto's granddaughter, his sole surviving heir, and she wants us to liquidate his estate!" Suddenly Mark wrapped his arms around Amanda, squashing her against his chest as he lifted her off her feet and swung her in a half circle, her ruffled hem billowing. With a shout of sheer jubilation he crowed, "Darling, we've done it—we've got the Gunderson job!" and his mouth closed hotly over hers.

He felt so good to hold. An eternity seemed to have passed since they'd last kissed—at least, since they'd last kissed out of pleasure, the pure exhilaration of the moment. Amanda returned Mark's embrace with delight, probing and nipping, savoring the taste of him, the unalloyed joy of his touch. For mindless minutes she clung to him, dazzled by his lovemaking, but then his equally dazzling words replayed in her brain, and reluctantly she lifted her head to gawk at him.

"You're not kidding me? We really got the Gunderson job?" she whispered breathlessly. Mark nodded. Amanda felt dizzy. She slipped out of his arms and sank onto the love seat. Touching her tender lips, she said, "I can't believe it."

The Gunderson job was a commission every antique dealer in northern Oregon had been eyeing covetously for months, ever since Otto Gunderson, last surviving child of a nineteenth-century lumber tycoon, passed to his reward at the age of ninety-six, leaving behind him a big white house five years older than he was and a treasure trove of Victoriana. His home was a rambling wooden cottage in the florid Queen Anne style, thick with gables and columns and spoolwork, located in the hills of Washington County, west of Portland, beyond the high-tech industrial developments local wags dubbed the Silicon Forest. Amanda had never been inside the house, but she'd driven past it on several occasions, and she had known the late owner.

Despite his great age, Otto Gunderson had been vigorous and quick-witted. Amanda had met him when he wandered into the store one afternoon, allegedly to inquire about repairing a Meissen figurine that had once belonged to his mother. Amanda had soon suspected he was less interested in the trinket than in having somebody to talk to. Because his call had happened to coincide with a lull in the day's business, Amanda had poured him a cup of coffee, and the two of them chatted. He told her about his house and its contents, and from there he segued into stories about his life. Amanda could tell he must have been a heartbreaker in his youth, a suspicion verified by some of the picaresque adventures he hinted at, yet regardless of his comparative health and his comfortable circumstance, he struck her as a lonely man, one who'd outlived two wives and all his children, leaving only a granddaughter who resided thousands of miles away. After that first visit, he had dropped by whenever he was in the area, and Amanda had always made time for him. She enjoyed seeing Otto, but a few months later, when she read in the obituaries that he'd succumbed to a heart attack in his sleep, quickly and without suffering, she had found it hard to grieve.

Shortly after the old man's death, when it became known that his heir intended to liquidate the estate once probate was complete, the Portland antique community began buzzing with rumors about which merchant would be awarded the lucrative assignment. Mark and Amanda had wanted it as much as anybody—a commission of such magnitude would elevate their reputation in the industry and could change Wexlers' Antiques and Collectibles from a thriving local shop to a dealership of regional importance—but she had not flattered herself that her brief acquaintance with Otto would influence the decision. Still, it had been impossible not to hope. After all, the Gunderson job would be the culmination of all she and Mark had ever worked for.

And now, amazingly, the job was theirs.

"I can't believe it," Amanda repeated giddily, almost giggling. "Do you have any idea what this is going to mean for us?"

"Well, it's going to mean a hell of a lot of work, for one thing," Mark drawled, but his eyes were dancing. "Mrs. Hendrix told me the contents of the house haven't been appraised since 1930, when Otto took out a twenty-thousand-dollar fire insurance policy."

Amanda whistled. "Can you even begin to imagine how much things much have appreciated in sixty years?"

"No, but I guess we're going to find out," Mark said. "She's having her attorney courier some papers and the keys to us, so that we can start mapping out our strategy, and then in a couple of weeks she and her husband are supposed to be flying out from Wilmington. While they're here they'll go around the place with us so she can choose the items she intends to keep for herself. But mostly, she told me, she's interested in realizing as much cash as possible out of the deal."

"In a way that's kind of sad," Amanda observed. "Not that I regret getting the job, of course, but when you consider how long the estate has been intact, it's almost a shame to break it up."

Mark shrugged. "That all depends on how you look at it. You have to remember that to the members of the Gunderson family, that house wasn't a museum and its contents weren't a collection. It was a home—Otto's home. His granddaughter's home is in the East. That's where she was born, that's where she's raising her own family, and, she told me, that's where she plans to invest the proceeds from her inheritance. I think that's a lot more practical than saddling her with a big house and a lot of furniture she doesn't want and can't use."

Mark paused. Smiling dryly, he added, "After all, darling, as beautiful as your parents' house is, would you really want to be stuck living there?"

"Caring for all those rose bushes, you mean?"

Mark's eyes gleamed. "Actually, I was trying to imagine us making love in Alden and Joan's bedroom."

Amanda tittered. "God, no! Anything—and *place*—but that."

For a moment the two of them gazed hungrily at each other, their minds meeting with a sensual purpose that was almost palpable. Remembering the flower still in her hand, which had miraculously escaped being crushed when Mark picked her up, Amanda brushed the blossom across her lips, then delicately stroked it over her chin and along the pale curve of her throat, trailing the lustrous petals down into the deep neckline of her lacy blouse. She saw Mark's nostrils flare.

"I do love that dress," he said huskily.

The telephone rang.

"Damn," Mark griped, sounding so disgruntled that Amanda laughed. Blowing her a kiss, he turned away and reached for the receiver. "Wexlers'," he announced crisply. His firm professional tone relaxed when the caller identified himself. "Oh, hello, Doug. How's it going? How's Warren?"

Amanda recognized the names of colleagues who operated a specialty shop—their particular area of interest was antique textiles and clothing—on the bottom floor of their house in the Sellwood district. Realizing Mark might be on the phone for some time, Amanda glanced at the rose in her hand and muttered, "I'd better find something to put this in." She stepped into the bathroom to look for a bud vase. While she filled the crystal flute with tap water, she watched Mark with pleasure as he lounged against the desk and admired the long, elegant line of his spine visible through his fine cotton shirt. She loved the feel of those bones beneath her hands as she clung to him in the darkness....

Above the hiss of the faucet she heard him say, "Yes, that's right, we just got the news ourselves.... No, we're both still a bit too dazed to start making any plans. We haven't been in the house yet, but I promise that when we do, we'll keep an eye out for anything you guys might be interested in." Amanda was carrying the filled vase into the office just as Mark murmured, "Thanks, I'll tell her. I know she'll appreciate the good thought. Give our love to Warren." Very carefully he set the receiver back into its cradle.

Amanda placed the rose in the center of the desk and surveyed it approvingly. The vivid coral-orange bloom gleamed like a jewel against the age-blackened wood. Rounding to Mark's side, she slipped her arm through his and snuggled close. "Word's out already? Honestly, NASA could learn something about communication from the dealers in this town. Sometimes I think people must use telepathy—or jungle drums."

When Mark did not respond to her teasing, Amanda rubbed her cheek sinuously against his sleeve, inhaling the clean aroma of starch and the subtle underlying fragrance of warm, masculine flesh. "Honey, you don't mind people finding out we got the commission, do you? Obviously it'll be quite a while before we're ready to announce sale dates, but in the interim a little word-of-mouth promotion won't hurt. The more publicity, the better. And considering what gossips Doug and Warren are," she added, "before the week is out we'll probably get calls from every dealer in the Northwest, possibly the entire Pacific Rim...."

Staring over the top of Amanda's head, Mark told her dully, "Doug asked me to pass on his good wishes and congratulations to you. He said it's really wonderful the way things are working out for the two of us these days, what with the Gunderson job *and* the baby."

Amanda lurched, her legs suddenly weak. She clutched at Mark's arm. Instantly he steadied her, but she still reeled with distress and dismay. She had forgotten. Oh, God, for a few ignoble, irresponsible, selfish moments she had been so caught up in her vision of professional success that she had actually permitted herself to forget the infinitely more important personal issues confronting her and her husband.

"While you were at your parents' house, did you talk to them?" Mark asked.

"Only my mother," Amanda said. "Father was playing golf with Jim Bishop."

Mark nodded. "I see. And how did Joan take the news?"

"Her reaction was about the same as yours."

"You mean she cried?"

"My mother never cries," Amanda said flatly. She added with a sniff, "Mother was upset, of course, but as usual she managed to contain her grief. You ought to know by now that her response to most crises is like a James Bond martini—shaken but not stirred."

The caustic tone in Amanda's last words surprised and alarmed her, and she fell silent, afraid to speak for fear her bitterness would spill onto Mark. She prayed for courage. When she thought she could keep her emotions under control, she rotated in Mark's arms, her body brushing his. The unaccustomed fullness of her denim jumper bunched into a thick pad over her stomach, forming a barrier between them. As she retreated far enough to allow the skewed fabric to fall free, she wondered drearily if the twisting of her dress was symbolic, sort of a half-baked omen that their child would always come between her and her husband.

She laid her palms flat on Mark's chest, feeling the firm, smooth skin beneath his shirt. "Darling, I—I—" she stammered, choking on the words.

He paled. "Don't say it."

"But I have to," Amanda insisted. "Avoiding the subject is pointless. In fact, silence is worse than pointless—it's stupid and dangerous. We have to talk." She swallowed hard. "I have to explain why I'm not going to terminate this pregnancy."

Mark's brow furrowed, and Amanda could tell he remained unconvinced that her choice was the best one. He searched her face urgently. "Please, dear, I know you're in a lot of turmoil right now. I know you're frightened of the . . . procedure—"

All at once the determined reasonableness of Mark's words was too much for Amanda. She exploded. "'Procedure!'" she shouted. "Goddamn it, you sound like a pamphlet for a junior high school hygiene class. This is abortion we're talking about!" With both hands she shoved him away from her.

She caught him off balance, and he stumbled backward against the desk, jarring it. The bud vase toppled over, and water sloshed onto the yellow pad with the comments Mark had written while talking to Susan Hendrix. Quickly he snatched up the notes. Wet ink smeared his shirt. While he lay sprawled across the desk, stunned, Amanda continued to rail, "Don't try to placate me with evasions, Mark Wexler. You want me to kill my baby! And no matter how firmly you or my mother or the doctor or anybody else is convinced it's the right thing for me to do, *I can't*!''

He clambered to his feet, shaking his head to clear it. His face was flushed, his chest heaving, but when he spoke he sounded unruffled. ''Did you say you can't have an abortion,'' he queried quietly, ''or you won't?''

Amanda lifted her chin pugnaciously. ''What difference does it make? It may be our child, but it's my body, and ultimately I'm the only one with the right to decide what will or won't be. . . .''

Her bravado faded when she eyed the ink stains on his shirt. Aghast, she cringed. Oh, no, what had she done? This was her husband, the man she loved and cherished, the man she'd never touched with anything other than tenderness and affection. What madness could have possessed her to lash out violently at him? Trembling, she whispered, ''Dear God, Mark, are you all right?''

He fingered the splotches and dismissed them. ''The shirt's a dead loss, but at least I have a spare handy. As for me, I'm fine. In case nobody ever told you, you hit like a girl.''

Amanda blushed. ''I—I'm sorry I pushed you. I've never struck anybody before in my life.''

''I know that.''

Somehow his arid calm was the ultimate humiliation.

''But do you know why I did it?'' Amanda pleaded, reaching for him, then letting her hands fall to her sides. ''Do you have any idea how it makes me feel when you reject your own child, when you think because our son isn't perfect, he's not worthy of living?''

"I never said that," Mark countered sharply, and the sudden edge in his voice made Amanda wonder if he was nearly as imperturbable as he pretended. He grimaced with distaste. "What do you think I am, some kind of Nazi?"

Gesturing helplessly, Amanda repeated, "I'm sorry. I assumed that was what you meant."

Mark shook his head. "No, that's not what I meant at all. You ought to know me better than that."

"Sometimes I wonder if I know you at all," Amanda said.

Mark gazed at her, and just for an instant a poignant, faraway look flickered in his eyes. Amanda had no idea what it meant. Then the wistful light faded, and she watched him square his shoulders with almost military precision. He took a deep, strained breath. "I have never, ever claimed only the perfect deserve to live," he declared. "What I said, and what I truly believe, is that there are worse fates than not being born." He regarded her somberly. "Please, Amanda, think about that before you make your final decision."

She sighed, weary and resigned. "I already have thought about it. I've thought about very little else since we talked to Steven. The words keep going round and round in my head. Am I being fair to the baby? Am I selfishly putting my own needs ahead of his? Those are terrible questions, and there don't seem to be any easy answers."

She lifted her hands in a gesture of appeal, an appeal for understanding. "I'm not being dogmatic, Mark. This isn't some kind of knee-jerk reaction on my part. No matter how much I want a child, even I have to admit that under some circumstances I'd probably opt for abortion. There are diseases, like Tay-Sachs, where the instant the baby is born, he starts dying a horrible, painful death. I don't see how I could condemn a child to a fate like that. But Down's syndrome is different, and no matter how I look at the situation, I keep running into the same wall—we don't know enough about our son's condition to pass judgment on the quality of his life.''

Amanda hesitated, knowing her next words would be irreversible. Once they were uttered, she would be committed to a course of action that could alter her life and jeopardize everything she treasured. Veiling her eyes with her lashes, she peeked up at Mark, trying to gauge his response, but his face remained stony, his expression impenetrable. He was deliberately shutting her out, Amanda thought sadly. Overnight her husband of ten years had become a stranger.

Finally, resolutely, Amanda plunged on. "I know you don't agree with me, Mark, but after a lot of thought and prayer I've concluded there's only one thing I can do. The only decision I can make and still be able to live with myself is to bear this child and then do everything in my power to ensure that his life is a good one.''

As soon as she spoke, the last bit of fortitude that had bolstered Amanda vanished, and her knees wobbled. Fumbling blindly behind her, she backed away from Mark until her legs bumped the love seat, and she sank gratefully onto the cushions to await his reaction. She did not wait long.

''Amanda, I can't accept your decision.''

''When it comes right down to it, you don't have much choice in the matter,'' she reminded him softly.

He shrugged, but the insouciant gesture did not match the tension in his face, which suddenly looked long and bony, with deep furrows grooving his taut skin. "I'm very sorry you feel that way," he said, "because even though I may not have any voice in your decision, I don't have to go along with it, either. I don't have to stand idly by and watch you make a disastrous mistake."

She gazed up at him, her eyes dark and defenseless in her white face. "So what are you saying?" she asked dreadfully. "Are you telling me that unless I have an abortion, you'll leave me? Is that what this is all about? Do I have to choose between you and my child? Are we—are we talking about *divorce*?"

Her sheer vulnerability tore at Mark, and he despised himself for the cruel dilemma he was forcing on her. His proud, strong Amanda, so fragile and yet so brave.... What kind of man was he to hurt her now, when she needed him most?

Against his will he remembered another woman in another lifetime, a pathetically young woman, bewildered and bereft, whose lanky blond hair framed a face still puffy from recent childbearing. Mark had only been ten years old, but even now he could recall the fear and despair in his mother's voice as she entreated helplessly in her native Biloxi accent, "Bob, don't go! We'll work things out somehow, I promise. Please, sugar, I need you—we all need you. How will we survive if you leave?" What Mark couldn't remember for certain was whether the man who had stalked through the kitchen, suitcase in hand, had paused long enough to answer her, or whether, as Mark suspected, his only response to her piteous pleas had been to bang the rusty screen door behind him as he stomped across the porch....

I am not my father, Mark told himself staunchly, shaking off memories that had tormented him for thirty-five years. No, by God, despite the haunting parallels in their situations, he was not Robert Wexler, sometime soldier and gardener, derelict husband and unfit parent. Regardless of how strongly Mark objected to Amanda's decision, how dubious he was of the future, he knew he would never simply abandon her to a fate she was incapable of coping with....

What he was far less certain of was whether Amanda might not eventually grow fed up with his insecurities and leave *him*.

Amanda asked, "Is this the end of us, Mark? Do you mean that because of this argument, you're willing to throw away the past ten years?"

"Damn it, I don't know exactly what I mean!" Mark declared, tired and exasperated. Sweat beaded on his high forehead, and tendrils of pale hair stuck to his skin and dangled in his eyes. Impatiently he scrubbed the damp strands back away from his face and wiped his wet palms on his trousers. "Lord, Amanda, can't you see I'm just as confused as you are? Everything's happening too quickly. I can't absorb all the changes. Twenty-four hours ago I had a perfect marriage and a rosy future—"

"But that doesn't have to change," she said pleadingly. "You can still have those things. At the moment our future looks rosier than ever, and our marriage—"

Mark shook his head. "Don't be naive, darling. The damage has already been done. Whether or not you have the baby is almost irrelevant now, because you and I are no longer the same people we were when we walked into Steven's office yesterday."

"I see," Amanda murmured, wondering why she wasn't screaming. "You're saying our marriage is kaput, just like that."

"No, I'm not! God, I wish you'd stop putting words into my mouth," Mark declared. "All I'm saying is that we have to work out some kind of compromise. If we can't, well, then—hell, maybe in a worst-case scenario separation would have to be considered, but I promise you nothing is going to happen 'just like that.' I don't want a divorce any more than you do. Besides, whatever our differences, there are an awful lot of practical reasons for us to stay together. If nothing else, neither of us is exactly in a position to give up this business we've built—"

Amanda recoiled as if she'd been slapped. "Oh, great," she cried, her voice rising perilously on a note of hysteria. "You'd stay for the sake of the store, but not out of loyalty to me? Thanks for nothing! If that's the way you feel, you can just take off now, and I'll manage on my own."

Mark let out his breath in a long, aggravated sigh. "I can't talk to you when you're like this," he muttered, pivoting, then he stalked to the window to stare out at the mall.

The atmosphere inside the office was so strained, so electric with tension, that the sight of pedestrians strolling casually along the sidewalks, enjoying the fine spring afternoon, seemed unreal. Mark spotted two girls in clown costumes handing out balloons and flyers to passersby and pointing them toward some unseen destination. From the direction they indicated, he guessed they were probably advertising one of the shops in the galleria a couple of blocks away. Belatedly he remembered he had a shop of his own to tend.

Mark scowled. He wondered why Sandra hadn't yet used the buzzer that signaled she needed assistance down in the showroom. Did the silence mean that business was so slack even an unseasoned clerk could handle it, or had her job skills improved more than he gave her credit for? Whatever the reason, it occurred to Mark that during the next few months, between Amanda's doctor's appointments and the demands of the Gunderson job, Sandra would be required to fill a far more important role in the running of Wexlers' than anyone could have anticipated when she'd been hired the previous January. He hoped the girl was equal to the task. Dear God, he hoped *he*—

Mark started, his thoughts invaded by a sound behind him, a soft noise he wasn't certain he'd ever heard before: a moist, snuffling moan of pain, punctuated by tiny explosive wheezes, quickly stifled.

At long last, Amanda was crying.

Holding his breath, Mark turned. He found her curled in a tight ball of misery on one end of the love seat, her feet tucked beneath her ruffled hem, her hands clasped over her mouth. She was shaking with the effort to smother her sobs. She gazed at Mark with huge, liquid eyes, like those of the figures in the waif paintings that had been in vogue when he was a teenager, but for a moment she seemed unaware that he was looking back at her. Then, when she became conscious of him, flags of crimson spread across her white cheeks, and she ducked her head to avoid his glance, but he could still see the moisture beading on her lashes. One after another the droplets pooled and dripped off to dissolve on her fingertips. Mark's heart wrenched with guilt. He had hoped she'd find release in tears, but now her grief was almost more than he could bear. His spirited, beautiful wife looked utterly desolate, utterly defeated—and it was all his fault.

Clearing his throat, Mark said, "Darling, you don't have to try to hide from me. I told you yesterday that it was all right to cry."

"You didn't tell me it would hurt so much," she choked out.

He flinched. "I'm sorry. I wish I knew something comforting to say."

She lowered her hands and lifted her wet, ravaged face to his gaze. "Say you won't leave me," she implored, the words dull and hollow sounding. "If you have to go later, I promise I won't try to stop you, but please, Mark, not now—not yet." She gulped and whispered, "Please don't make me have my baby alone."

Mark stared, stupefied that the woman he loved could actually believe him capable of such callous behavior. With a groan he flung himself onto the love seat beside her. "I won't go till you kick me out," he growled, and he pulled her onto his lap, his arms both shackle and shield.

They clung together. Mark could feel her soft breasts cushioned against him, their ripe fullness tantalizingly novel. In his embrace she felt so warm, so womanly, and yet, in spite of the pounds she had gained, she remained too delicate, too insubstantial for the vital role she played in his life. He buried his face in the curve of her neck, her cameo earring cool against his cheek. He inhaled deeply, breathing in her unique perfume. There was an elusive quality about Amanda, something as ethereal as that indefinable fragrance that filled his nostrils, as necessary to him as air, as evanescent as the dawn. He could savor her sweetness, but he had never been able to capture her essence.

Mark lifted his head and framed her face in his hands. "How could I ever leave you?" he asked, brushing aside with his fingertips the moisture that lay on her bruised eyes like dew on crushed violets. "Don't you realize how much I need you, how much I love you?"

Amanda sniffed blearily. "You hardly ever say it."

"I know," Mark admitted with a sigh. "I'm not very good at words—certain words, anyway. I have this mental block, I guess. It's always been much easier for me to show love than to talk about it."

"Then show me," she whispered with a despairing urgency that troubled Mark. "I have to know how much you need me. Make love to me." Stretching her face to his, she kissed him hungrily and tugged at his shirt.

Mark hesitated. He could feel the yearning in her as her teeth and tongue teased his mouth. When her skillful fingers unhooked his buttons and his lapels gaped, the faint erotic pull and scratch of her nails on his bare skin sent sharp tingles of desire darting through him, but he was reluctant to react. Amanda grew more aggressive, nipping at him, inviting his lips to part for her invasion. Still Mark held back. Her excitement—or desperation—worried him.

He thought he understood the reckless melancholy driving her, the urgent need for reassurance, but he wasn't sure impromptu sex was the appropriate outlet for such feelings. He was perfectly aware of the aphrodisiac quality of violent emotion, but considering the mental roller coaster the two of them had been riding for the past twenty-four hours, it seemed that what they needed more than anything at the moment was rest—quiet, tender, undemanding time together, filled with the kind of love that would cleanse and heal. Anything crude or selfish was bound to exacerbate the conflicts already existing between them.

"Hey, you," Amanda murmured, slipping her fingers inside his shirt to caress the plates of hard, taut muscle defined beneath his smooth skin, "how about cooperating a little?" She found his flat nipples and pinched delicately. Mark gasped. "I can feel your heart pounding," Amanda purred. "That's more like it." Her hands drifted lower, toward his belt.

Struggling for control, he captured her wrists and cautioned her gently, "Dear, I don't think this is the time or place. Sandra could signal us at any moment—"

"If she does, we'll ignore her. We're in charge, remember?" Amanda reminded him, squirming provocatively.

Mark found breathing increasingly difficult. "We're supposed to be careful—no acrobatics or rough stuff," he said, trying to sound reasonable. "This couch is probably too small for what you have in mind."

"You don't know what I have in mind." Amanda twisted free of Mark's grip and resumed her delicious exploration. "I'm not interested in acrobatics or rough stuff. I just want to love you. I want to touch you—like this. I want to know you're here so that I can touch you." She spread his shirt open and pressed her breasts against his bare chest. Even through the thickness of her clothing her nipples were hard and inviting. "Sweetheart, I want you to touch me back," she urged. "I have to feel your hands on me. Otherwise—" she paused, a faint line appearing between her eyes "—otherwise, after all the other unbelievable things that have happened, I might begin to wonder if you're real, too."

Her ingenuous admission destroyed the last of his defenses. "Oh, God, Amanda, I'll show you how real I am," he groaned, and fumbled for the zipper on her dress.

She lay across his lap naked to the waist, her blouse and bra flung across the back of the love seat, her denim jumper bunched at her hips as Mark caressed her body. He cupped her full breasts in his palms, his thumbs sketching circles around the darkened, crinkled areolas. He observed, "Your nipples used to be like little pink rosebuds. They've changed."

Amanda arched against his hands. "The rosebuds have gone forever, alas," she quipped throatily. "Now I'm just plain old brown."

Mark shook his head. "Not old, not plain. Beautiful." Sliding one arm beneath her back, he lifted her so his mouth could close greedily over first one breast, then the other. When he spoke again, his voice shook. "Beautiful," he repeated, "and delicious."

Amanda's eyes were murky. "I know something even more delicious," she said intensely. She stroked him, feeling his arousal. "Mark, I need you inside me."

He sighed. "I need me inside you, too, darling, but I'm not sure I know how to manage it on a love seat."

Amanda grinned. "You've got to be kidding. Could this be the same man who once had his wicked way with me on the side of a cliff halfway up Multnomah Falls?" It had been a sweltering summer day during the first year of their marriage, and they'd driven up the Columbia Gorge for a picnic. Their lovemaking, spontaneous and reckless, had proved much more fulfilling in theory than in actual practice, but despite sunburn, insects and sharp pebbles in awkward places, the erotic interlude remained one of their most treasured intimate memories.

Mark reminded her, "We were a hell of a lot younger then, Amanda—and you weren't pregnant."

She blinked. Fearfully she asked, "It's not the pregnancy that's holding you back, is it? Now that we know about the baby, does my body turn you off?"

Shaking his head slowly, Mark pressed Amanda's palm over the front of his trousers. "C'mon, honey, does that feel as if you turn me off? I just don't want to hurt you, that's all."

"The only way you'll hurt me is by making me wait any longer," she murmured, and she caught the tab of his straining zipper and eased it down purposefully.

AFTER THEY FINISHED, after the force of her climax left Amanda spent and weeping in Mark's arms, after only the red flush on his cheeks remained as evidence of his own convulsive response, Amanda lay limp and half-naked on the love seat and watched her husband dress. Just as their lovemaking had reached its shattering conclusion, the buzzer from the showroom sounded, signaling the intrusion of the outside world. Now, instead of holding each other and basking in the afterglow, Mark was wrestling with the cardboard box in which his clean shirt was packed, while Amanda looked on and felt abandoned.

Mark dropped the torn box into the wastebasket atop the shirt that had been ruined with ink, then he began extracting pins from the folded one. He fumed, "I have never for the life of me understood why it's necessary to use eighty-seven straight pins in one plain dress shirt!"

"I can do that for you," Amanda offered dully.

"No, thanks. I'm almost done," he muttered, extracting another pin. "Finally, I think that's— No, damn it, there's another one!" He yelped with pain and paused to suck a spot of blood that bloomed on his fingertip.

Amanda said, "Next time I'll tell the laundry to put your shirts on hangers."

"Good idea." He shook out the shirt, and the fresh, clean smell of starch wafted through the office. Mark poked his arms into the sleeves and fumbled with the buttons. The buzzer sounded again. He grimaced and jerked on his trousers. "God, I'd better get down there in a hurry, or else Sandra's going to be banging on the door to find out what's wrong."

"Just be grateful she didn't need us ten minutes ago," Amanda murmured.

As he adjusted his belt, Mark barked humorlessly, "Yes, thank God. That would have been—" He broke off. Lifting his head, he gazed at Amanda. His brows came together as he noted her flaccid posture, her forlorn expression. He asked, "Darling, are you all right?"

She lifted her shoulders. "I'm fine. Don't worry about me. In a second I'll get myself dressed and join you and Sandra downstairs."

Mark's frown did not soften. "I'm sorry for the rush," he said. "This wasn't the way I wanted it."

Amanda nodded. "I know. Don't blame yourself. I was the one who insisted."

Still Mark hesitated. His gaze slid over Amanda's supine form. A sensual light gleamed in his eyes when they lingered on her bare breasts and the long white thighs exposed by her disheveled skirt. He took a deep breath. "As quickies go," he told her, "that one was pretty spectacular."

"You were wonderful," Amanda said. "You always are. At least that hasn't changed." She bit her lip. "Of course, when you come right down to it, I suppose nothing's changed between us."

"Sex never changes anything, no matter how good it is," Mark reminded her. "Did you really think it would?"

Amanda sat up. "No, of course not. But I can dream, can't I?" She waited until she heard Mark's footsteps disappear down the stairwell, then she reached for her bra and began straightening her clothes.

CHAPTER SIX

AFTER WRITING NOTES on Amanda's chart, Steven gazed thoughtfully at her and declared, "I think you're making a serious mistake."

"So does Mark," Amanda said. "So do my parents."

Steven shook his head. "I'm not talking about your decision to go ahead and have the baby. What I'm concerned about is the time between now and then. You say you don't plan to tell anyone about the baby's condition until after he's born. That worries me."

"Why—because you think I'm still trying to deny the situation?" Amanda asked. "It's not like that at all. It's just that I have enough on my mind right now without having to cope with rude questions. Simply being pregnant at my age draws a lot of funny looks. As for talking about the baby's condition, well, after the way my family reacted, I figure most people who find out are either going to pity me or else expect me to justify my decision. Neither option is very appealing."

"You could tell people to mind their own damn business," Steven suggested lightly.

Amanda shrugged. "If I keep quiet, I don't have to tell them anything."

"But that's just the problem," Steven countered. "Certainly I understand your wanting to protect your privacy, but I also understand why it's not healthy to keep news like this bottled up inside you. Every pregnant woman has fears and concerns that should be voiced. Because of your situation, you have more than most. You need an outlet, someplace where you can talk freely and frankly." He thought for a moment. "Have you considered getting in touch with a support group? There are organizations specifically for the parents of Down's syndrome children. I'm sure you and Mark—"

"Mark won't even talk to me about the baby!" Amanda snapped. "I hardly think he's going to be interested in baring his soul to strangers."

The doctor seemed startled by her waspish tone. "I'm sorry to hear that," he said. "Problem pregnancies put a strain on even the strongest marriages, but of all my current patients, I'd have guessed you and Mark were the couple most likely to weather this situation."

Smiling sardonically, Amanda told him, "That's funny. I'd have agreed with you."

Steven's gray eyes were sympathetic. "If that's the way things really stand between you two, then I'm not going to try to comfort you with platitudes. But I'd like you to consider what I said about getting in touch with a support group. You could go alone if you have to. In fact, if you suspect you might be raising this child without your husband, there's even more reason for you to contact these people."

Amanda sighed. "I'll think about it."

"Do that," Steven said briskly. "Also, if you haven't done so already, I want you to go to the library and get some books on Down's syndrome—*recent* ones, I mean. Check the copyright dates. Progress is being made in this field all the time, but the literature doesn't always keep pace. I certainly don't want you reading some relic from the early seventies that says 'mongoloids' are ineducable and all you can do is shove them into an institution—'' He caught himself. ''Sorry. Even doctors are allowed to lose their objectivity once in a while.'' Glancing again at her folder, he noted, ''Before you leave the office, tell the receptionist I want to see you again in two weeks.''

''So soon?''

Steven explained, ''Usually I don't need to check my obstetrical patients more than once a month for the first six months, but under the circumstances, I think I ought to keep a closer eye on you—or rather, on the baby. Your health is excellent, but we're going to have to monitor the fetus's progress very carefully.'' He hesitated, watching her expression. ''For what it's worth,'' he told her, ''you ought to know that in spite of all the advice you're getting to the contrary, you aren't the first woman—or even my first patient—to make the choice you've made.''

Amanda brightened. ''You knew someone else who went ahead and had her baby after the same diagnosis? How'd it turn out?''

Steven's voice was absolutely neutral. ''Sorry, Amanda. That's privileged information.'' He moved to leave. At the door he looked back at her. ''One last thing...''

''Yes?''

''I know I promised there wouldn't be any platitudes about you and Mark, but please remember, four and a half months is a long time. Lots of things could happen between now and October.

AMANDA SPENT AN HOUR in the library, and when she returned to the shop, laden with books, she found Sandra in charge. The clerk was showing a selection of glass paperweights to a customer, and while the woman wavered, unable to decide, a couple entered the store to inquire about a mission-style pie safe they'd spotted through the window. Amanda dumped her books and papers onto the Edwardian settee and stepped forward to wait on them. By the time the couple left, promising to "think about it"—a phrase Amanda had long since learned meant they didn't want to pay the price but were reluctant to admit it—Sandra's shopper had departed with three of the paperweights.

Filing away the receipts, Amanda complimented Sandra on her successful transaction. "You're showing quite a flair for this business, dear. You certainly outsold me."

The teenager beamed. "It was easy. The lady really wanted them all for her collection. She told me she'd just gotten her income-tax refund and was in the mood to splurge."

"So you let the customer talk herself into the sale?" Amanda asked. "Excellent. As long as she doesn't feel she's been pressured into buying something she can't afford, she'll be able to enjoy her purchase and think of it as an investment, as well."

"She seemed to like the store a lot," Sandra added. "She said she'll be back again as soon as she accumulates some more mad money."

Amanda laughed. "That's great—sheer music to a merchant's ears." She glanced around. "Speaking of merchants, where's Mark? In the storage room or upstairs in the office?"

Sandra shook her head. "Mr. Wexler left on an errand. He told me he needed to run out to Hillsboro."

"Oh," Amanda said. "Ted must have called him about some new find."

Like all antique dealers, Mark and Amanda stocked their store from a variety of sources. Some of their merchandise was acquired through private sales, and the two of them personally attended estate auctions and the major buying shows held in the East each fall. But they also relied on "pickers" like Ted, a student who spent his spare time at garage sales and church bazaars, scouting out bargains that he in turn resold to dealers like the Wexlers. Mark, who had supported himself in the same way while he went to college after his stint in the army, joked that sooner or later the young man was bound to become a full-fledged dealer himself, and probably a major competitor. For the time being, however, Mark and Amanda always welcomed Ted's calls. They valued his excellent taste and discerning eye because they knew that whatever he showed them would eventually earn a good profit.

Amanda asked, "Did Mark say when he'd be back? It'll be fun to hear what kind of goodies Ted has unearthed this time."

"Mr. Wexler said he probably wouldn't be gone more than a couple of hours," Sandra answered. "Did you need him right away?"

"I picked up some stuff at the library that I wanted to show him."

The girl said, "Yeah, I gathered you must have made an extra stop or two on your way back from the doctor's. Find anything interesting?"

"Some. In addition to—in addition to several books I needed, I decided to look for material on the Gundersons. When we put together the catalog for the auction, we'll want to include some background information on the house and the people who lived there. Buyers always seem to respond better if they have some idea of the history of the items they're bidding for.''

"Can't Mrs. Hendrix fill you in about her family?" Sandra asked.

"Only very superficially," Amanda replied. "Apparently her father and grandfather weren't particularly close, so she never got much of a chance to know Otto. She can only remember being in his home once, when she was a small child. On the phone she did tell me that when she and her husband fly out here soon, she'll look through her family's papers for anything that might be of help. In the meantime I decided to see what I could discover elsewhere."

"And you got lucky?" Sandra pressed.

"I'll say," Amanda drawled. "This morning when I asked the research librarian about the Gundersons, he went straight to the microfilm file. He dug up a profile the historical society published many years ago about Otto's father, the lumber tycoon, and there were even newspaper clippings from turn-of-the-century society pages, with photographs of Mrs. Gunderson standing regally in front of the 'parlor suite crafted especially for her by the Herter Brothers of New York.'" Amanda shook her head in wonder. "My God, if it turns out that parlor suite is still intact, then we've lucked into something even bigger than we thought. A couple of years back, one Herter cabinet by itself sold for nearly forty thousand dollars at Sotheby's."

"Wow," Sandra breathed, her mouth an O of appreciation. "Just think what the commission on a sale like that would be."

Amanda laughed. "I do, I do. That's one reason I wish Mark were here. I want to show him the articles the librarian copied for me."

Sandra asked, "While we're waiting for Mr. Wexler to get back, would it be all right if I looked at the clippings?"

"Certainly. Help yourself." Amanda waved carelessly in the direction of the sofa where she'd dropped her books. It wasn't until she saw the clerk pick up the top volume on the stack that Amanda recalled that most of the material she'd checked out of the library was not about antiques.

She held her breath as she watched Sandra stare at the title in her hand, a guide for raising Down's syndrome children. The girl set it aside without comment. The second book was about educating the "developmentally delayed." Sandra frowned thoughtfully. The third book was a mother's memoir....

When Sandra looked at Amanda again, her expression was veiled. Carefully she ventured, "Mrs. Wexler, would you mind me asking you a personal question?"

Bracing herself for pity or horror—or both— Amanda admitted reluctantly, "You don't have to ask, dear. I hadn't planned to say anything about it, but last week Mark and I learned that our baby will be born with Down's syndrome."

Sandra nodded. "My big brother, Georgie, has that," she said.

Amanda gasped, stunned by the girl's matter-of-fact tone. "I beg your pardon?"

"Haven't I ever mentioned my brother before?" Sandra asked, puzzled. "That's funny, I thought I had. Georgie's twenty, and he's about my favorite person in the whole world, a really sweet guy without a malicious bone in his body. He's the one who gave me the jasmine perfume I like so much."

Amanda croaked, "Yes, but—"

Sandra continued blithely, "Georgie still lives with Mom and Dad and me, but he's going to trade school, learning furniture repair, and as soon as he gets a regular job, he hopes to be able to move into a group home. There's one not far—"

Abruptly the girl broke off. Staring at Amanda with round, remorseful eyes, she said contritely, "Oh, gosh, I'm sorry, Mrs. Wexler. I must really sound insensitive. I don't mean to. You have to remember, I've known my brother all my life. I guess that's why it never occurred to me to mention how special he is. To me he's not somebody with a condition called Down's syndrome—he's just Georgie. I love him, and *that's* what makes him special. Sometimes I forget other people don't see it the same way." She gnawed her lip. "I am sorry to hear about your baby, Mrs. Wexler. That's really tough."

Touched by the girl's concern, Amanda agreed gruffly, "Thank you, Sandra—and you're right, it is tough. I'm only just beginning to realize *how* tough."

Sandra's russet-colored brows came together as she peered at Amanda. Scooping the books off the settee, she said, "Why don't you come sit down for a few minutes, Mrs. Wexler? You look sort of washed-out."

"I feel that way, too," Amanda admitted. Gratefully she sank onto the space Sandra had cleared. Tilting her head back over the top of the sofa, she closed her eyes and massaged her temples with her fingertips. "Being pregnant at my age is no picnic to begin with," Amanda declared with a yawn, "and the mental strain isn't helping much, either."

After a moment her lashes fluttered up again, and she smiled at her clerk. Clasping the girl's hand, Amanda said, "Sandra, I have to confess, I've done you an injustice. Since you started working for us, even though you've proved yourself to be very bright and capable and hardworking, I've tended to think of you as just a teenager. But you're much more than that. You may be young, but you're mature and compassionate, and I really appreciate how sweet you're being to me. Considering how worried I am about people finding out, it's sort of ironic that you should be the first person outside my family to hear about the baby."

"Maybe it's fate," Sandra said. "Mom is always telling the group that she's firmly convinced parents of D.S. people have a special guardian angel to guide them to the help they need."

Amanda asked, "What group is that?"

Sandra said, "It's an outreach program my folks are involved in—actually, I guess Mom founded it. It all started years ago, when Georgie's pediatrician called my mother and asked if she'd talk to another woman who'd just had a Down's syndrome baby. He said the other lady was taking the news really hard and she needed somebody who understood how she felt, so she could work out her feelings. Mom met the other woman, and talking did seem to make her feel better. Before long my dad and the lady's husband got involved, and the next thing you know, the doctor started referring other people to them. It all just sort of blossomed."

"It's great that they were able to help each other," Amanda commented.

"My parents are great people," Sandra said, smiling fondly. "Dad's an accountant, but he donates a lot of time to the Special Olympics, and even though Mom insists she's 'just a housewife' who's only trying to do what's best for her son, she attended night school to earn a degree in special education. Last year she and

Dad and Georgie went to the state capitol to testify at a legislative hearing about funding the disabled. They got their pictures in the paper and everything."

Amanda said, "You must be very proud."

Sandra beamed. "I am."

Touched by the girl's obvious love for her family, Amanda queried diffidently, "Forgive me for asking a question like this, Sandra, but doesn't all the attention your brother gets bother you? Since I am an only child, I'll admit I don't understand sibling relationships very well, but it sounds as if most of your parents' time is devoted to Georgie and his problems. Don't you ever feel . . . well, don't you ever feel jealous?"

"My parents devote a lot of time to me, too," Sandra returned. "Last summer, after I graduated from high school, my mother took me and my best friend to New York for a week, and we saw Broadway plays and visited the Statue of Liberty and shopped in Bloomingdale's—it was fantastic! And when I told Mom and Dad that I wanted to work for a couple of years instead of starting college right away, even though they were disappointed, they both said I had to do what was best for me. They said the most important lesson they'd learned raising Georgie and me is that everybody is unique and it's wrong to try to force people into molds."

Amanda thought of the tension that had always existed between herself and her own parents, tension due to her failure—or outright refusal—to fit the mold they'd selected for her. She'd always been too emotional to suit Alden and Joan. As a child she'd been clinging, demanding attention at inconvenient moments, such as when they were about the leave the house for yet another of their many social obligations. As a young adult she'd seemed impractical to them, willing to break off an engagement to a wealthy young man of impeccable breeding for no better reason than that she'd discovered he bored her, in bed and out. And now, as a woman approaching middle age, her parents found her to be stubborn almost to the point of irrationality, with her determination to go through with this "doomed" pregnancy....

Amanda said to her clerk, "You're a lucky girl to have such wise parents."

All the praise appeared to make Sandra faintly flustered. "Yeah, Mom and Dad are pretty neat," she admitted, shrugging uncomfortably. She gazed thoughtfully at Amanda. "Do you think you and Mr. Wexler would like to talk to them? I know they'd be happy to help. I could call them for you."

"Thank you. I'd like that very much," Amanda said, but as she spoke, she realized that Mark's willingness to cooperate was far less certain.

Her suspicions were confirmed later that afternoon, when Mark returned from Hillsboro.

They were seated on opposite sides of the partners' desk with Mark's notebook between them, while he described the garage full of bric-a-brac and collectibles the picker had shown him and explained his notes and calculations. Amanda stared at the pen moving point by point down the list. Mark concluded, "Because there's so much, Ted told me he's decided to sell the merchandise in one lot this time, rather than piece by piece, which means in order to get any part of it, we'll have to invest more money than we originally intended. Still, he has some good pieces, and considering how hot American Primitive is these days, I think we could move it all in a hurry. I told Ted I'd call him back tonight with a bid, after I'd discussed it with you."

Mark paused, awaiting Amanda's response. When she did not speak, he pressed, "Well, what do you think?"

She blinked. "What do I think about what?"

Laying down his pen, Mark asked, "Haven't you heard a word I've said?"

"Sorry," Amanda murmured. "I guess I let my mind wander." Without realizing what she was doing, she hugged herself, wrapping her arms protectively over her belly.

Mark frowned. "Darling," he said in a tone that seemed to oscillate between compassion and impatience, "I know it's difficult for you to think about anything except the baby these days, but we do have a business to run, remember?"

Hurt, Amanda countered stiffly, "I haven't forgotten about our business. What about all that background material on the Gunderson house I just showed you? How can you look at that and then imply I'm letting you down?"

"I didn't claim you were letting me down," Mark insisted. "You've never let me down. I love the stuff you dug up about the Gundersons—but I'd love it even more if I thought your heart was in the job."

"I can't help it if I seem a little preoccupied at times."

Mark clucked impatiently. "I know, dear, I know. Under the circumstances it's probably unrealistic for me to expect you to be anything but preoccupied with the baby. It's just that after all those years of wanting the same things, virtually thinking the same things, suddenly we seem to be on completely different wavelengths, and I'm not sure how to deal with the situation."

Relieved that Mark had finally given her the opening she needed, Amanda insisted urgently, "But there are people who can help us. Something happened this afternoon that I intended to tell you about as soon as you returned from Ted's, but we got sidetracked. At my appointment today, Steven said you and I ought to talk to other people who have gone through the same thing we're going through. There are programs available for the parents of Down's syndrome children, and he suggested we get in touch with a support group. I told him I'd think about it. Then, by the most amazing coincidence, I discovered that Sandra's parents head up a group—"

"Sandra, our clerk?" Mark interrupted in bewilderment.

Amanda nodded eagerly. "It turns out her brother has Down's syndrome. So Sandra telephoned her mother—her name's Stephanie Pollard, and she sounds like a lovely person—and Stephanie suggested that tonight you and I should meet her and Gordon someplace for coffee—Gordon is Sandra's father—and we'll get acquainted and decide whether we think the group might be helpful...." At Mark's lowering expression, Amanda's voice trailed off. "You don't like the idea," she concluded glumly.

He shook his head. "If you're proposing that we get on intimate terms with an employee's family, then no, I don't like the idea. Apart from the fact that I find the idea of spilling my guts to strangers thoroughly distasteful, I can think of a whole lot of reasons why such an arrangement would be neither wise nor workable."

Amanda's eyes narrowed. She said, "I never realized that you were a snob, Mark."

"I'm not a snob—I'm just being practical," he retorted tightly. "No way in hell could we discuss deeply personal concerns with Sandra's parents without it affecting our relationship with the girl here in the store. There's always trouble when you try to mix your private life with business."

"You and I have been doing it successfully for years," Amanda reminded him.

"That's true," Mark murmured, his smile sardonic, "but lately we've been having trouble, haven't we?"

Amanda shivered. Taking a deep breath, she inquired, "So I gather you won't go with me to meet the Pollards tonight?"

"That's right," Mark said. "I'd prefer you didn't go, either, but if you think these people can do you some good, then I won't try to stop you—not that I could ever stop you from doing anything once you made up your mind."

"At least you know me that well," Amanda muttered, surprised to hear the acid in her voice. She squared her shoulders. "Very well, I'll go by myself and make your excuses."

Patches of hot, indignant color bloomed on Mark's cheekbones. "You'll do no such thing!" he snapped, half rising from his seat. Emphatically he told her, "*Nobody* makes excuses for me, Amanda—not even you. If the Pollards ask where I am, tell them I said thanks very much for their concern, but I prefer to deal with my problems my own way."

Amanda refused to retreat from Mark's anger. She commented dryly, "You know, that statement would be a lot more convincing if you showed any sign of dealing with your problems at all."

Mark's flush deepened, and his expression grew shuttered. Subsiding into his chair, he jerked his calculator out of his pocket and slammed it down on the blotter. He began reviewing the computations he'd made in his notebook.

Amanda bit her lip, her eyes burning as she watched her husband pointedly ignore her. She wondered why it was that she'd never noticed before what an effective wall the partners' desk formed between them.

WHEN AMANDA ARRIVED at the coffee shop, half a dozen people were milling around the lobby, marking time until they were seated. Amanda searched the crowd, uncertain whether her clerk's mother and father were among them. All at once a couple who appeared to be in their late forties stepped toward her, their hands outstretched in greeting. "Amanda, it's so good to meet you at last," the woman exclaimed. "Sandra's been raving about you for months."

Amanda wondered how the Pollards had managed to identify her so quickly, until she realized that all they had to do was watch for a middle-aged pregnant woman. For her own part, Amanda could now recognize definite similarities between Sandra and her parents. Stephanie Pollard was a graying blonde with her daughter's round face and chunky figure and the same engaging grin. Her husband, Gordon, was taller and thinner, a retiring-looking man in a somber business suit, but the vivid fringe encircling his natural tonsure made it clear from whom Sandra had inherited her red hair.

Amanda shook Gordon's hand, but when she turned to the other woman, to her surprise Stephanie wrapped her arms around her and hugged her as if they were old friends—and to Amanda's even greater surprise, she found herself hugging Stephanie back. In that embrace from a stranger Amanda felt the warmth and caring and understanding that had been denied her by the people who supposedly loved her, and suddenly she was clinging to Stephanie and shaking with emotion.

Endless moments later, remembering where she was, Amanda broke away and stepped back, glancing around with embarrassment to see if anyone else in the restaurant had witnessed her outburst. "I'm sorry," she mumbled, wiping her eyes. "I didn't mean to fall to pieces that way. I don't usually go around causing scenes in public."

"You didn't cause a scene," Stephanie assured her, her smile kind. "I promise you, nobody even noticed."

Gordon nodded benignly. "That's the great thing about places like this. Everyone minds his own business." His gaze skirted past Amanda toward the door. "I suppose your husband is parking the car?"

Amanda shook her head. "I'm sorry, but Mark couldn't come with me. He—" She started to invent some diplomatic excuse, but then she broke off, unwilling to lie. Inhaling raggedly, Amanda said, "Mark told me to tell you that he appreciates what you're trying to do for us, but he doesn't want to get involved in a support group right now. He says he prefers to deal with his problems on his own, but to be perfectly frank, I just don't think Mark is ready to face the fact that our child has Down's syndrome."

"When do you think he will be ready?" Stephanie asked.

Amanda shrugged, her expression bleak. "Maybe never," she murmured, the loneliness and finality of the word tearing at her.

Stephanie and Gordon exchanged glances. Gordon laid a firm, supportive hand on Amanda's shoulder and suggested gently, "Let's have a cup of coffee and talk."

That evening, while Amanda sat in a corner booth and conversed with Sandra's parents, she realized for the first time how isolated she'd felt since making her decision to have the baby, how desperately she'd needed a sympathetic audience, somebody who would hear her out without passing judgment or reminding her of the "easy" solution to all her fears and concerns. So far, the closest she'd found to an impartial listener was Steven Rhodes, and though the doctor continually assured her that he would do everything in his power for Amanda and her child, she had no idea how he felt about her decision on a personal level. Her parents, having accepted that they would never have the kind of grandchild they craved, seemed to regard her decision as a monumental faux pas, a tragic and irresponsible blunder that would discredit her family and alienate her from polite society. And Mark . . .

"Don't give up on your husband yet," Stephanie told Amanda. "Stress is inevitable in any relationship involving a handicapped child. Be patient with Mark— give him time. Maybe he does need to work out the situation in his own way. At least the two of you have a few months to prepare yourselves. It won't be the way it was for us, with the news thrown at you without warning."

From his wallet Gordon produced a recent photograph of his two children, a studio portrait of Sandra in a party frock, looking pretty and grown-up, and her older brother, a short young man in a suit and tie. George's hair was a darker red than Sandra's, and he had his mother's light eyes, but except for the heavy horizontal fold of skin on his eyelids and the rather flat bridge of his nose, he looked remarkably like his sister.

"You have attractive children," Amanda murmured, handing back the photograph.

Gordon smiled lovingly. "Thank you," he said. "You should have seen Georgie when he was born. He was the most beautiful baby, with big blue eyes and tiny red ringlets all over his little pink scalp. I remember standing next to Stephanie's hospital bed, holding him, thinking, this is my firstborn son. We named him George Raymond Pollard II, in memory of my older brother, who had died in Vietnam. I was so proud. The only thing that puzzled me was how floppy Georgie felt in my arms, sort of limp and unresponsive, not the way my sister's kids had been when they were babies, but I decided I just wasn't used to newborns." Gordon paused, his face grim. "Then the pediatrician came in."

Amanda watched Stephanie pat her husband's arm to comfort him, and she could sense the anguish the couple still shared, even after twenty years.

Gordon swallowed thickly before resuming his story. "I've never forgotten that moment—not that a moment like that is easy to forget. I still don't understand why the man told us the way he did. Maybe it was standard procedure in those days, or maybe he thought he had to be cruel to be kind, but what the doctor said seemed vicious and dehumanizing. He stared at me holding my son, and he announced baldly, 'We just got the tests back. That's a mongoloid you and your wife have there, and if you're smart you won't get attached to it. It'll never be more than a vegetable, so put it away someplace and forget you ever had it.'"

Amanda recoiled in horror, but Gordon appeared in control of his emotions once more. Calmly he continued, "Poor Steph became hysterical. The doctor had to summon a nurse to sedate her. And all during the commotion I just stood off to one side, still holding my beautiful infant son and trying to understand why God had cursed us. I distinctly remember thinking that perhaps the name was jinxed, that by calling my son after my dead brother I had inadvertently cast some evil spell on him, and I wondered if I could break the spell by gently placing my fingers around the baby's throat and squeezing...."

Amanda stared, tense with dismay and disgust, unable to believe she was sitting in an ordinary, unpretentious restaurant, listening to an ordinary, unpretentious man explain how once upon a time he had actually considered strangling his own child. "That's—that's a revolting story," she whispered shakily.

"Of course it is," Stephanie said, reaching across the table to catch Amanda's icy fingers in her own, "and we didn't tell it to you to upset you. The point of the story is that Gordon didn't hurt the baby, and we didn't let the doctor's prediction become a self-fulfilling prophecy by abandoning our son in an institution. Sanity prevailed. But in moments of crisis—and let's be honest, being told your child has Down's syndrome is about as traumatic a crisis as any parent can face—people are apt to think or say or do things that are completely out of character. Adoring fathers can contemplate murder, compassionate doctors can bandy words like 'vegetable,' and loving husbands—" Stephanie sighed. "Well, sometimes loving husbands do leave their wives."

"And sometimes they come back again," Gordon reminded Amanda. "So please, try to be patient and understanding with Mark. I know that must seem like an impossible order right now, when all your hopes and fears are centered on the child growing inside you. But at least you do have the child, you can feel him—you know he's real. Until the baby's born, your husband's relationship with him will remain problematic at best. That's nature. That's a fact in every pregnancy, no matter how untroubled. In a difficult case like yours, you have to remember, the only reality Mark can center on is you—and who knows what fears he's suffering right now?''

BY THE TIME Amanda finally returned home, Mark was already in bed, reading. He sat propped against a mound of pillows, and light from the lamp on the nightstand spilled in a golden circle over him, gilding his hair, burnishing his smooth, naked body down to the sheet draped across his thighs. When Amanda stepped into the bedroom, Mark laid the thick book facedown in his lap and smiled at her, his expression reserved. ''How was your evening?'' he asked.

''It was fine. I like Sandra's parents.'' Amanda put away her handbag and tugged off her cardigan. As she folded it, she inquired with measured courtesy, ''And how was your evening?''

''Very quiet,'' Mark replied, his tone equally polite, equally unrevealing. ''I was actually able to get started on the Ludlum thriller I bought ages ago. It's a good, fast read. I'm halfway through it already.''

''That's nice,'' Amanda murmured. She began to undress, slipping out of her long top and stretch-waisted slacks with swift, methodical movements. When she had stripped down to her underwear, she paused to regard her reflection in the mirrored closet doors, grimacing at the plain white cotton panties and bra encasing her increasingly bulky figure. Amanda had always loved luxurious, alluring lingerie, and her biggest gripe against maternity wear was that the only undergarments available seemed to be sturdy and utilitarian to the point of ugliness. Maybe the manufacturers assumed that pregnant women were beyond allure. Amanda huffed in annoyance and removed the remainder of her clothes.

As she bundled up her discarded clothing, Mark announced suddenly, "Before I started reading, I did something I've been meaning to for several months now." Amanda glanced up, puzzled. He told her, "I made an appointment to have a cellular telephone installed in your car tomorrow."

Her eyes widened. "Why did you do a thing like that?"

He shrugged unconvincingly. "It seemed like the thing to do." Amanda continued to stare. Finally Mark blurted, "Okay, I admit it, I don't like you being where I can't reach you! You drive all over northern Oregon in this job. The thought of you getting stranded somewhere, unable to call me...or a doctor..." His voice faded and he shuddered.

Amanda blinked. "Oh, Mark," she murmured.

He said tightly, "I know you think I don't care about what you're going through right now, but you're wrong. I worry about you. I worry about you all the time."

The naked fear in his face stunned her. Quickly she averted her eyes, unable to face that raw emotion directly. Noting the clothes still wadded in her arms, she muttered, "Excuse me while I dump this mess in the hamper." She ducked into the dressing room. When she reappeared in the doorway, he was watching for her, his gaze hot and intent on her nude body. She padded self-consciously across the bedroom, aware of him following her every movement.

When she opened a dresser drawer to fetch her favorite silk nightshirt, he whispered throatily, "Please don't put on a nightgown."

She forced herself to meet Mark's hungry stare. He was caressing her with his eyes, touching every part of her, from her face and ripe breasts to her rounded belly with the peculiar brown line that was forming between her navel and the delta of dark curls beneath.... Amanda sighed. "Darling, I love you, but I'm very tired."

"I only want to hold you," he said.

A dimple formed in her cheek. "I'll bet." She closed the dresser drawer and climbed into bed.

She fell asleep in the crook of his arm, her face nuzzled against his chest, her tender lips curved in contentment. Mark sensed her smile and thanked God that there remained one way in which he was able to make her happy, since he seemed to be failing her in every other way. Despite his behavior, which had to strike her as bigoted, almost irrational, at least the two of them were still able to communicate sexually. At least his insecurities had not yet driven her from his bed.

She snuggled closer, her breasts cushioned against his side, a slim leg draped across his thighs. Mark stroked the elegant line of her spine, the curve of her small bottom. Even in slumber she was warm and soft and succulent in his arms, and she exuded a subtle, honey-sweet fragrance that intoxicated him. Without her unique perfume to fill his nostrils, Mark thought, he might forget how to breathe.

He could not bear to lose her.

Not the way he'd lost the others.

CHAPTER SEVEN

"THIS IS A WONDERFUL HOUSE," Amanda told Susan Hendrix and her husband. Amanda and Mark were standing with the other couple in the entry hall of Otto Gunderson's old home. Sunbeams streamed through the stained glass fanlight over the big front door, sparkling on dust motes, casting carnival-colored light on the worn green carpet and faded beige walls.

Susan glanced around, her expression skeptical. "If you say so," she muttered, wrinkling her nose at the musty air. "It looks—and smells—pretty decrepit to me."

"That's just because the house has been closed up since last winter," Amanda said, smiling tolerantly. "Your grandfather's executors kept the gas and electricity connected so the pipes wouldn't freeze, but apart from a routine security check now and then, the place hasn't been opened for months. You'll like it much better once it's been aired and cleaned."

Since receiving the keys to the property, she and Mark had been inside several times, first with an attorney to make a videotaped survey of the interior, and later with an independent appraiser to begin cataloging the contents. Although Mark remained surprisingly noncommittal, Amanda had fallen in love with the house. Everything about it appealed to her: the big rooms and long hallways, the elaborate staircase with lyre-shaped balusters and the ornate light fixtures that dangled from high, bordered ceilings. Despite somebody's misguided effort in years past to "update" the decoration by painting over the rich wallpaper and covering the parquet flooring with drab wall-to-wall carpeting, Amanda could see the inherent style and quality of the architecture. Once upon a time the Gunderson family manor must have been quite a showplace. With some imagination and a comparatively modest outlay of cash, the right person could make it a showplace again.

And Otto's granddaughter was obviously not the right person. As soon as Amanda met Susan Hendrix—a chic, sleek brunette in a Liz Claiborne suit—she had guessed the woman would not be attracted to the antique splendor of her ancestral home. Susan and her husband, Philip, a computer expert, both appeared to be in their early thirties, and they were obviously too forward-looking, too modern in outlook—too *young*— to find much appeal in the rococo excesses of a bygone era.

Buffing the mahogany wainscoting with her fingertips to raise a shine on the dull wood, Amanda continued, "You mustn't be put off by the fact that the interior needs serious refurbishing. What you have here is a diamond in the rough."

Philip frowned. "Very rough, you mean. When we were viewing that tape you sent us, I got the impression some of the rooms hadn't been painted in decades."

"Judging by the avocado-and-gold color scheme, probably not since the early sixties," Mark observed.

Susan nodded. "You may be right about that. I can't remember exactly, but it seems to me that the one time I was here before, when I was a very little girl, the house looked about the way it does now."

"God knows how much it's deteriorated since then," her husband grumbled. "Your grandfather must have really let it run down."

"Not necessarily," Mark said. "Appearances can be deceptive. Even though Otto may have neglected the decoration, he kept the house itself in repair. When the appraiser and I were looking it over, we discovered that the basic structure is remarkably sound for a building its age. The roof is solid. The plumbing and wiring are good, even if they are outdated. A person would have no trouble living here."

"I'm glad to hear it," Philip said. "It'll make unloading it that much easier."

"There's no chance you might hang on to it?" Amanda asked.

Susan shook her head. "No chance at all, I'm afraid."

What a pity, Amanda thought, squelching the words before she could speak them aloud, but the other woman seemed to hear her silent admonition.

"I know I must sound mercenary and heartless," Susan admitted frankly. "You two probably think I'm only interested in the money I can realize out of my grandfather's estate, and in a way, I suppose you're right. But the fact is, I scarcely knew my grandfather. Living in the East, I've always been closer to my mother's family. Besides, relations between Otto and my father were strained before I was born—I'm not exactly sure why, but I suspect Dad didn't get along well with Otto's second wife—so I never had much opportunity to form an attachment. When Dad died in that boating accident and Otto came for the funeral, we tried to comfort each other, but we were strangers. I'm truly sorry the man was lonely, but there was no way Phil and the girls and I could have moved out here to keep him company."

"I'm sure Otto never would have expected you to," Amanda reassured her. "I can't pretend that I knew him very well, either, but in our few conversations he impressed me as being intuitive and practical. I think he'd approve of your plans for your inheritance."

The other woman smiled and slipped her arm through her husband's. "It's true, the money will make a big difference to us. We should finally be able to get Phil's software company going."

"If you're trying to raise capital, then I think you're going to be pleasantly surprised by the results," Mark said. He indicated the briefcase he was carrying. "I have the appraiser's notes here, as well as some rough estimates. Do you want to see them now, or would you care to go through the rooms first?"

Turning to his wife, Philip suggested, "Sue, why don't I stay down here and look over the papers while you and Mrs. Wexler go ahead with the grand tour? I know you spotted some things on the tape that you said you might want to keep as mementos."

When the two women were out of earshot, Susan regarded Amanda with a rueful smile. "You'll have to excuse Phil for not sounding more enthusiastic. He's a dear man, but he's even less sentimental than I am. Besides, I think he finds unused houses a little spooky."

"Lots of people do," Amanda murmured. *Even Mark,* she added to herself, recalling her husband's peculiar reaction the first time they'd entered Otto's old home. The attorney who accompanied them on that initial tour had been a brisk, no-nonsense sort. Amanda would have liked to linger over each newly discovered treasure, but the lawyer had insisted they work methodically and efficiently. When he headed for the first room they were to document, Amanda trooped dutifully after him, video camera in hand, pausing only when she realized Mark was not alongside her. She looked back. Her husband was still standing in the vestibule, gazing with a frozen expression up the length of the steep, narrow staircase. When Amanda called his name, he turned and stared at her, his face blank and gray, as if he'd forgotten for a moment who she was. His eyes were haunted.

"You say you're looking for keepsakes," Amanda noted to Susan as the two women strolled through the house. "When you were watching the tape, was there anything in particular that caught your attention? If Victoriana doesn't appeal to you, there's a lot of furniture from later periods that you might like better."

Susan's brow furrowed. "I don't think I'll want any of the furniture," she decided. "None of it really strikes me as fitting our taste or life-style. But what I would like to see are some of the smaller items I spotted—knickknacks and porcelain, for instance—"

"Oh, there's some lovely porcelain," Amanda told her. "You have some fine pieces of Meissen that I understand originally belonged to your great-grandmother, as well as some Lowestoft and Wedgwood. And if you like kitsch, there's quite a collection of souvenir plates and memorabilia from World's Fairs, everything from the 1915 Panama-Pacific International Exposition to the one in Montreal."

"Really? How delightful," Susan exclaimed.

Seeing her enthusiasm, Amanda relaxed, grateful to have discovered at last something that interested her client. Since taking on the Gunderson job, she was amazed at how proprietary she'd become about Otto's

worldly goods, and how surprisingly—and illogi-
cally—resentful she felt that his heirs viewed his estate
only in terms of the cash to be realized from its sale. She
said, "Of course, most of the really good porcelain is
displayed in the parlor or the dining room, but there are
little pieces scattered throughout, even in the nursery."
She paused. "Would you like to see the nursery? It's my
favorite part of the house."

"I wonder why," Susan drawled, glancing with an
indulgent grin at Amanda's maternity smock. "Sure,
I'd love to see it. Lead the way."

As they climbed the stairs to the second floor,
Amanda told the younger woman, "Even though the
children's quarters obviously haven't been used in decades, they've been maintained carefully. There's a
beautifully hand-embroidered coverlet on one bed, and
the closets are full of toys. The first time I stepped inside, despite the dust and the must, I had the feeling that
the little boy who played with those toys was liable to
come bounding back into the room at any second."

"I see what you mean," Susan murmured, her voice
oddly subdued as she surveyed the nursery, from the
crib in a curtained alcove to the student desk and
chalkboard to the easel with a crude crayon sketch of a
sailboat still tacked to it. Amanda had the feeling that
for the first time the other woman was relating to her
surroundings, viewing the place not for its profit potential but as an integral part of her heritage. "There's
a lot of love here," Susan whispered.

"Yes," Amanda agreed quietly, understanding. The
room vibrated with love, as if the emotion were an energy field emanating from the very walls. Amanda had
sensed it the first time she stepped inside. Despite half
a century of disuse, the Gunderson nursery still ra-

diated more love than she'd ever experienced in her own childhood.

Susan swallowed hard. "I didn't expect it to be like this, considering what rotten terms Dad and Otto seemed to be on for as long as I can remember...." Delicately she touched the name scrawled at the bottom of the yellowed drawing. The dry paper crumbled beneath her fingertips. "My—my father drew that picture," she stammered, choking back tears.

To allow her client some privacy, Amanda turned away discreetly and pretended a sudden interest in the baby furniture in the alcove. The crib, with its matching dresser and change table, did not deserve the intense scrutiny she was giving it. Despite its age, the set was not especially valuable. The pieces were machine-made of pine with a dark mahogany varnish that had deteriorated through the years. When Amanda jiggled the dresser, she could feel it give slightly, indicating the glue had weakened. Considering the nursery suite's shabby appearance and lack of style, it was unlikely to command much attention at the auction, which was a shame, Amanda thought, because the wood was still sturdy and all the hardware intact. With that fake finish stripped away and the joints reinforced, the set would be both attractive and functional. She wondered if Susan might have any use for it.

But when the other woman regained her composure and Amanda asked her about the crib, Susan laughed. "Thanks, but no thanks. The day our younger daughter started school, I fell on my knees and shouted hosannas of thanksgiving for my deliverance. There aren't going to be any more Hendrix babies." She caught herself, obviously worried that she'd been tactless, given Amanda's condition. Quickly she amended, "I love my kids, you understand, but between raising them and trying to help Phil get his business off the ground..." She shrugged. "It's hard to imagine just how many hassles a couple of healthy, rambunctious youngsters can give you."

It's even harder to imagine how many hassles a not-so-healthy youngster can give you, Amanda said silently, annoyed by Susan's innocent remark; then fiercely she squelched her irritation. If she expected to be any kind of mother to her disabled son, the first thing she had to do was develop a thicker skin.

Amanda said aloud, "You don't have to explain, Susan. I just wondered whether you might want to keep the nursery suite for yourself or someone you know. With a little refurbishing it could provide years more service, but I really don't think it'll bring what it's worth at the auction."

Susan shook her head. "I'm sorry, but I don't need the furniture, and I can't think of any of my friends who'd want it badly enough to warrant the cost of shipping it back east. As far as I'm concerned, you can give the set to the first person who offers you whatever the appraiser valued it at."

"That sounds reasonable," Amanda said, flipping open her memo book. "I'll make a note to include it with the other items we sell from the store. In the meantime, is there anything here in the nursery that you do want to keep for yourself?"

Susan's expression softened, reminding Amanda that her client was not a cool, avaricious Yuppie but a young woman who had lost a great many people she loved. Susan ventured wistfully, "I don't suppose there's any way we could take down that drawing of my father's without it disintegrating, is there?"

Amanda smiled gently. "We can ask Mark. If he doesn't know how to do it, then I'm acquainted with several other dealers who specialize in preserving old documents. One way or another, we'll save the picture for you. I promise."

STANDING BEHIND AMANDA, Mark laid his hands on her shoulders and said, "Hey, you, didn't your mother ever tell you it's not good for your eyes to spend so much time staring at a computer? You need to take a break now and then."

Blinking blearily, Amanda glanced away from the monitor, where she'd been working on the catalog for the Gunderson sale. Although for years she'd maintained their store's inventory and accounts on a computer, composing the sales book marked her first venture into desktop publishing, and she was finding the task challenging and frustrating in about equal measure. "What time is it?" she asked with a yawn, relaxing in her swivel chair and stretching her arms over her head.

Mark's face loomed above her. "It's nearly two," he told her, peering at her upside down, his brows a slash of concern where his mouth should have been. He caught her chair and tilted it backward until Amanda's feet left the ground.

"Careful!" she yipped, flailing dizzily.

Mark murmured, "Calm down, I'm not going to let you fall." Delicately he caressed her tired eyes with his lips, his warm breath fluttering her lashes. Amanda grew very still. She waited for his mouth to touch hers, but instead of kissing her, he abruptly righted her chair again and began to knead the tense muscles corded at her nape. "You've been up here typing away for hours."

Despite the delicious pressure of his fingertips, Amanda could not relax. She felt disgruntled and worried. "Why didn't you buzz me?" Ordinarily noon was their busiest time of day, when workers in the surrounding office buildings took their lunch breaks, although as the Rose Festival approached, they were seeing more and more tourists in the store. "Haven't we had any business?"

In Mark's hazy reflection on the computer screen she could see him shrug. "We've had lots of business. But Sandra and I were able to handle things."

Frowning, Amanda persisted, "Are you sure? I could have helped out."

"I told you, we were able to handle it," Mark repeated. "Now be still and let me massage your neck. You're coiled tighter than a watch spring."

Obediently Amanda settled back into her seat, but she remained unconvinced. "Well, if you're really sure..." she muttered dubiously, the words dying in a groan of pleasure as Mark prodded a particularly sensitive spot. Under his expert hands some of the physical stress began to leach from her body, but despite his reassurances, she could not shake off the mental strain that plagued her.

Lately Amanda had grown tetchy about doing her full share of work. Given the fragile state of their personal relationship at the moment, she did not want Mark to have any reason to claim she was failing him in their professional partnership, as well. Not that he'd ever blamed her in any way—on the contrary, his manner toward her was attentive in the extreme. That cellular telephone had been only one example of his solicitude, albeit an ironic one, since, as the days warmed and her pregnancy advanced, she was spending less and less time with her body crammed behind the wheel of her sedan. Her weight was rising daily, while her energy level, ordinarily very high, was ebbing. As much as she enjoyed scouting for merchandise, driving enervated her. The long trips out to the Gunderson estate, where she was involved in the herculean task of tagging, listing and photographing every single item in the house, left her completely exhausted. Although she would have died rather than admit it, she was beginning to entertain serious doubts about whether she was going to be able to continue working until the estate auction, which was not scheduled for another three months.

After extensive discussions with Susan and Phil Hendrix, they'd settled on a fall date. Although Otto's granddaughter and her husband were naturally eager to obtain their money as soon as possible, Mark had been able to convince them that profits would be substantially greater if adequate lead time was allowed for the extensive preparation and publicity an estate sale of this magnitude warranted. Amanda had already sent announcements to the major antique trade journals, and in a few weeks she'd order advertising space in newspapers throughout the Northwest.

Despite her determination to hide her chronic fatigue from Mark, he had noticed it. One evening while she lay slumped on their sofa, drained and aching, Mark had studied her white face with alarm and finally hazarded, "You know, I've been thinking. It might be a good idea to hire a second clerk, at least during the festival. Sandra could use some help in the showroom."

Amanda's lashes flew up, and she levered herself onto her elbows. "I thought I was supposed to be in the showroom with Sandra," she said dangerously. "I thought we agreed we wouldn't hire another clerk until I go on maternity leave."

Mark took a deep breath. "I've also been thinking it might be a good idea for you to consider starting your maternity leave sooner than we'd planned."

Amanda had exploded with a bitchy vehemence that astonished and embarrassed her in retrospect. "Why?" she demanded, instantly forgetting her own qualms. "Are you hinting I've let you down on the job? Are you saying I'm not doing my share, that I'm making more work for you and Sandra?"

With more patience than her paranoid raving deserved, Mark answered, "It's only a thought. We both know you can't continue working indefinitely, and I'm sure your doctor would approve of you getting more rest. Considering how tired you become—"

"That's only because it's been getting warmer," Amanda snapped. "You know hot weather always bothers me."

"I think it's the standing on your feet all day that's bothering you," Mark persisted, "not to mention running up and down the stairs at that damned house."

"I can't help it if Otto didn't install an elevator," Amanda grumbled petulantly. "As for working in the store, I'll sit down if I have to, but I refuse to use my pregnancy as an excuse to do less than my half."

Mark scowled, but his tone remained mild. "Amanda, there's no reason for you to pretend you're one of those peasant women who supposedly labor in the fields till they drop their babies in the dirt and then get up and resume the plowing. You're allowed to take time off to rest." He paused. "But if you really do believe it's too soon to hire extra staff, we'll make some other arrangement. How would you feel about taking over my share of the paperwork? You'd be doing me a favor—you know how I hate bookkeeping—and you'd be able to set your own pace and relax whenever you needed to. In return, I could fill your shift on the sales floor."

Amanda remained skeptical. "You wouldn't mind putting up with Sandra's dithering?"

"It seems to me the girl dithers a lot less than she used to," Mark commented.

At last Amanda had sighed. "Very well," she conceded with ill grace, "if you insist, we'll try it your way for a while. But this is only a temporary arrangement, you understand, just until I get some of my energy back. I don't want you thinking I'm ready to quit work yet."

"Of course not, darling," Mark had crooned, and Amanda had recognized his soothing tone as the same one he'd used on a cranky child.

Now, peering over Amanda's shoulder at the computer screen, Mark noted with approval, "You're really whipping right along on that catalog. I'm impressed by how quickly you've learned to use this new software."

"Mostly it's just a matter of common sense and reading the manuals," Amanda said, shrugging. The movement made her wince.

Mark resumed the massage. As he rubbed the stiffness from her taut muscles, he chided her, "Amanda, even though I'm delighted by the progress you're making, you are supposed to be taking things easier these days. It doesn't do much good to switch to a desk job if you wind up exhausting yourself more than if you were working the sales floor.''

''I'm not exhausted,'' she retorted defensively. ''I'm just stiff and uncomfortable from sitting so long.''

''Then how about getting some fresh air and exercise?'' Mark suggested. ''I missed lunch, too. Now that things have slacked off a little downstairs, we could walk over to the Yamhill Market for something to eat.''

Amanda hesitated, rubbing her cheek against the hand on her shoulder while she gazed at the computer. ''A break sounds wonderful,'' she admitted wistfully, ''but I really had hoped to get two more pages keyed in before I quit this afternoon.''

She felt Mark's irritation return. ''Why the big rush?'' he demanded in clipped tones. ''You have plenty of time before the deadline on getting the pasteups to the printer.''

''I just want to do my part while I still feel up to it, that's all,'' Amanda insisted. ''By the time September rolls around, I'm not going to be much use to anybody.''

''Maybe so,'' Mark said, ''but I really wish you had let me contract out the catalog rather than taking on the job yourself. It would have been a lot easier for you.''

Amanda countered, ''The work's not hard, just exacting. Besides, think of the overhead. The money I save by doing everything myself will partially offset the cost of my replacement.''

Mark swore under his breath and rotated her chair so that she faced him. ''Damn it, Amanda, you know perfectly well we can afford to hire extra help!'' he reminded her grimly. ''Even without the Gunderson commission, Wexlers' isn't exactly a shoestring operation.''

"Of course not, but—but—" She sighed in resignation. "Please, let's don't argue. Can't you accept that I want to do as much as I can while I'm still able? I've been working all my adult life. I thrive on work, I *enjoy* my work. It's all well and good to say I should relax more, but the fact is, without my job I'd be climbing the walls inside a week."

Mark's expression gentled. "But this pregnancy is taking so much out of you."

Amanda patted her stomach. "Oh yeah?" she muttered. "You wouldn't say that if you'd seen the scales this morning." Her lips curved ironically. "Darling, I'm forty-two years old. I never expected it to be a piece of cake."

Shaking his head, he squatted beside her, his eyes level with hers. There was a faint gleam of silver in the lock of fair hair that drooped over his forehead, and she could see fine lines scoring his brow, lines deeper and more numerous than they'd been a few months earlier. If Amanda was feeling her age, then so was Mark. Soberly he told her, "If we live to a hundred, you'll still be one of the youngest people I've ever met. But I'm very concerned about you."

"I know," Amanda said. Stroking her husband's cheek, she repeated softly, "I know you worry about me. I promise I'll try to pace myself better, but please don't make me quit my job."

"Eventually your own body is going to force you to slow down," Mark reminded her darkly.

She nodded. "But by then, if I'm lucky, I'll have something—some*one*—else to occupy my time."

Mark did not reply. He rose to his feet and stalked back to the partners' desk, but not before Amanda had glimpsed his anguished expression. She wondered what he was thinking as he pretended to sort through the envelopes and magazines piled on her blotter. She wondered if he had guessed that the real reason she insisted on working until she was numb with fatigue was because that was the only way she knew how to keep her mind off the schism between them. Despite Mark's solicitude, she was all too aware that he still had not accepted her decision to have the baby. He continued to refuse to meet the Pollards, and the couple of times Amanda had tried to discuss setting up a nursery, he had changed the subject. The rift caused by his unwillingness to talk grew wider daily.

Oddly, the one place where they still seemed to communicate at all was in bed. They continued to make love as frequently as before her pregnancy, perhaps even more often, but now there was an element of desperation in their passion, a tacit, melancholy admission that the mystical empathy they'd once shared no longer united them, and the only satisfaction they could give each other now was physical. For Amanda, it was not enough.

And apparently Mark was as miserable as she was. She knew he often remained awake after he thought she'd fallen asleep. Many nights, while she feigned slumber, she could hear him pacing in the study. The audible evidence of his distress did not gratify her. She loved Mark—she had always loved him—and he loved her. Sometimes—only sometimes—lying awake in bed, listening to the restless sound of his agitated movements echoing through the dark condominium, she dared to ask herself whether she wasn't wrong to sacrifice that love for an uncertain future.

Abruptly Mark tossed the mail he'd been glancing through back onto the desk. Facing Amanda again, he asked, "Well, do you want to go out for lunch or don't you?"

Hastily she answered, "Yes, I'd like that very much." She turned back to the keyboard long enough to type in the save command. After switching off the computer, she pushed her ungainly body out of her swivel chair and stood up, listing to one side as she rubbed her aching back. She yawned elaborately. "You're right, I do need to get out more. Staying cooped up in this stuffy office is beginning to make me claustrophobic."

Mark's mood lifted. "Then let's take a walk. It's a gorgeous day today, and the fresh air will help you work up an appetite."

Amanda picked up her handbag. "Would you mind a tiny delay on the way to lunch? I want to pop into that maternity shop two blocks over. In their window I spotted a dress that would be perfect for Mother's dinner party."

"Of course I don't mind," Mark said, slipping his arm around her thick waist as he escorted her toward the door. "You know I enjoy seeing you in pretty clothes. Of course, by the same token, I hope you don't mind being adventurous cuisinewise. Unless you're violently opposed to the idea, I'd like to try out that Greek café in the market. I have a sudden craving for stuffed grape leaves."

"Oh yeah?" Amanda teased. "I thought I was the one who was supposed to have weird cravings."

Mark's grin was expansive. "This is the nineties, remember? Husbands and wives share everything now."

If only I could be certain that were true, Amanda thought as they headed down the stairs. If only she knew whether in "everything" Mark was including the

most important thing a husband and wife could share—
the life of their child.

WHEN MARK AND AMANDA returned from lunch, replete with moussaka and laden with fresh produce
they'd picked up at the market, the store was full of
customers. In the children's area, Sandra was demon-
strating a cast-iron mechanical bank to one couple,
while in other parts of the showroom more people
milled impatiently. Amanda looked at her husband. "It
would appear we got back just in time."

"Right," Mark muttered, nodding toward the front
of the shop, where a pair of adolescent boys in De-
peche Mode T-shirts were smirking their way through a
collection of old magazines. Because of the nature of
the business, few teenagers wandered into Wexlers'
Antiques and Collectibles, and those who did were
usually girls looking for costume jewelry. While Mark
and Amanda welcomed customers of all ages, through
the years they'd learned that it was prudent to keep a
watchful eye on some of the younger ones. Mark said,
"I'll see what those guys are up to."

Amanda glanced in the direction of the dining display, where three people were examining a small gate-
leg tea table. "And I'll get the others," she concurred.
Detouring into the back room long enough to drop off
her purse, the groceries and a dress box from the maternity boutique, she smoothed her hair with her hands
and bustled across the showroom. "May I help you?"
she asked with brisk good cheer, but her professional
smile warmed with real pleasure when two of the three
turned to her and she recognized the stocky blond
woman and the tall, balding man with the vivid red
fringe.

"Stephanie, Gordon—how delightful!" she declared, greeting Sandra's parents with a hug. "What brings you here today?"

Stephanie said lightly, "Oh, we decided it was about time we saw our daughter's workplace with our own eyes. Last winter, when you first hired Sandra, she made us promise faithfully that we wouldn't embarrass her by dropping by—"

Gordon interjected, "What she actually said was 'I'm not six years old and I don't need Mommy and Daddy checking up on me to make sure I'm doing my job right.'"

Everybody laughed. Then Stephanie finished, "After dutifully biding our time all these months, listening to her rave about the store, Gordon and I figured we've earned the right to visit."

"Of course you have," Amanda replied firmly. "You should have come ages ago, regardless of what Sandra said. Has she had an opportunity to show you around yet?"

Gordon shook his head. "That couple she's waiting on now walked in right behind us, so we're trying to stay out of her way while she takes care of them."

Amanda's gaze flicked back toward the clerk and her customers, who were consulting a well-thumbed Kovel's price guide, a sure sign of serious collectors. "It does appear as if Sandra will be busy for a while yet," Amanda agreed. "We'll wait a few more minutes, and if she's not free then, I'll be your tour guide myself. In the meantime—" she looked past the Pollards to the front of the store, where Mark was bagging an old *Saturday Evening Post* for one of the teenagers "—in the meantime," she repeated, her tone marginally less positive, "at long last you'll have an opportunity to meet Mark."

If Sandra's father heard the faint hesitation in Amanda's voice, he gave no sign. "That's great. We were hoping your husband would be here, because there's someone we want you both to get acquainted with, as well." He turned to the third member of their party, a young man who was still bent over the tea table, and gestured for him to step forward. When the young man stood between Gordon and Stephanie, Gordon wrapped an arm lightly around his shoulders and announced proudly, "Amanda, I'd like to introduce you to our son."

The resemblance between Sandra and her brother was even more pronounced in person than it had been in the photograph, Amanda realized, surveying the youth with an intensity she hoped wasn't obvious. Neatly groomed in jeans and a green polo shirt that set his auburn hair ablaze, Georgie Pollard was short, about the same height as his sister, and, like her, he gave the impression of being slightly overweight, although Amanda suspected some of that fleshiness was an optical illusion caused by his squat neck and stubby fingers.

Gazing at Georgie, Amanda wondered suddenly how tall her own child would be. When she first became pregnant, she had fantasized about a lanky six-footer with dark hair and blue eyes, who would slouch adorably as he stood at the podium to deliver the valedictory address to his graduating class at Stanford.... Her image of her son who resembled a young Jimmy Stewart was only one of the pipe dreams she'd had to discard when she learned of her baby's condition. Down's syndrome people, she knew, were usually small in stature with a tendency toward obesity, just as Georgie was.

Still, Amanda wondered wistfully, since she and Mark were both taller and slimmer than the Pollard parents, was it foolish to hope their child would grow to at least medium height? Impatiently she discarded the thought. If she'd learned one thing during the past few months, it was not to make assumptions about the future. Besides, she added fairly, there were worse fates her son could suffer than to look like Georgie Pollard. The young man was not unattractive. In fact, apart from that distinctive fold of skin that gave his pale eyes the illusion of being slightly slanted, there was very little outward indication that Georgie was other than perfectly normal.

If anything, Amanda decided, it was Georgie's expression that set him apart from other people, the guileless warmth of his smile. She knew he was twenty years old, but he seemed much younger. When she extended her hand to him, he accepted her greeting with an ingenuous delight that struck her as not so much childlike as . . . innocent. Amanda remembered how Sandra had once described her brother as being totally without malice. Amanda could believe it. Georgie radiated a sweetness, a naïveté almost breathtaking in its purity. Despite his age, he appeared to be untouched by life.

Considering the heartaches in store for any child born in these times, Amanda suddenly wondered if such purity of emotion might not almost be a blessing.

Huskily she said, "I'm very happy to meet you, Georgie. Sandra's told me a lot about you."

He beamed. "Sandy's told me a lot about you, too." He spoke slowly, hesitating as if considering each word individually before uttering it. "She says she really likes working for you and Mr. Wexler." His voice, while low pitched, had a peculiar roughness to it, a blurring of tone that reminded Amanda of the speaking voices of certain deaf persons. Recalling from her reading that Down's syndrome children were especially susceptible to ear infections, she wondered if he'd suffered a hearing loss when he was younger.

While Amanda talked to Georgie and his parents, out of the corner of her eye she saw the teenage boys saunter through the front door, and a moment later she heard firm, familiar footsteps approach. Murmuring an excuse to the Pollards, she turned to her husband. "Don't tell me those kids actually bought something," she said, chuckling with forced heartiness.

"Believe it or not, one of them was hunting for a magazine published the week his dad was born. He wanted it for a Father's Day present."

"Really? How imaginative," Amanda declared. "I guess there's hope for the younger generation after all." She paused. Inhaling raggedly, she caught Mark's sleeve. "Now that you're free for a moment, there are some people here I'd like you to meet," she told him, and she nudged him over to Sandra's family.

She had to give her husband credit for being a good actor, Amanda thought as she made the introductions. With her fingers curled lightly around his arm, she could feel him stiffen, but none of his tension showed in his face. His smile was congenial as he welcomed Stephanie and Gordon and assured them their daughter was a real asset to the business. When he greeted Georgie, his friendly expression remained firmly in place.

Not that Amanda had truly imagined Mark would be overtly discourteous, of course. His impeccable, almost courtly good manners—a heritage from that tragic southern girl who had been his mother—had been too deeply instilled in him ever to falter, no matter how sorely he was tested. But when Amanda considered Mark's bewildering behavior of the past few months, his apparent prejudice against the developmentally delayed, she realized that she would not have been surprised if he had suddenly concocted some excuse to duck out of this meeting.

Instead, Mark chatted quite naturally with their guests. Stephanie commented on the weather being perfect for the upcoming Rose Festival, and when Gordon referred to the accounting firm where he was employed, he and Mark discovered they had mutual acquaintances there. After Sandra's customers completed their transaction and left the store, she joined the group. The conversation remained light, innocuous, the smallest of small talk. Nobody mentioned Amanda's pregnancy, and nobody hinted at the real reason behind the Pollard family's visit to the shop.

Then Mark turned to Georgie and said cordially, "A while ago I noticed you inspecting that little teak table behind you. It's one of my favorite pieces in the store. Do you like it, too?"

The young man shrugged uncomfortably. "I don't know. I think it's too nice."

Amanda, who was still holding Mark's arm, could feel the frisson of negative emotion—confusion, distaste, pity, she wasn't certain which—that shuddered through him in reaction to Georgie's apparently nonsensical remark. But once again Bonnie Wexler's childhood training prevailed, and Mark's expression revealed none of his true feelings. His face was inscrutable as he murmured, "I'm sorry. I don't understand what you mean."

Georgie glanced at his parents and sister, who all smiled back encouragingly but remained silent. Watching the byplay among them, it occurred to Amanda that Georgie's family probably always insisted on his speaking for himself, even though Amanda was sure there often had to be times when it would be tempting, as well as faster and more convenient, for one of the others to step in and take over the conversation. She'd never considered before that teaching someone to assume responsibility for his own words was an essential part of teaching him to assume responsibility for his life. There was so much she needed to learn if she hoped to raise her child to maturity and independence....

Mark repeated patiently, "I'm afraid I don't understand what you mean about that table being too nice, Georgie. Yes, it is a fine piece of furniture. Why is that bad?"

The young man's brow wrinkled as he struggled to explain. "I need something for my class, something small like that table, or maybe a chair. But it's got to be old and scratched so I can fix it up again. That table doesn't need any fixing."

Light dawned, and Mark relaxed. "Oh, now I see. You're looking for a piece of furniture you can practice restoring, right?"

"I need it Monday," Georgie replied, his relief at being understood almost palpable. He scanned the showroom sadly and sighed. "I've been looking and looking, and I can't find what I want. Sandy told me you might have something here I could use, but everything is too nice."

Mark said, "I'm sorry, but unless an item is very rare, we hardly ever stock pieces that aren't in good condition. It's just too much hassle—"

"Wait a minute, Mark," Amanda interrupted. "Do you remember that job lot we bought from Ted a few weeks ago? Wasn't there a little lingerie chest that we decided was too beat-up to display?"

"Yes, of course, I remember that chest," Mark said, scrubbing his cheek with a fingertip. "It's Japanese, with a lacquer finish so crazed you can hardly tell what color it was originally. The drawers are falling apart, but all the pieces seem to be there. I think it's in the corner of the back room."

"Well, don't you think that might be exactly the sort of thing Georgie is looking for?" Amanda persisted.

Mark grimaced. "I don't know. Lacquer is so difficult to work with...." He regarded Georgie sternly. "Do you think you could put drawers back together and restore a lacquer finish?"

With dignity the young man told him, "I'm learning how to fix all kinds of furniture. My teacher says I'm good."

"Fine," Mark said. "In that case, why don't we go take a look at that chest? It's not doing us any good, so if you can use it, you can have it."

Hesitating, Georgie glanced questioningly at his parents. Gordon said, "It's your decision, son."

"Okay," Georgie declared with an eager nod. His face glowed. "Mr. Wexler, I'd like to see the chest, please."

Mark gestured toward the rear of the store, to a door near the office stairs. "The storage room is back this way," he said, leading the way. Georgie plodded after him.

Breathlessly Amanda watched the two men disappear from sight. Her heart was pounding. While she knew it was unrealistic to pretend an instant rapport had developed between her husband and the youth, at least Mark had been tolerant and patient. She wondered if she dared be optimistic for the future.

She turned to the Pollards, her eyes glossy with unshed tears. "I didn't know what to expect," she whispered hoarsely. "After the way Mark's been behaving lately, I was afraid that if he ever met your son, he might not be...polite."

"Oh, really? You expected him to call Georgie names?" Stephanie drawled. Her teasing tone faded when she saw how upset Amanda remained. Giving Amanda's shoulder a reassuring squeeze, Stephanie reminded her gently, "Your husband is a compassionate man, dear. I could tell that the instant I saw him. One look at Mark, and I knew he'd never deliberately reject anyone just because they're different."

Still wary of hoping for too much, too soon, Amanda stammered, "But—but if Mark is so compassionate, why has he been so stubborn about meeting you two? How can he be so sweet to Georgie when he refuses to talk to me about—about our own baby?"

Gordon said firmly, "The answer to that question is easy, Amanda. Your husband is a good, caring man, but he's also human and he's scared—as he has every right to be. As much as Steph and I love our son, as proud as we are of his progress, neither one of us will pretend the past twenty years have been easy. Mark's just having trouble facing up to what lies ahead for you two."

Stephanie said, "But perhaps tonight Mark has made the first step in the right direction. Don't you agree, Amanda?"

"Maybe," Amanda whispered, staring at the storage room door. She wondered what Mark and Georgie were saying to each other in there. She wondered if her husband's conversation with the Pollards' son was making him any more confident of the future, any more willing to accept his own son.

"Maybe," she whispered again. She wrapped her arms around her waist, hugging herself and her child.

CHAPTER EIGHT

AMANDA'S MOTHER'S REPUTATION as an outstanding hostess was well deserved, and among Portland's elite, invitations to the party she gave annually during the Rose Festival were prized. This year's affair was no exception. The house on Cumberland Road was bedecked with the cream of Joan's flowers, their heady perfume drenching the air, their colors so breathtaking that the vivid formal gowns of the guests seemed dull by comparison. The menu was sumptuous, a gourmet delight, and after dinner the lead soprano from the Portland Opera entertained the gathering with a recital of light classics. She concluded with a witty pop medley that segued from "The Rose" to *"La Vie en Rose"* and "Second Hand Rose," and when the applause died down, the guests began to filter through the house and out into the gardens. Mark and Amanda, who'd sat together during the music, separated. He became engrossed in a conversation about golf with Jim Bishop and several other men, while she drifted down the corridor to the library, where she settled into a comfortable chair beside the empty fireplace and slipped off her silver high-heeled sandals. Cheryl discovered her there, rubbing her stockinged toes together.

"Aha, caught you!" Cheryl cried when Amanda tried to tuck her feet beneath the handkerchief hem of her long blue skirt. As Cheryl flopped into the armchair on the opposite side of the hearth, she shook her blond curls in mock reproach and chided her friend, "Don't you know pregnant women aren't supposed to wear anything but orthopedic oxfords with sturdy arch supports?"

Amanda grinned. "Well, if I didn't know before, I certainly found out tonight. My feet are killing me." She sighed and shrugged her bare shoulders. "Actually, I do know better. This is the first time in weeks I've put on heels. Lately I've taken to wearing sneakers with just about everything—but somehow I really couldn't see teaming this dress with a pair of Reeboks."

Cheryl surveyed her approvingly. Amanda was wearing a silk gown of deceptively simple cut, with layers of ultramarine chiffon flowing from tiny jeweled straps that sparkled like the diamonds in her ears. "That's a spectacular dress," Cheryl commented. "Very sophisticated. You're lucky. Maternity clothes are so much nicer now than they were back in my childbearing days. Everything then was sort of sickeningly adorable, all frills and teddy bear prints. I guess the idea was to wear something till the baby was born and then make nursery curtains out of it."

Amanda chuckled. "Oh, Cheryl, you know that's not true. I remember when you were expecting your oldest girl. You looked perfectly fine."

"But you look beautiful," her friend countered. "In fact, I think it's almost obscene for a pregnant woman to look as good as you do. Don't you realize this reproduction business is supposed to inflict at least a little wear and tear? I swear, you seem younger every time I see you."

"I certainly don't feel younger. Sometimes I think I must be about a hundred years old."

"Fatigue just goes with the territory, hon," Cheryl commiserated, "but don't worry, in a few months you won't be pregnant anymore—and then you'll learn what *real* exhaustion is all about!" She paused. After a moment she asked, "Seriously, Amanda, how are you? Is everything okay with you and the baby?"

Amanda studied her manicure. While she picked at an imaginary rough spot on a cuticle, she pondered her reply. She knew Cheryl's question was an honest one posed out of genuine concern for her welfare, a question that deserved an equally honest answer. Cheryl was a caring, compassionate woman, and they had been friends too long for Amanda to dissemble. Continuing to hide the truth made Amanda feel underhanded, especially since she knew Cheryl was bound to feel hurt when she learned—as she inevitably would—that Amanda had misled her about the baby. On the other hand, Amanda also knew that the moment was wrong. A dinner party in her parents' home was hardly the appropriate occasion for earthshaking revelations.

Staring intently at her nails, Amanda equivocated, "My obstetrician says I'm doing fine."

If Cheryl noticed the ambiguity of that remark, she was too diplomatic to comment. Instead, she said, "That's great. Despite all the aches and pains, in a woman's life nothing quite measures up to the magic of being pregnant. When I remember how special I felt in those days, I almost envy you the experience."

Amanda smiled skeptically. "Oh, really?"

Cheryl laughed. "I said 'almost.' You know I'm very, very happy for you and Mark, but frankly, considering what's involved in starting a family at our age, I'm equally happy that Jim and I aren't the ones doing it!"

"Did we hear somebody take our names in vain?" Jim called, strolling into the library alongside Mark.

Amanda glanced up, catching her breath at the sight of her husband. Even after ten years, she still loved to look at him. Like all the other male guests at the party, he and Jim were both handsomely attired in black tie, but evening wear suited Mark especially well. The severe tailoring emphasized his height and bearing, and the stark contrast of snowy pleated shirt and somber suit was a perfect foil to his fair coloring. Compared to Mark, Jim looked slightly ill at ease, uncomfortable—which was ironic, considering that Jim had lived in upper-middle-class luxury all his life, while Mark had not owned a tux until after he and Amanda were married. . . .

Clearing her throat, Amanda said, "What brings you guys in here? I thought you were back in the other room arguing the merits of that new golf club in Lake Oswego."

"Your mother made us break up," Mark explained lightly. "She said she hates parties where all the men and women separate into little groups, and she was depending on us 'boys' to set a good example."

With a chuckled aside, Jim noted, "I just love your mother, Amanda. She's the only person I know who can make me feel fifteen again."

Mark finished, "Anyway, dutifully obeying our hostess, Jim and I decided it was time to find out where you two had disappeared."

Jim sank onto a hassock at his wife's feet, while Mark crossed the room to Amanda and perched on the arm of her chair. Stroking her hair absently as he spoke, he asked, "So what have you been talking about? When we walked in here, the conversation sounded fairly intense."

Before Amanda could respond, Cheryl said with a grin, "Oh, like you, we were just following time-honored tradition. While you 'boys' were discussing sports, we 'girls' were talking about your upcoming blessed event. I guess pretty soon I'm going to have to start making plans to give Amanda a shower."

Feeling Mark's hand falter in its rhythmic movements across her head, Amanda said, "That's a lovely idea, Cheryl, but don't you think I'm a little old for a baby shower?"

"It's the baby's age that counts," Cheryl drawled. "After all, no matter how old you are, your child is still going to need diapers and a layette and all the usual accoutrements—and when you consider how many shower presents you must have forked out over the years, it's only fair to get a few back. Besides, don't you think it would be fun to see some of the old gang again? It seems like ages since we got together."

Amanda bit her lip. "I—I guess so," she murmured, wondering where she'd find the strength to endure a baby shower. Steven Rhodes and the Pollards all insisted that few things could help her through these difficult months as much as the support and encouragement of the people closest to her. But if Amanda still lacked the courage to tell Cheryl, arguably her best friend, the truth about the baby's condition, how was she supposed to face a bevy of school chums with their congratulations and their happy reminiscences about their own childbirth experiences?

"I guess a shower would be fun," Amanda repeated slowly, without conviction, "but only if you promise not to make any plans just yet. You know how small our condo is. I have no idea where I'd put a bunch of baby presents." Leaning her cheek against the silky sleeve of Mark's jacket, she forced a smile. "For that matter, we aren't altogether sure yet exactly where we're going to put the baby."

Jim suggested, "Maybe it's time for you to contemplate getting some place a little roomier. Your condominium is perfect for just the two of you, but when you have kids, you have to start thinking about things like houses with yards—"

"And schools," Cheryl added earnestly. "Even if you expect to send your child to private school, you need to make sure your neighborhood schools are good, too, in case your plans change in the future."

Jim added, "That's true. And, of course, good public education will increase the resale value of your house, as well. That's one great thing about the area where we live—"

"Speaking of which," Cheryl declared, "I know of a lovely home that just went on sale only a block away from us. If you'd like to see it, I could—"

Mark held up his hand, signaling a halt to their friends' excited comments. "Wait a minute, you two! Aren't you getting a little ahead of us? We barely mention that we need a handy spot for the crib, and already you've found us a house in the suburbs. Don't you think you ought to slow down a bit?"

Chagrined, Cheryl shrugged. "We're just saying it would be nice if you guys lived closer to us, that's all."

"I know," Amanda agreed quietly. "I'd like very much to be closer to you, too. But we really haven't thought that far into the future. The mere fact of the baby has changed so many things for us that right now we're trying to take life one step at a time."

Jim nodded. "You're probably wise. It was traumatic enough having kids early, the way Cheryl and I did, but at least it was more or less what we'd always expected. I can't imagine what it would be like to start a family in your forties. You must feel a trifle unsettled at times."

Completely discombobulated, Amanda thought with arid humor, wondering how her friends would react were she to reveal exactly how unsettled her life had become in recent weeks. She said nothing.

In the lull that followed, instrumental music, sweet and rhythmic, floated down the corridor from the other end of the house. Amanda cocked her head to listen. "More rose songs?"

Cheryl commented, "It sounds like dance music to me."

In confirmation of her remark, Alden suddenly appeared at the library door. He was wearing an old-fashioned but impeccable evening suit, with a crimson rosebud on his lapel. "Ah, there you are, Amanda," he declared. "Your mother asked me to find you young people and let you know there's dancing in the solarium."

Glancing at her husband and friends—all patently middle-aged—Amanda suppressed a smile and said politely, "Thank you for telling us, Father."

Alden hesitated. "Are you all right, child?"

"I'm fine," Amanda answered in surprise. "Why do you ask?"

Her father's grizzled brows came together. "After the way you vanished following the entertainment, I thought perhaps you weren't feeling well."

Amanda wriggled the bare toes protruding from beneath her skirt. "My feet are a little tired, that's all."

He scowled. "Maybe you should lie down for a while."

"That's not necessary, Father," Amanda replied quickly. "I'm okay, really."

Obviously unconvinced, Alden muttered, "Well, if you're sure...." He sighed. "If you're up to it, I know it would mean a lot to your mother if you'd mingle more. People have been inquiring about you, and we wouldn't want them to get the idea that something was wrong."

"I'm sorry," Amanda murmured, wondering if only she could hear the subtle emphasis in her father's last words. In the weeks since receiving the results of the amniocentesis, Alden and Joan had adopted a curious attitude toward Amanda and their unborn grandchild. In private they made it clear to her that they felt she was being selfish and utterly wrongheaded in proceeding with the pregnancy, that by doing so she had elected a course that would have disastrous repercussions in the family for generations. On the other hand, knowing her decision was now irreversible, in public they awaited the baby's birth with a sort of stiff-upper-lip dignity, the way Amanda imagined they'd behave if she was to become involved in some egregious scandal. She might have found a certain pathos in her parents' attitude, if only she wasn't convinced they were still secretly hoping for a miracle—or a blessed release.

Amanda repeated, "I'm sorry, Father. I didn't mean to be rude. I don't know whether I'll dance or not, but we'll join you in the other room in a few minutes."

"Please do," Alden said sternly. He paused, and his expression softened as he added parenthetically, "You all really should come see the solarium. I realize the music may not be exactly what you youngsters like, but there's a full moon tonight, and we've turned off the lamps so that the moonlight streams in through the glass on the people who are dancing. The effect is quite lovely. In fact, it's rather...romantic." Then, grimacing as if he'd said something gauche, Alden nodded abruptly and bustled down the corridor.

In the library the four people seated around the fireplace stared at each other. Cheryl exclaimed, "My goodness, girl, I had no idea your father could be so sentimental."

"Neither did I," Amanda muttered darkly. "He must be swept up in the mood of the party. He certainly never acts that way with me—"

Suddenly Mark squeezed Amanda's arm. "Well, darling," he asked briskly, "shall we show your parents what well-brought-up children we are and go dance?"

Amanda glanced uncertainly at her husband, assuming his suggestion was merely a tactic to divert the conversation from the increasingly ticklish topic of her familial relationships. But gazing into his face, she saw that he was beaming back at her, his expression candid, with none of the furtive desperation she'd glimpsed lately whenever he thought she was not watching him. She gulped. Perhaps her father was not the only one to have succumbed to the romantic atmosphere of the party.

"Dance?" Amanda echoed, the word catching in her throat. "Do you really want to dance?"

"If you're not too tired, I wouldn't mind," Mark said. "It's been ages since we've been on a dance floor together—not since the cruise, in fact—and Joan and

Alden's pianist is a hell of a lot better than that character on the ship."

"You mean the one you bribed not to play?" Amanda whispered huskily. Her eyes grew drowsy with erotic memories. Still she hesitated, her mouth dry. Wetting her lips, she reminded Mark, "But I—I've changed since the cruise. You may not be able to get close enough to put your arms around me anymore."

With mothlike delicacy Mark dipped a fingertip in the sheen of moisture on Amanda's mouth. "I've managed so far, haven't I?" he murmured, his tone heavy with meaning.

Across the room Jim coughed. When Mark and Amanda both started, jerking their heads in his direction, he lifted his brows comically and leered. "Hey, you two, don't you know what that kind of behavior can lead to?"

Cheryl clapped her husband's shoulder. "Not much point in warning them now, dear. From the looks of Amanda's waistline, I'd say your lecture is about five months too late."

THEY DANCED IN THE SOLARIUM until the moon was a memory and on the eastern horizon the glaciers atop Mount Hood shimmered in the nacreous light of dawn. After parting with the Bishops, Mark carried Amanda home, where they fell asleep in each other's arms and did not stir until almost noon. When they awoke, still bathed in the romantic aura of the evening before, they made sweet, ardent, fulfilling love. They spoke little. For once words seemed unnecessary. It was only when they recalled the concert tickets they held that they dressed reluctantly and headed downtown for Sunday brunch at one of the hotels overlooking the Willamette and the Rose Festival Center stretched along Waterfront Park.

From the restaurant window Mark gazed down at the greenbelt, where tall trees were overshadowed by the dark, massive hulls of the U.S. and Canadian navel vessels moored at the river's edge. He could see crowds of people clambering over the ships and streaming down the gangplanks to the carnival ashore. Fair rides whirled like giant kaleidoscopes, and vivid banners fluttered in the breeze. Every few moments a helium balloon would tear loose from a child's fingers somewhere and shoot upward, a dot of color dancing against the bright sky. In the caged cars atop the tall Ferris wheel, which was about level with the window where Mark and Amanda sat, teenagers waved and spun dizzily.

Glancing across the table at his wife, who was wearing the blue denim jumper he liked so much, Mark asked suddenly, "What would you think about going to the carnival this afternoon instead of the symphony?"

Amanda looked up in surprise from her crab quiche. "Why the sudden change of plans?"

Mark shrugged. "As much as I love music, all at once it struck me as too beautiful a day to spend cooped up in an auditorium."

"You may be right about that," Amanda murmured, following his gaze out the window. She smiled. "If you'd prefer to walk around instead of going to the concert, that's fine with me. I don't think I've been to a carnival since I was in college."

"I'm not sure that I've ever been to one," Mark said.

Amanda laid down her fork and stared. "You're kidding. Not ever?"

He pondered. "I don't think so. I've been to amusement parks, and, of course, I was working at the

World's Fair in Seattle when I got drafted—but if we're talking about a traveling carnival like the one set up down there in the park, then no, I don't think I've ever been to one. Although..." He scowled with concentration. Gesturing vaguely, Mark muttered, "I have this very faint recollection, sort of a frozen image, of being someplace with my parents, someplace with lots of bright lights and noise and crowds. I guess it must have been a carnival set up in a field, because I can recall scuffing my shoes in the dirt and clinging to Mom's hand while Dad swung a big wooden mallet at one of those ring-the-bell games. They were both laughing—" Mark broke off with a grimace. "My God, if I'm really remembering as far back as I seem to be, neither one of my folks would have been half the age I am now." He glanced across the table at Amanda, who was regarding him quizzically. "Why the funny look?"

She said, "I was just thinking how strange it sounds to hear you refer to your father. In all the years we've been together, I don't think you've mentioned him a dozen times."

"There's nothing to mention," Mark declared tersely. "He didn't stick around long enough for me to build up much in the way of fond memories." He paused, his expression enigmatic. "Did I ever tell you I tried to find him once?"

Despite her astonishment, Amanda did not blink. "After your mother died?"

Mark shook his head. "Under the circumstances I imagine the Spokane police would have tried to contact him then, but if they had any luck, I wasn't there to hear about it. I'd already hit the road to avoid having Mrs. Tedesco climb into my bed again...." He exhaled roughly. "I'm talking about years later, when I was in the army. At this late date I can't even remember what prompted me to make the effort. Plain old curiosity, I suppose. It's not as if Dad and I would have had anything constructive to say to each other. But whatever the reason, I bribed one of my buddies who was a records clerk to put through a request to Washington asking for any current information on a veteran named Robert Wexler. Eventually they responded with a list of about a dozen Robert Wexlers, and yes, one of them was my father, but the last address shown was where we'd been living when he walked out on Mom."

Diffidently Amanda ventured, "If you're still interested in locating him, it might be easier now than it was in the early sixties. His record must be in a data bank somewhere—Social Security, for example. He'd be retirement age now, assuming—" She broke off, not wanting to say the words.

Mark finished the sentence for her. "Assuming he's not dead, you mean? You don't have to be tactful, Amanda. I have considered that possibility."

She winced. "But if your father did die, as his next of kin surely you would have heard somehow."

"Not necessarily," Mark dismissed. "For years I was just as rootless as my old man apparently is. In any case, it doesn't really matter. As far as I'm concerned, I've been an orphan since I was fifteen." Abruptly he reached for the check. "Have you finished eating yet? We're wasting that beautiful afternoon we promised ourselves we'd enjoy."

They did not refer to Robert Wexler again, and as they strolled through the carnival, enjoying the sights and sounds of the merrymakers, Mark's good humor returned. Amanda noticed that the uncharacteristic frankness that had prompted him to mention his father in the first place seemed to remain with him. She wondered if his mood was an extension of the night before or merely a product of the balmy weather—or perhaps an answer to the smiles of the people around them. Mark appeared relaxed and content, more open and unreserved than he'd been with her in months. He held her hand and they wended their way through the crowds milling around the rides and game booths—slowly, Mark adjusting his long stride to the awkward duck-footed gait Amanda was beginning to adopt as her weight increased. Passersby noted her condition and beamed on them, and Mark grinned back, his expression warm and full of masculine pride.

When the heat and the din began to tire Amanda, they left the amusement area and headed for the relative peace of the riverbank, strolling along the walk until the barkers' cries and the amplified circus music were far behind them and only an occasional shrill whoop from a nearby playground disturbed the quiet. Resting her elbows on the floodwall, Amanda was gazing out over the dark water, absorbing the soothing rhythm of its flow, when a girl in a long patchwork skirt scurried past, headed in the direction of the carnival, a basket of flowers and ribbons on her arm. Mark raised his head and stared after her. Amanda looked at him, puzzled. "What's the matter?"

"Nothing's the matter," he said with a laugh. "Wait here just a minute, and I'll be right back." While Amanda watched in bewilderment, Mark loped after the girl carrying the basket. Quickly he concluded his negotiations, and a moment later he returned to Amanda with a garland of white and yellow roses woven into a fragile, fragrant coronet with silky streamers. "Flowers for my lady," he murmured, settling it precariously on her dark hair.

Amanda's eyes widened in amazement. When she moved her head, she could feel the wreath shift unstably, and one of the ribbons dangled against her cheek. "For heaven's sake, Mark." She laughed, her fingers fluttering nervously on the garland as she tried to steady it. "I can't wear flowers in my hair."

"Of course you can," he drawled. "They go perfectly with your denim jumper and sandals. We can pretend it's 1969 and we're back at Woodstock."

"I wasn't at Woodstock, and neither were you," Amanda reminded him dryly. "But the mere fact that we could have been is proof positive that I'm too damn old to be going around decked out like a superannuated flower child." She started to remove the roses, but Mark captured her fingers.

"Please, Amanda," he urged quietly, "I want you to wear them."

Her hands fell back to her sides. "But I feel so silly."

"You look beautiful," he whispered, smoothing the flossy tendrils of dark hair disarranged beneath the garland. "Like a bride."

"A pregnant, middle-aged bride?" Amanda quipped hoarsely, her mouth dry as she gazed up at him.

His eyes gleamed, blue-hot. "*My* bride," he murmured. He bent his head to hers—

A child's voice, screechy with outrage, pierced the air. "Hey, dummy, get away from there!"

As Amanda watched, Mark's face went white. He pivoted in the direction of the cry.

At the edge of the nearby play area were parked two bicycles with gaudy helium balloons tethered to their handlebars. A small dark-skinned boy dressed in shorts and an Indiana Jones T-shirt was clinging to one of the bikes while he stood on tiptoe and tried to clutch the balloon strings that skittered in the breeze. Although he appeared to be only about five years old, he was wearing glasses, and, intent on his quest, he did not see the two slightly older boys bearing down on him.

The first boy to reach him yanked his arm and bellowed in his ear, "Hey, dork, I said keep your stupid hands off my bike!"

The younger child reeled, gaping at his attacker with eyes that were slightly crossed behind his thick lenses. He smiled vaguely. Then one of the balloons bobbed into his field of view. "Mine," he cried, fumbling again for the string just beyond his grasp.

The third boy entered the foray. "No, stupid, they're *ours*," he taunted, "so you just get lost!" He elbowed aside the smaller child, who stumbled against the bicycle and knocked it off its kickstand. It toppled into the second bicycle, and both overturned in a heap on the grass with a loud metallic clatter. One of the balloons popped.

The oldest boy squealed, "Now look what you did, you dummy!" and furiously shoved the smaller child, who landed on top of the fallen bicycles. His glasses fell into the dirt. Wailing with panic, he flailed blindly for them and began to cry.

Mark swore under his breath and sprinted across the lawn, Amanda in his wake. Inserting himself protectively between the distraught child and his assailants, Mark growled, "All right, you guys, that's enough. Leave him alone."

The two boys recoiled, staring up apprehensively at the fierce, towering stranger who had suddenly materialized in their path. In the sternest tones Amanda had ever heard him use, Mark reprimanded them. "You ought to be ashamed of yourselves, picking on somebody smaller than you."

The ringleader tried to bluster indignantly, "But—but he messed with our bikes and broke my balloon!"

"He wasn't hurting anything until you grabbed him," Mark said.

The boy sniffed and beetled his brows. "I don't like retards touching my stuff."

"Yeah, mister," his cohort chimed in. "We know this kid. He's blind as a bat and so stupid sometimes his mama keeps him on a leash. My sister says—"

"Enough!" Mark shouted. "I don't want to hear another word from either of you. Now just take your things and go play somewhere else."

The two boys exchanged glances. One took a deep breath, as if preparing to blurt out some final charge, but Mark glowered and shook his head slowly. All at once the boys scooped up their bicycles and sped away, skidding in their haste.

Grimly Mark watched them leave, then he turned to Amanda. She was kneeling on the ground, brushing grass from the little boy's clothes and gently resettling his glasses on his nose. As she looped the earpieces into position, one of the ribbons on the wreath she was wearing fluttered toward him. His wet brown eyes widened with delight. "Pretty," he cooed. Amanda held very still. He tugged at the silken streamer and turned it over in his fingers, examining it intently. By the time he released it, his tears were forgotten.

When Mark assisted Amanda to her feet, the child was clinging trustingly to her free hand. She glanced at her husband and asked under her breath, "Now what? Where are his parents? We can't ask him—he's barely verbal. Do you suppose he could have wandered away from the carnival?''

"I'm not sure," Mark muttered, his gaze sweeping the greenbelt. "Those little hellions claimed they knew him, so at a guess I'd say he comes from somewhere in the immediate—" He broke off, nodding toward a path on the far side of the playground. A young black woman was racing through the park, jerking her head frantically in all directions. Mark waved and caught her attention.

"Oh, thank God!" she gasped, her words muffled against her son's small, squirming body as she swept him into her arms and hugged him hard. "We were at the water fountain, and I turned my back for *one second*..."

Trying to sound wiser than she felt, Amanda murmured, "Sometimes a second is all it takes."

"Don't I know it!" the younger woman declared with a sigh, her fear slowly subsiding. "Kids this age are always a handful, but this little guy has them all beat...." Her voice died in a strangled whisper. Studying Mark's and Amanda's faces as if trying to ascertain how much they'd noticed, she cleared her throat and explained gruffly, "I'm afraid he's severely retarded." Amanda nodded, her expression sober. The boy's mother shuddered. "I was so terrified. When I think of the road on one side of the park and the river on the other..."

Amanda patted her arm and consoled, "Don't think about it. He's safe now. Apart from a slight tumble, nothing happened, so the two of you might as well go on and forget about everything but enjoying the rest of this beautiful day."

"I guess you're right," the young woman agreed. She let the wriggling boy slide down out of her arms. When he settled on his feet, she clasped his hand securely and they started to walk away. Glancing back over her shoulder, she called, "Thanks again!"

"Don't mention it," Amanda replied, a smile pasted on her lips. She waved at the departing pair, then she turned to Mark. He was gone.

Shading her eyes against the sun, Amanda scanned the park until she spotted Mark's rapidly retreating figure in the distance on the embankment. He was stalking away from her, the space between them increasing with each swift, churning stride. Even from the back she could tell by the tense tilt of his head, the rigid set of his spine, that he was blazingly angry.

Mystified by his abrupt departure, she called his name. He did not seem to hear her. She tried to catch up with him, or at least come within shouting range, but after running only a few steps she halted in frustration, flushed and panting, a stitch in her side. She leaned against the floodwall, and while she gasped for breath, she was suddenly conscious of the surreptitious, hastily averted glances of passersby. All at once Amanda had a vision of the grisly spectacle she was likely presenting at the moment: a fat, wheezing, red-faced woman in a too-youthful dress, with the added fillip of flowers in her hair. It was definitely time to leave the park, she thought sardonically. The halcyon afternoon, so full of warmth and sharing, had been spoiled completely by that unpleasant incident with the little boys, and now Amanda just wanted to go home.

She looked for Mark again, but a swarm of sightseers had clustered at the wall to watch a yacht pass beneath the Morrison Bridge, and she could not pinpoint him in the crowd. She wondered where he was headed. His erratic behavior was both baffling and annoying.

She knew he had been upset by that incident in the playground—as anyone would have been—but he had no right to take out his indignation on her. It wasn't her fault those kids had gotten into a scuffle.

Covering her hot face with her hands, she cursed silently. She was beginning to feel exasperated enough to collect the car from the hotel parking garage and leave her husband behind to fend for himself, except that they'd driven downtown in his Volvo, and she wasn't carrying her spare set of keys. Short of hailing a taxi, she had few options other than to remain where she was until he deigned to come back. With a sigh she searched the area for a shady park bench.

By the time Mark returned to Amanda, he had been gone less than a quarter of an hour, but her impatience made the interval seem endless. In chilly silence she watched him approach. When he stood directly in front of her, his expression unreadable, she folded her hands across her stomach and gazed up at him.

The tense stillness stretched between them until finally Mark took a deep breath and said, "All right, I apologize for running off the way I did. That was...rude."

"That was a lot of things," Amanda observed, her tone curt. "I'm not sure 'rude' is even one of the more important ones."

"I needed a moment to sort a few things out. I have some feelings I'm having trouble dealing with."

"And talking to me wouldn't help you deal with them?" Amanda asked.

He shook his head. "I can't talk to you. I don't understand you anymore. It is utterly incomprehensible to me that any woman could deliberately choose to expose her own child to ugly altercations like the one we just witnessed between that pathetic little boy and those two young hoodlums."

Amanda winced. She stared into her husband's cold, accusing eyes and tried to recall the ardor with which he had looked at her less than an hour before, when he had placed the wreath on her hair. Had that look been real, she wondered poignantly, or had it been a product of her own fevered longing and lingering euphoria from an overdose of moonlight and roses? Reality or illusion, it was all gone now, evaporated like the loving affinity once so strong between them, vanished like her hope. The tall blond man looming over her was a stranger.

Despite her anguish, she refused to be cowed. Marveling at her own composure, she said quietly, "I haven't *chosen* our son's fate, I've *accepted* it. There is a difference." She paused to inhale raggedly before adding, "And just for the record, maybe you should remember that occasionally all youngsters, even perfectly normal ones, are teased cruelly by their playmates. It's a fact of childhood."

Mark's forbidding frown did not change. "That's easy for you to say," he grated. "You had the most overprotective parents in the world. They never even let you smudge your clothes— God forbid that you should do something as common as getting into a fight! You wouldn't be so quick to dismiss such scenes if you knew what they can lead to."

His bitterness rattled her. She had never realized before that he resented the difference in their upbringings. Determined not to show her hurt, with spurious calm she queried, "And I suppose you know more about childhood squabbles than I do?"

"Yes, I think I can safely say that's true," Mark countered aridly.

Amanda waited. "Well?" she pressed.

"Well what?"

She could feel her temper rise. "Well, are you going to explain that last remark," she demanded, "or do you just plan to keep me dangling? If that's what you have in mind, I might as well tell you now that I'm sick and tired of games." Her eyes flashed with dark lightning. Intensely she said, "This juvenile I-know-something-you-don't-know routine has no place in our relationship, Mark. After ten years, I deserve better. *We* deserve better. So for Pete's sake, quit equivocating and tell me what the hell you're talking about!"

She watched him struggle. She did not know what conflict raged inside him, but it appeared to be a brutal one. His eyes clouded and he squinted, as if he were trying to shut out images that assailed him. The planes of his lean face looked gaunt, taut and as sallow as parchment, and across his brow were slashed deep grooves like battle scars. When he spoke, his usually resonant voice sounded dry and sere, shriveled with pain.

He croaked, "You really want to know what I'm talking about? Okay, I'll tell you. I'm talking about Marilyn,"

"Marilyn," Amanda echoed through pursed lips. She nodded tightly. "I've always suspected that name meant more to you than you claimed. Who is—was—Marilyn? And don't try to feed me some fairy story about old movie stars."

Mark smiled without humor. "Actually, the reference to Marilyn Monroe wasn't a total fabrication, because that's who she was named for. She was blond and beautiful, just like my mother's favorite actress, and Mom figured the name would be a kind of good luck charm. For a whole lot of reasons that turned out to be a very ironic choice."

Perplexed, Amanda scowled as she tried to sort out the information Mark was giving her. She had not yet reached the correct conclusion when he sat down beside her and took her hand in his. With leaden precision he explained, "Marilyn was my baby sister. I was ten years old when she was born and my father left us. I was fifteen when my mother lovingly tucked her into bed with her Raggedy Ann doll and then blew out the pilot light on the gas wall heater, in order to put them both out of their misery."

CHAPTER NINE

IF HE CLOSED HIS EYES, he could still picture the squalid apartment, the one with the movie stars' pictures pasted in a clumsy collage across the bare cupboards of the alcove that passed for a kitchen. In the area that served as a living room when the sofa bed was folded away, the only bright spot was a faded, curling poster from the film *How to Marry a Millionaire* thumbtacked to the wall over a tipsy table ornamented with a brass vase and a gaudy plaster candlestick from Tijuana. More than once Mark saw his mother wistfully arrange a handful of wildflowers in the vase and light a single fat candle, as if that tattered sheet of glossy paper were an icon of some goddess of glamour and romance, adored yet ever unreachable.

The candlewick had been cold and black that afternoon, and instead of the dusty-sweet fragrance of wild mustard, the room had reeked of gas. Mark could remember the weight of the policeman's callused hand on his shoulder as he gently nudged the shaking boy back to make way for the coroner's men; he remembered, too, that when the two covered stretchers were carried down the front steps of the apartment house to the ambulance waiting at the curb, one of the onlookers gawking on the sidewalk removed his cap and muttered, "God, that's tough."

Mark also remembered the officer's questions, compassionate yet insistent as he pressed for information. Was Mark absolutely certain he'd found nothing, no note or message from his mother to explain why she'd done it? Mark's response had been equally insistent, almost hysterical. No, no, there'd been no note. There'd been nothing at all. Why should there be? It was an accident, an accident.

But most of all Mark remembered the oppressive weight of the scrap of paper wadded in his jeans pocket, a single, crumpled sheet of cheap juvenile stationery, yellow with blue bunnies, and the equally childish handwriting that began, "Forgive me, Mark. I know this will be hard on you, but you have to believe me, it's better this way...."

Amanda's fingers lay flaccid and cold in her husband's while she stared in the direction of the festival center, her gaze focused on a distant pennant fluttering atop one of the cruisers anchored upriver. When she spoke, her voice sounded equally remote.

"Your sister," she murmured, not looking at Mark. "You had a sister, and you never told me about her."

"I never told anyone about her," he said.

"Why not?" Amanda asked. "What was wrong with her?"

There was an undercurrent of strain in his words, like the tension of an ungreased wheel. "Mom contracted German measles during her pregnancy. She was hardly sick—at first she thought it was only a light cold on top of morning sickness—but seven months later her baby was born profoundly deaf."

Shivering, Amanda laid her free hand on her belly and muttered, "Deaf. That was all?"

"There was some brain damage, too," Mark said harshly. "Though the doctors weren't sure of that at first. This was the fifties, remember? A lot of the tests we take for granted didn't exist yet. All the medical people could do was observe, and they observed right away that something was wrong with Marilyn because she didn't respond to outside stimuli the way normal babies did."

Amanda's fascination with the flags on the naval vessels did not abate as she persisted, "And on the basis of those observations, your father deserted his family and your mother killed herself and her own child?"

"My father deserted his family because he was a selfish, no-good son of a bitch," Mark shot back bitterly, but as he spat out the words his tone altered, the hostility fading to dull resignation. "At least, that's what I've been telling myself for thirty-five years. Now I'm not so sure anymore. Mom and Dad were both practically still kids themselves, and it had never been a happy marriage. Not that I'm trying to justify what he did, but maybe—maybe the prospect of raising a handicapped child was simply more than he could deal with."

At last Amanda turned to Mark again. Peering steadily at him, she asked, "And how do you justify what your mother did?"

Mark shook his head. "I don't. I'll never be able to forgive her for being so weak—but I do understand. She got into a situation she couldn't handle. Doctors advised her to put Marilyn somewhere where she could get special education, but Mom refused. She wanted her daughter with her.

He sighed wearily. "Maybe things would have been different if Dad had stuck around—I don't know. All I do know is that we lost everything when he left. The little bungalow we lived in, the pickup he drove, those all came with his gardening job, and once he was gone, Mom and the baby and I had to make way for the gardener who replaced him. Poor Mom had no job, no education and no family to turn to—apparently her parents had disowned her when she became pregnant with me. If it hadn't been for the housekeeper, we would have ended up on the street. But Mom had helped out from time to time, whenever an extra hand was needed for things like serving at parties, so the housekeeper talked the owner into letting her stay on as a maid, and the three of us moved into a single room off the garage. I think it had been used to store tires or something. I suppose I ought to have been grateful for a roof over our heads, but I hated that place. I hated the dark, tarry smell, like old rubber, that always seemed to be in the air, and I hated the way there was no place I could go to escape the sound of Marilyn crying. She cried all the time when she was an infant—perhaps she was in pain, I truly don't know—and as much as I loved her, that constant noise used to drive me crazy. The only thing worse was listening to my mother's muffled sobs when she thought I was asleep...."

Mark's voice trailed off, and he grimaced in disgust. "God, I don't want to talk about this. It sounds like a bad soap opera." He glanced at Amanda. She was gazing at him with dark, hooded eyes, her expression unrevealing as she waited for him to continue. After a moment he took a deep breath and said angrily, "The point of this dreary story is that we didn't even get to keep that smelly storeroom for very long, just until Marilyn was a toddler. She was still beautiful, but by then her deficiencies were glaringly obvious, and one fine day the owner's son, a boy about my age, decided to make fun of her. He called her a dummy." Mark paused, trying to shut out the tormenting memory of those childhood taunts.

Amanda said, "But your sister couldn't hear him."

"I could," Mark rasped.

She nodded. "Let me guess. You beat him up, right?"

Shrugging, Mark corrected her. "It'd probably be more accurate to say he beat me up. He was bigger than I was, and I was the one who ended up with the broken nose—not that any of that mattered to his parents. My mother still lost her job." He rubbed the bridge of his nose as if the ancient fracture pained him. "Things went downhill even faster after that. Mom tried to find another job as a domestic, but let's face it, even in those days damn few people wanted live-in maids, especially ones with handicapped babies. We ended up in a series of seedy apartments while Mom cleaned offices at night. I tried to take care of Marilyn, but I was just a kid myself, and whenever she was sick, which was often, Mom had to miss work. We struggled along that way for a couple of years. It was a lousy way to live, but in time I sort of adapted to it. When I started high school and got a part-time job at the Tedescos' grocery store, I actually thought things were looking up a little—" He broke off. After a moment, he said dully, "I guess Mom never did adapt. When I found her—them—I also found an envelope pinned to the pillow on my cot. In it were two locks of hair, her wedding ring and all the money she had in the world—$4.67. There was also a note saying she was sorry, but she'd tried as hard as she could and she'd finally realized that my sister would have been happier if she'd never been born."

Mark fell silent. Empty and enervated, he slumped against the back of the bench and studied Amanda's profile as he waited for her to speak. She was having difficulty dealing with his revelations, he could tell. Beneath the festive coronet she'd obviously forgotten, her magnolia-pure complexion was ashen, her cheeks pinched and hollow. And those striking dark eyes he loved so much looked as opaque as obsidian. As he watched, she slipped her hand from his grasp and crossed her arms over her breasts, hugging herself. She trembled visibly. He shouldn't have told her, Mark thought with compunction. No matter how hard she pressed him, he ought to have kept quiet. Considering the delicate state of her emotions in recent months, he ought to have spared her the additional burden of his sordid secrets. For a woman of her tender sympathy—

Amanda said, "How dare you?"

Mark blinked, uncertain he'd heard her correctly. "Darling?"

"Don't call me darling!" Amanda snapped, and with growing dismay Mark realized that what he'd mistaken for shock was in fact indignation and something perilously close to dislike. "How dare you keep such a secret from me?" she demanded, her voice quiet but shaking with betrayal.

Stunned by her attack, Mark countered, "I—I just didn't want to upset you."

"Upset me?" Amanda choked out. "What could possibly upset me as much as finding out that we've been together for over a decade without you divulging what was obviously the pivotal event in your life? What else don't I know about you?"

"Not much," Mark muttered. "Nothing that matters anymore, anyway."

Amanda refused to be mollified. "If you think a tragedy like your sister's death doesn't still matter a very great deal to you, then I'd love to know exactly what you do consider important." She shuddered. "Mark, what happened to your baby sister was terrible and senseless, and I'm truly, truly sorry for her and for you—but I'm even sorrier that you saw fit to hide it from me. I feel as if you've been lying to me for years. I'm your *wife*, damn it. I have a right to share your pain."

"But it wasn't just my pain," Mark reminded her. "There was my mother's memory to be considered."

Amanda grimaced. "Oh, yes, your mother—that poor, self-sacrificing little blossom crushed by a cruel world."

Puzzled by her tone, Mark said, "I suppose that's a fairly accurate description of her."

"A partial description, you mean." Amanda sighed. "I guess it's wrong of me to pass judgment on your mother without having known her. Maybe she really was everything you've ever claimed her to be, and it's pretty obvious that she must have been desperate and depressed. But still, it's hard not to view her as also being selfish and manipulative and in love with her own fantasies."

Mark shook his head in bewilderment. "I don't understand what you're saying."

"You don't see it, do you?" Amanda pressed. "Do you truly believe your mother was thinking solely of your sister when she set up that melodramatic little deathbed scene for you to discover, complete with locks of hair and confessions about babies who should never have been born? Good Lord, it's a wonder she didn't leave *Madame Butterfly* playing on the phonograph!"

Mark swallowed thickly. With reluctance he admitted, "Okay, it's true that psychologically Mom was a very extravagant woman—too much so. She would have made a good actress. Possibly if she'd been a little more down-to-earth, she would have seen that there were alternatives. It's horrible to speculate that murder and suicide could have somehow struck her as romantic.... Surely that's reason enough in itself to show some compassion."

"For her?" Amanda queried fiercely. "Maybe I would, if she'd shown some compassion for *you*. But she not only left you, she left you to find the bodies. That's obscene and unforgivable! Maybe even worse than what she did to your sister."

Rubbing the vein pulsing in his temple, Mark said, "Then if you understand that, perhaps you'll understand why I've never been exactly eager to tell you about that part of my past before. I never meant to lie to you, Amanda—except maybe by omission."

Amanda's eyes narrowed. "You lied deliberately at the genetic counseling session. When Steven Rhodes asked about your medical history, you told him and me both that you had no brothers or sisters and no knowledge of any birth defects in your family."

Blanching, Mark declared raspily, "I didn't think any purpose would be served by mentioning Marilyn. Her problems stemmed from my mother's German measles—they weren't hereditary. I promise you, if there had been any history of hereditary problems, I would have said something."

"I don't believe you," Amanda said. "I think you'd put up with anything to avoid breaking your precious silence. I think you'd rather jeopardize the health of your own child than risk having to admit that when it came to the crunch, your mother didn't care about what happened to you any more than your father did.''

Mark winced. ''That's an ugly thing to say.''

''It's an ugly thing to have to say,'' she told him, ''but I guess I'm just tired of being diplomatic. For months now, ever since we found out about the baby, you've been behaving...peculiarly, not at all like the man I thought I knew and loved. I've tried to make allowances. I convinced myself you were having more trouble dealing with the news than I was, that you were scared about the future—a perfectly understandable reaction. When I'd see how kind you are to people like Georgie Pollard or that little boy here in the park a while ago, I'd remind myself that you're a sensitive, caring man, and even if it took time, sooner or later you'd accept our child and learn to live with his condition.''

Amanda fell silent, moistened her lips before she continued. ''But I've been fooling myself, haven't I? Thirty-five years ago you wiped your sister out of your mind, and ever since then you've been pretending she never existed—and now that's what you want me to do with our son.''

Levering her thick body off the park bench, she stood up ponderously and positioned herself before Mark, her feet spread for balance. Despite her clumsiness, she faced him with a dignity so regal it was a rebuke. She started to speak, but she was distracted by a gust of breeze from the river that caused the ruffled hem of her denim prairie dress to flutter and the satin ribbons on her headdress to ripple. Her eyes widened with surprise and chagrin. Reaching up, she carefully removed the wreath and handed it to her husband. As she smoothed her hair, with equal care she murmured, ''Thank you for the roses, Mark. It was a charming gesture, but I think I'm too old to wear flowers in my hair."

She paused. Then she said, "I truly am sorry about your sister, Mark. Her death was a calamity, one you've obviously never recovered from. But after all these years you ought to have figured out that you can't ease your pain by pretending it didn't happen. Your sister was real, Mark, and however much you may wish it was different, our son is real, too. In fact, as far as I can tell, the only thing that isn't real is our marriage."

This time it was Amanda who stalked away.

WHEN THE YOUNG, expertly groomed secretary spotted Amanda struggling with an armload of bundles and shopping bags, she jumped up and bustled across the office to help her. "Oh, my, Mrs. Wexler, you have been busy," she said as she relieved Amanda of several cumbersome sacks and stacked them next to the desk. "It looks as if you've been to every baby boutique in the downtown area."

"Most of them," Amanda admitted ruefully, yawning and rubbing her back. "I probably overdid it a little."

The younger woman said solicitously, "Then, here, why don't you sit down and rest? I'm afraid Mr. Bishop is running a few minutes behind schedule this afternoon. May I get you something to drink while you wait? We have coffee or iced tea."

"Tea sounds wonderful," Amanda agreed, collapsing luxuriously into the soft cushions of the couch and flexing her tired feet. When the secretary returned with a tall, frost-beaded glass, Amanda accepted it gratefully. "Thanks, I needed that," she said with a grin as she savored the cold beverage. "You'd think I'd have had enough sense to pace myself in this heat, but today was the first time I did any serious shopping for the baby, and there are so many wonderful things to buy, it's hard to stop."

The younger woman nodded. "Yes, I remember how easy it was to go overboard when I was expecting my little girl." She glanced at her wristwatch. "I'm sorry, but I really don't know how much longer Mr. Bishop will be with his other client. Shall I find you a magazine?"

Amanda shook her head. "No, thanks, I have some stuff of my own I need to look through." Opening her handbag, she pulled out a nursery furniture catalog and several glossy brochures and began to thumb through them.

The afternoon Mark and Amanda spent at the Rose Festival had proved to be a turning point in her pregnancy, the day she reluctantly acknowledged that her husband was so crippled by his past that he might never be able to give her and her child the emotional support they needed. The anguish that admission cost her was almost unbearable, yet she knew she dared not succumb to it. She would not be like Mark's mother, devastated by the contrast between her dreams and reality. For the sake of her child, she had to be strong. Yes, dear God, yes, she loved Mark and she needed him desperately, but her baby needed her more.

She studied the advertising pamphlets with growing frustration. For months she had delayed setting up a nursery in the condominium, rationalizing her procrastination by saying she was too involved in preparing for the auction to shop for cribs and layettes. In fact, she'd been waiting for Mark to express some interest in the project; she'd hoped that if they worked together, somehow the shared task would help Mark bond to his unborn son. Now Amanda knew she could wait no longer. If providing a snug bower for the baby was to be her responsibility alone, then she needed to do it before her advancing pregnancy rendered her physically incapable of handling the job. The problem was, now that she was actually shopping for a nursery suite, she couldn't find anything she liked.

She stared at a photograph of some contemporary Italian furniture—sleek, blond and very expensive—that one of her friends had recommended. The Euro-chic styling struck Amanda as cold and pretentious. Another nursery suite, faux Victorian, was so poorly constructed it was laughable. Amanda tucked the brochures back into her purse. What she really wanted for her baby, she knew perfectly well, was something simple and sturdy and straightforward—like the old crib and dresser and change table she'd spotted in Otto's house. She'd probably have to buy a new crib that would conform to modern-day safety standards, but the other pieces were definitely appealing....

Amanda was just asking herself wistfully whether any of the furniture restorers Wexlers' relied on—crafts-persons who were usually booked up a year in advance—might possibly have time to refinish the Gunderson suite before the baby arrived, when suddenly Jim Bishop appeared.

"Hi, hon," he greeted, assisting Amanda to her feet and hugging her warmly. "How's the little mother?"

"The little mother is getting bigger every day," Amanda responded with a smile. "By October I'm going to be the size of a Sherman tank."

"Nonsense. You're going to be more beautiful than ever," Jim assured her. He escorted Amanda into his private office and settled her into a comfortable chair facing his desk. Returning to his own seat, he toyed with a pencil while he studied her quizzically. After a moment he ventured, "You know I'm always delighted to see you, Amanda, but I have to admit I was a little surprised when my secretary told me you'd made an appointment. This is the first time either you or Mark ever consulted me in a professional capacity. I thought Wexlers' legal affairs were handled by the same firm that represents your father."

Amanda nodded. "They are, but that's business, and what I want to talk to you about is personal. I need you to write me a new will. When Mark and I were first married, we made out wills leaving everything to each other. Now, with the baby coming, I want to change mine to make sure my child will be taken care of in the event of my death."

Jim chuckled indulgently. "Amanda, honey, you're not going to die."

She stiffened. "Don't humor me, Jim. This isn't some whim brought on by my pregnancy. I'm perfectly serious." She took a deep breath. "While we're at it, I also need to discuss the ramifications if Mark and I decide to break up our partnership."

Jim grew very still. Quietly he asked, "Your partnership in the antique store, or in your marriage?"

"Maybe both," Amanda answered.

Her friend rolled his eyes. "Damn," he swore bitterly. "Talk about news I didn't want to hear…. In case I haven't told you this before, Amanda, you and Mark are two of my favorite people in the whole world. Are things really so bad between you?"

She gestured helplessly. "Things are . . . unsettled between us," she admitted, and then, squaring her shoulders, she explained why.

By the time Amanda finished talking, Jim was chewing on his pencil, his expression grim. "There's no chance this could be some ghastly mistake, a lab error or something?"

"No," Amanda responded patiently. "The situation is all too real. My baby has Down's syndrome. That's a fact, one I've accepted and Mark hasn't. So you can understand why it's vitally important that I know my son will be taken care of, no matter what happens to me—or to Mark and me."

"Of course. I'll be happy to do what I can for you, but you do realize, don't you, that you can't just make unilateral decisions about the baby's future? He's Mark's child, too. Whether or not you two stay married, Mark has rights—"

"Which he'd probably be delighted to relinquish," Amanda interjected acidly.

She could tell her tart tone surprised Jim. Shaking his head sadly, he said, "I don't believe that, Amanda, and I'm not sure I think you really believe it, either. Your husband is a good man. No matter what happens, he'll always make sure his child is provided for."

Amanda cried, "But I don't want my baby just to be 'provided for'—I want him to be loved!"

Jim's answering smile was full of irony. "Unfortunately, my dear, try as we might, love is something us lawyers haven't yet figured out how to write into a legal document."

He fell silent. After a moment he said, "I guess I owe you an apology, Amanda. I thought you were being overemotional. Whenever Cheryl was expecting, she'd have spells of being terribly temperamental—hormones, I guess. I'll never forget one night when she was about eight months along with our oldest girl and I was still clerking.... She threw a chocolate pie at me because I forgot to tell her I'd be working late and by the time I got home the meringue had fallen...." Jim paused again. When Amanda did not smile at his anecdote, he straightened in his chair and cleared his throat. "Of course, now that I'm aware of the circumstances, I understand your concern. You're wise to consider the future, especially since someday there may be very large sums at stake—"

"If you're delicately referring to my father's estate, then don't count on it," Amanda interrupted tightly. "He may decide he doesn't want to take a chance on his money going to someone who can't handle it."

Jim nodded. "In that case, I'll try to draw up papers that will prepare for any contingency. Naturally I want to help you any way I can—short of representing you in a divorce action." He grimaced. "If it comes to that, then I'll have to refer you to one of my associates. You and Mark are both too close to me personally for me to take sides. But, of course, I hope it won't come to that."

Amanda sighed. "From your lips to God's ears," she murmured, consciously echoing one of her father's favorite expressions. She just wished she had Alden's faith in the words' power to influence the Almighty.

"Mr. Wexler, would you mind if I left work a little early this afternoon?" Sandra asked diffidently. "If it's going to cause a problem—I mean with Mrs. Wexler out of the store—then of course I'll stay as long as you want me to, but I've already finished everything you told me to do, and business is a little slow...."

Mark shrugged. "If you want to take a couple of hours off, that's all right with me, Sandra. Amanda will be back sooner or later, and in any case, this near closing time I don't anticipate a sudden surge of business too big for me to handle on my own." He paused, smiling. "You never ask for time off. What's so special about tonight—a hot date?"

"I wish," Sandra replied with a dramatic gesture, ruffling her russet curls. "Unfortunately, it's nothing so fun. I have some shopping to do, and I want to finish in time to get home before my brother does. Mom and Dad went camping at Crater Lake, and Georgie likes someone to be there when he returns from school. Otherwise, he worries." Grimacing, she confided, "Actually, I haven't had a real date in quite a while, not since I broke up with my boyfriend last Easter. The guy was really nice at first, but then he started griping about Georgie being around all the time. I told him if he didn't like my brother, he could take a hike."

Mark studied the girl thoughtfully, considering for the first time that there were certain parallels between her family situation and what his own had been when he was a child. "Forgive me for asking, Sandra, but didn't it bother you to have to choose between your boyfriend and your brother?"

She shook her head. "There wasn't any choice. When that jerk complained about Georgie, I realized he wasn't the person I thought he was."

"But surely at some level you must have resented having to make that decision at all?" Mark persisted. Aware that Sandra was regarding him oddly, he sighed an declared, "I'm sorry for asking such personal questions. You must think I'm being morbidly nosy. It's just that, well, I'm worried about the future for Amanda and the baby and me. I see your happy family and I hope that the three of us will be able to function as well as you do, but frankly, I have serious doubts."

"Oh, I'm sure you worry too much," Sandra said, but Mark was not mollified.

Clearing his throat, he admitted hoarsely, "When I was a boy, I had a baby sister who was born with birth defects. She only lived till she was five—I was a few years younger than you are when my sister...died—but she spent her whole life in misery and pain, and the strain of coping with her illness destroyed my family."

"And you think that's what will happen to you and Mrs. Wexler?" Sandra asked.

"That's what I'm afraid will happen," Mark answered dully.

The girl was quiet for several moments. At last she admitted, "Oh, Lord, Mr. Wexler, I wish I knew what to tell you. You should be talking to Mom and Dad— they're the ones with counseling experience. Unfortunately, they're out of town this week. In the meantime, all I can do is repeat what Mom's always saying, which is that there are no givens in this world. Being born normal certainly doesn't guarantee happiness, and being other than normal doesn't have to mean a lifetime of grief, either."

"I wish I could believe that," Mark said.

"Maybe in time you will," Sandra told him. Glancing at her wristwatch, she noted, "Well, if I expect to finish my shopping before Georgie gets home, I'd better fly. Thanks for letting me off early." She grabbed her handbag and scurried away.

Wexlers' Antiques and Collectibles was closed for the day by the time Mark finally heard Amanda's footsteps echo up the stairwell. Seated at the partners' desk, he lifted his head to listen. Her labored tread was so different from the quick, graceful gait with which she used to fly up the stairs that it might have been another woman. The noise worried him. She sounded so weary, so... burdened. He'd give everything he had to be able to lighten her burden, but she refused to let him help her. In Amanda's opinion he no longer had the right.

Despite Sandra's reassurances, Mark knew the rift between him and his wife was widening daily. She'd begun to separate herself from him the moment he told her about Marilyn. He'd seen it in her face that afternoon in the park, in the warm brown eyes that had grown increasingly colder and more distant with each word. To Amanda his reticence was something furtive and ugly, a confirmation that he'd been shamed and repelled by his handicapped sister, just as she was convinced he was ashamed of the child she now carried. When he'd appealed for understanding, Amanda had rejected his pleas outright. Why should she believe him this time? she had countered with inexorable logic. He'd already admitted lying to her and her obstetrician.

It was that final deception she found impossible to forgive, Mark realized morosely. Eventually Amanda might have come to accept his reasons for never telling her about his sister, if only he had not deliberately lied during the genetic counseling session. The irony was that at the time Steven Rhodes had queried him about his family background, Mark had barely been conscious of twisting the truth. The questions had seemed so routine, so cut-and-dried, and after all, he had indeed been an only child for all but five of his forty-five years. Since the circumstances of Marilyn's pathetically short life could not be duplicated, there had seemed no point in resurrecting ancient tragedies. But

Amanda viewed the situation differently. To her the only thing that mattered was that Mark had lied. The fact that his falsehood was in no way connected with the baby's condition was irrelevant. As she saw it, he would have jeopardized the health of their unborn child for his own selfish purposes, and by doing so he had henceforth waived the right to comment on her behavior. The chasm between them widened.

God, he missed her. It seemed absurd to say that he was lonesome for a woman who was almost always literally in the same room as he was, yet that was how Mark felt. Physically Amanda remained close at hand, but mentally she'd never been farther away. That argument in the park had finally brought about the thing Mark had feared from the moment she told him she was pregnant: all her emotions were now wrapped up in her baby, leaving no room for her husband. She and Mark talked but did not communicate; they shared a bed but did not make love. Mark still hungered for Amanda as much as ever, still craved the comfort and satisfaction only her warm, welcoming body could give him, but now whenever he approached her, she retreated as if leery of even the most casual caress. He had not touched her in weeks.

Amanda appeared in the office door, weighed down with packages. Mark jumped up from the desk. He was almost prepared to wrestle her load from her, but she let them drop to the floor without protest. Sinking onto the love seat, she leaned her head back against the cushions and closed her eyes, one hand at her throat as she struggled to catch her breath. Mark watched her anxiously.

Her appearance bothered him. She looked so haggard lately, her lovely face bleached and slack with fatigue. Despite the weight she'd gained, her features remained finely drawn, her eyes shadowed, and her long lashes drooped against cheeks that were sunken and bloodless. He knew she hadn't been sleeping well—hell, neither of them had enjoyed a decent rest in an eternity, not since the night of Alden and Joan's party—but recently Amanda had been more agitated than ever. Her increasingly bulky body seemed to make repose impossible, and often when she did finally drift into slumber, Mark could hear her whimper softly, as if in pain. The sound reminded him chillingly of his mother's muffled sobs.

Whenever he dared question her, she grew hostile and defensive, protesting heatedly that Steven said her pregnancy was progressing normally. Despite her insistence that a woman her age was simply bound to experience more discomfort than the average expectant mother, Mark was not reassured. He knew Amanda's body in sickness and in health, and what she was experiencing at the moment was not health. She did not look well. Mark thought he probably ought to telephone her doctor.

The one reason he hadn't consulted with Steven already was because he knew Amanda would resent his "interference." Not that her anger would be anything new, Mark acknowledged wryly. At times he was convinced that she was determined to find fault with anything he did in reference to the baby. When she declared that it was time to start setting up the nursery and he told her to pick whichever room in the condominium seemed most convenient for her, she accused him of indifference. Contrarily, when he indicated that for his own peace of mind he wanted to check out the maternity wing at the hospital Steven recommended for the delivery, Amanda said he was meddling. Nothing he did seemed to please her, and while Mark recognized that their uniquely stressful situation was bound to contribute to her mood swings, he was troubled that there might be something organically wrong, as well.

Aware that he was risking yet another rebuff, Mark tried to broach the subject tactfully. "That must have been quite a shopping trip," he observed, glancing at her packages. "I had no idea you were going to try to do so much in one afternoon. Did you find everything you wanted?"

"Yes and no," Amanda murmured with a yawn. She reached for one of the shopping bags as if to show him its contents; her hand dropped away. She said, "I bought basic items for the layette—nightgowns, receiving blankets, little undershirts—but there are other things I don't know about yet. Bottles, for example. If at all possible I want to breast-feed the baby, but Stephanie told me that babies like mine aren't always able to nurse naturally, so I may need bottles, but I'm not sure whether I should go ahead and get them."

With hooded eyes Mark glanced at Amanda's swelling bosom and pictured her naked to the waist, a small, downy head pressed to her breast. The image was so potently erotic that he felt his body harden. He had to touch her, even if she rejected him. Half expecting a snub, he sat beside her on the love seat and took her limp hand in his. To his surprise and relief, she did not jerk away. Gently he stroked her palm and wrist, relishing the feel of her soft flesh against his as he said huskily, "I'm sure you'll be able to nurse the baby if you want to."

"I hope so," Amanda murmured, oblivious to the effect she was having on her husband. She continued,

"Then there are diapers to think about. How am I supposed to know how to choose diapers? Some people recommend disposable and others swear by cloth...."

Her voice faded, and Mark could tell she was loopy with exhaustion. Looking down at the hand he held, he noted with dismay how clearly the blue veins showed through her translucent skin. When he surreptitiously checked her pulse, he was perplexed to discover that despite her lassitude, her heart was pounding erratically.

With care not to disturb her, he edged closer. "I wish you'd try to take things a little easier, Amanda. I worried about you being gone the whole afternoon. We still have plenty of time left to shop for diapers and baby bottles. You shouldn't try to do it all in one day."

"I know," she conceded dully, leaning her head against his shoulder, "but the layette wasn't really what I went shopping for. I just sort of picked it up along the way. What I was hunting for was nursery furniture. I can't even begin to redecorate the spare bedroom until I know which style of crib and dresser and such we're going to have."

Languidly she relaxed against him, her perfume filling his nostrils. Her nearness was like a drug. Mark struggled to keep his voice casual as he continued the conversation. "Did you see anything you liked?"

"Not really," she murmured in a dreamy voice. "Most of what I looked at was overpriced junk, and the rest was too yuppified for my taste."

"I'm sorry to hear that. I know how eager you are to get started on the nursery. Of course, if you can't find what you want locally, we can always drive up to Seattle—"

"I've already found what I want," Amanda said.

Mark scowled. "I don't understand."

Amanda stirred slightly. "I've decided I want to buy the nursery suite from the Gunderson house—with the exception of the crib. We'll want one that conforms to safety standards."

His surprise was so great that he forgot to temper his tone. "That pile of rubbish?" he exclaimed in disbelief. "Good Lord, Amanda, the stuff's probably not even safe."

He felt her stiffen. "I checked out the crib carefully," she told him. "I measured the distance between the slats to make sure they conform to current standards. You don't think I'd risk hurting my child, do you?"

"Of course you wouldn't," he soothed her quickly. "But darling, darling, there's no need to economize. We can afford better."

His effort at appeasement came too late. He had broken the mood, and their momentary rapport was at an end. Amanda raised her hand from his shoulder and slipped her hand free from his grasp. "I wasn't thinking about money," she countered, "even if Susan Hendrix is willing to practically give the set away."

"She's selling it for what the appraiser listed it at," Mark pointed out.

"Appraisers are blind," Amanda said scornfully. "Most of them remind me of the classic definition of a cynic—someone who knows the price of everything and the value of nothing."

Mark observed, "If failing to see the attraction in a rickety crib that's definitely seen better days makes the appraiser a cynic, then I have to plead guilty, too. The nursery suite is old, yes, by you're not talking about the sort of fine craftsmanship that appreciates with age.

This is serviceable, machine-made furniture that didn't amount to much when it was brand-new sixty years ago, when Otto's children were infants. There's nothing inherently valuable about it.''

"There's love," Amanda said. "That crib positively vibrates with it. I feel certain the children who slept there in the past felt loved and safe—the way I hope our own child will feel."

Mark's brows peaked, punctuating his skepticism. "I never heard of furniture having karma before. It sounds very poignant, but don't you think our baby will feel a lot more loved and safe in a bed that doesn't look like a junk-store reject?"

"I'm not stupid, Mark. I know the suite needs work," Amanda rejoined. "I have no intention of buying it until I've located somebody who can restore it for me before the fall."

"Lots of luck! If you remember how long it took us to get that secretary in our front hall refinished—"

Heatedly Amanda insisted, "I'm going to find someone. Now that I've unearthed the furniture I want for my baby, nothing is going to stop me from—"

Suddenly she collapsed back against the cushions on the love seat. Blotches of red painted her sallow cheeks, and her head wobbled dizzily.

"Good God, Amanda!" Mark exclaimed in alarm. "What's the matter?"

Breathing hard, she covered her face with her hands and mumbled into her palms, "Nothing's the matter. I'm just a little woozy, that's all."

Gently he pried her fingers apart and studied her features. "No, that's not all," he declared sternly, his mouth tightening into a grim line as he stared into her eyes. "You've made yourself sick, wandering around downtown all afternoon in this heat. I thought you promised me you'd try to take things easier, now that you've finished composing the auction catalog. Have you forgotten it's summer, and you're almost seven months pregnant? Honestly, if you won't moderate your activities, then I guess I'll have to do it for you. I never should have let you go shopping by yourself."

"You couldn't have stopped me," Amanda told him. She paused, inhaling raggedly. Then she added, "Besides, I didn't spend the whole time outdoors on my feet. For over an hour I was seated in a nice, air-conditioned office."

Mark frowned. "You went to see your doctor?"

"My lawyer," Amanda said.

Caught off guard, Mark said in a puzzled tone, "Why did you do that? We haven't needed any legal advice since the time that importer falsified the provenance on the—"

With frigid emphasis, Amanda repeated, "I said *my* lawyer."

Mark rocked back as if struck. He could feel the blood draining from his face, seeping into some bottomless void in his gut. He gulped dryly, trying to speak, but no sound issued from his throat.

Watching him struggle, Amanda cried, "You told me ages ago that we might end up separating. Did you expect me to just sit around waiting for you to drop the other shoe? I have to protect myself. I have to protect the baby!"

With an effort so hard it was physically painful, Mark forced out the word, "For heaven's sake, Amanda you know I'd never—"

The telephone rang.

Mark and Amanda both jumped, startled by the intrusion of the outside world. "Oh, hell, talk about great timing," Mark grumbled, blinking owlishly, as if he'd been wrenched from a dream—or a nightmare. He noticed with surprise that while he and Amanda had shredded each other verbally, the sun had begun its descent behind the western hills and the office had become cloaked in shadow. He glanced at his wife. She was huddled at one end of the love seat, her arms wrapped with difficulty around her knees. Even in the fading light he could see that she was trembling.

The electronic bell shrilled again. "Aren't you going to answer that?" she asked faintly.

Mark squinted balefully at the telephone. "Why bother? If it's important, they'll call back. Besides, at this hour it's probably just a wrong number, anyway."

"It might be somebody who couldn't reach us at the house."

Recognizing that she was grasping for any excuse not to pursue their quarrel, Mark shrugged. "Whatever you say." He went to the desk, switched on the lamp and cleared his throat. Picking up the receiver, he announced briskly, "Wexlers'."

The voice on the other end of the line was low pitched and halting, its peculiar dissonance more pronounced than usual because the speaker was in emotional distress. "Mr. Wexler, can I talk to Sandy, please?"

Mark said, "I'm sorry, Georgie, but your sister isn't here now." Out of the corner of his eye, he saw Amanda grow alert at the boy's name.

Georgie sniffled and pleaded, "Are you sure Sandy isn't there? I really need to talk to her. It's important."

"Sandra left early to do some shopping, Georgie. It probably just took her a little longer than she expected.

I'm sure she'll be home any moment now." Covering the mouthpiece with his palm, Mark muttered to Amanda, "I don't know what to do. Sandra told me her parents are down at Crater Lake, and Georgie sounds as if he may be crying."

"Oh, no," Amanda murmured. "Here, let me speak to him." She clambered up from the love seat. Mark pulled out her desk chair and handed her the receiver. Tucking it under her ear as she sat down, she said, "Hi, Georgie, this is Mrs. Wexler. I'm sorry Sandra's not here right now, but, as Mr. Wexler told you, I'm sure she'll be home before long." She wet her lips. "Georgie, dear, you seem really upset. While you're waiting for Sandra, is there any way I can help you? Can you tell me what's wrong?"

Mark watched Amanda's expression darken with dismay as she listened to the boy. Nibbling the tip of a fingernail, she asked, "Are you absolutely sure you understood them correctly?...I see. Well, did they give you any reason why they're closing the school?...A note? Would you mind reading it to me?" After another long pause, she said sadly, "I think the word is 'appropriation,' Georgie. It means money, money from the government. Apparently there isn't any more."

She tried to sound upbeat, despite the bad news. "Gosh, I'm sorry. I know how much you've been counting on this. I wish I could think of something to say to make you feel better. Would you like Mr. Wexler and me to drive over and keep you company until your sister arrives...No?...No, of course that's fine, as long as you're sure you'll be all right. When Sandra gets home, tell her I said to call us if you two need anything. In the meantime, Georgie, you take care of yourself, and I promise if I get any bright ideas, I'll let you know. Bye." Carefully she hung up the phone and gazed blankly at her desk calendar. "Goddamn it!" she blurted.

"So what happened?" Mark asked.

Amanda heaved a disgruntled sigh. "It's so unfair. You know that vocational-training program Georgie's been in?"

"The one where he's learning furniture finishing and repair?"

Amanda nodded. "The last time I talked to his mother, she told me that Georgie was only a couple of months away from completing his schooling. According to Stephanie, Georgie is one of their prize pupils. Once he's earned his certificate, the next step in the program should be to place him in a real job, where Georgie could start earning a salary and his employer would get a subsidy for hiring him."

"You said the next step 'should' be to put Georgie in a real job. I gather something's happened?"

"As far as I can tell," Amanda explained drearily, "it sounds as if the plug's been pulled on the whole project. Georgie said that when he went to school this morning, everything was fine, but at the end of the day the director passed out letters to all the students and told them he was sorry but today was the last day."

Mark's eyes widened. "That's a hell of a way to treat a bunch of mentally disabled kids."

"That's the way I feel, too," Amanda agreed, "but you know how it is with government funding. Some bureaucrat somewhere probably decided the money could be better spent building another bomber." She rubbed her forehead as if it ached. "That poor boy. All he wants is a job so he can live halfway independently in a group home, and now that dream has been crushed.

And naturally this *would* happen when Gordon and Stephanie aren't on hand to deal with it.''

"His sister's there," Mark reminded her. "Sandra's perfectly capable of helping her brother till their parents return from their camping trip."

"But I want to help, too," Amanda said. She fell silent, considering. After a long moment she glanced at the address wheel on her side of the desk and ventured, "Mark, how many people do we know in the furniture restoration business?"

He shook his head firmly. "No, Amanda. If you're thinking what I presume you're thinking, then please just forget it right now. I realize you've grown very fond of the Pollards in the short time you've known them, but I don't want you mixing their problems with our business."

"You don't think any of our contacts would be interested in hiring Georgie?" she asked.

Mark said brusquely, "To be perfectly honest, offhand I can't think of anybody who'd be terribly eager to hire a retarded workman—not unless he came with the added sweetener of a government subsidy."

Amanda's face reddened. Tightening her delicate jaw stubbornly, she stated in clipped tones, "If that's true, then most people must be terribly shortsighted. I have faith in Georgie's work—".

"I wasn't aware that you'd ever actually seen any of the boy's work," Mark pointed out.

"That's not important," she retorted heatedly. "Georgie has confidence in his work, and I have confidence in him—so much so that I'm going to hire him myself." She rose unsteadily to her feet and seemed to grow more agitated with each word. "If I can't find him a full-time job, at least I can give him a temporary one.

I'm going to buy that baby furniture from Susan Hendrix, and I'm going to have Georgie fix it up for me. Then you'll see. Then you'll—''

Mark stared at her, aghast. Amanda's flush had deepened as she'd ranted, and her voice had edged toward hysteria. Her gestures were wild and disoriented; Mark could see an irregular pulse throbbing in her temples. She swayed dizzily, but when he grabbed her shoulders to steady her, she flailed at him, and he dragged her against him, pinning her arms to her sides. As he struggled to subdue her, she squirmed, the maddening friction of her soft body both titillating and heartbreaking. In anguish, Mark cried, ''Damn it, Amanda, calm down! You have to be quiet. You're hurting yourself. You'll hurt the baby!''

Suddenly she grew still. Her panting breath was hot on his face as she stared at him with bleak black eyes. ''What difference does it make to you if I hurt the baby?'' she croaked bitterly. Then she fainted.

CHAPTER TEN

THE AIR WAS COLD AND STILL, oddly tasteless except for the subtle tang of disinfectant and denatured alcohol. Amanda glanced with dull curiosity at the sterile white drape cocooning her bed. Somewhere beyond that featureless barrier she could hear the rattle of a metal cart fading into the distance, and a disembodied voice as antiseptic as the air requested somebody to please report somewhere. Amanda frowned. In the back of her mind she knew those sensory details added up to something—something surprising—but she felt too lethargic to work out the equation. She closed her eyes. When she opened them again, the drape had been pushed away, revealing a semiprivate hospital room. The other bed was unoccupied, but at Amanda's side stood a man in a long white coat, a stethoscope tucked into the pocket. His intelligent gray eyes were grave as he gazed down at her.

Amanda's lips felt dry and chapped. She motioned toward the covered jug on her bedside table as she croaked, "What happened?"

"In medical terms," Steven said laconically, pouring ice water into a tumbler, "your blood pressure shot up and you went bonkers."

She raised her head to sip through the straw he held for her, and she noticed the IV bag dangling over the bed. She lifted a weary hand high enough to observe the tubes taped to her arm. "What's this?"

Steven shrugged. "Just some saline solution. The mixture was a little more interesting last night, but once we got you stabilized, we put you back on good old salt water."

"'Last night'?" Amanda glanced toward the window. From her supine position she could see the tip of one of the downtown high rises jutting massively into the bright sky, the sun glinting on its eastern face. She wrinkled her forehead in confusion. "How long have I been here?"

"About fifteen hours. You collapsed in your office around seven, and Mark called the paramedics."

She shook her head. "I don't remember. I don't remember anything I did or a single word I said—"

"That's all right," Steven remarked. "People rarely say anything memorable in these situations."

The blankness worried her. She persisted, "But how could I lose most of a day? I do recall meeting my—a friend in the middle of the afternoon, and then I did some more shopping for the baby—" She broke off, and her eyes grew round with alarm. Struggling to push herself upright, she fumbled at the coarse sheets mounded over her belly and cried, "Oh, my God, the baby! Is he—is he—"

Catching her hands and nudging her back against the pillow, Steven told her sternly, "The baby is all right. We did an ultrasound last night, and he appears to be okay—no thanks to you."

The doctor's censuring tone was so at variance with his usual dry humor that Amanda could only gape at him dreadfully. "What do you mean? What have I done?"

Steven said grimly, "You've let yourself become overtired and run-down and totally stressed out, that's what. I couldn't believe it when they called me in last night and I saw how much your condition has deteriorated in the short time since your last checkup. You once told me you'd be willing to spend the duration of your pregnancy in a hospital bed. If you're not careful, you may just get a chance to prove you meant that."

He swore testily. "Honestly, Amanda, of all my patients, I assumed you'd be the one with enough sense not to try to play Supermom, especially considering how much you want this baby. You're a middle-aged woman expecting her first child under uniquely trying circumstances. Where the *hell* did you get the idea that you could be pregnant and yet not have to make changes in your work and life-style?"

With real trepidation Amanda recalled all the friendly hints and gentle admonitions she'd been receiving lately, not just from Mark but from family and acquaintances, as well—advice she'd chosen to disregard. Was it possible that in her arrogant determination not to accept help from anyone, she had actually endangered the baby? If that was so, then she didn't think she'd ever be able to forgive herself.

Weakly she admitted, "I know I probably should have quit work a long time ago. Mark wanted me to, but I wouldn't listen to him. I told myself remaining on the job was less stressful than sitting at home brooding about all my other problems."

"Well, it looks like you were wrong, doesn't it?" Steven snapped.

Amanda felt her eyes smart. Too frail to fight back tears, she blinked wetly and gulped. "So—so what happens now? Do I really have to stay here in the hospital till the baby's born?''

Taking pity on her, Steven relented and shook his head. ''If you'll promise to behave yourself, I'll let you go home tomorrow, once I'm sure your blood pressure is going to stay down. But when I say you have to behave yourself, I mean it. I'm not ordering bed rest, but I want you off your feet as much as possible. Take lots of naps. You can read, watch TV, knit or whatever, but I don't want you working anymore, not even at the computer. Visitors are okay as long as you don't try to wait on them. In a couple of weeks, after I've checked you again, maybe I'll give you the green light to go out for dinner or a movie one evening, but I don't want you to interpret that as permission to run yourself ragged all over again.''

''But what about shopping?'' Amanda protested. ''There's so much I still have to get for the baby.''

Steven said severely, ''Contrary to popular belief, a newborn's needs are pretty basic—a full stomach and a dry bottom and a warm place to sleep. Everything else is more for the parents' vanity than for the child. You can wait until later to do your shopping, or until Mark has time to do it for you.''

His expression darkened. ''Speaking of Mark, you ought to know he's been quietly going insane with worry about you. While you're considering the sin of pride and what your stubbornness has been doing to you and the baby, you might give a thought to your husband, as well.''

Amanda looked stricken. ''Poor Mark, I forgot all about him,'' she exclaimed. ''Where is he? Is he here?''

Steven pointed to a hard plastic chair next to the bed. ''He was right there all night long, watching you sleep.

Finally, around sunrise, I told him to go home and get some rest himself. I thought it was going to take a couple of orderlies to drag him away from you."

He paused. After a moment he grimaced and said, "You know, Amanda, no matter how much I care about my patients, I've always made it a rule never to become involved in their personal lives, but for you, I'm going to break the rule. There's something I have to say—namely, your husband loves you."

Amanda's eyes widened. "I know that," she murmured. "I've always known that."

"Then I'd advise you to take better care of that love, if you don't want to alienate him completely. Your irresponsible actions are hurting Mark as much as they're hurting you and the baby. Talk about people looking haggard—he's even more run-down than you are!"

Amanda recalled the evidence of strain in her husband's features. Daily intimacy made it both harder and easier to notice change. When Amanda looked at Mark, she always tended to see the handsome, vigorous thirty-five-year-old she'd married, but lately shadows had bruised his deep-set eyes, the long grooves bracketing his nose and mouth had seemed deeper, and there were scattered strands of silver in the reddish-gold hair at his temples. For the first time it was possible to believe that he was closer to fifty than forty.

Amanda gulped. "I've never wanted to alienate Mark. It's just—it's just that sometimes it's hard to think of anyone else, knowing all the extra love this baby needs...."

"Are you positive about that, Amanda? Some women are so wrapped up in their children that the fathers become irrelevant. I know how desperately you've wanted a baby. Now that you have what you want, are you sure you aren't using the Down's syndrome issue as an excuse to ease your husband out of your life so you can concentrate on motherhood?''

Deeply shocked, Amanda gasped. "Are you implying that Mark and I would be having just as many problems even if the baby were perfectly normal?"

"The thought has occurred to me," the doctor commented.

Shaking her head vehemently, Amanda cried, "That's a terrible thing to say! Damn it, Steven, of course I haven't...." The words died in her throat, and she sank back against the pillow, confused. "I don't know," she mumbled uncertainly. "I guess I never considered that possibility before."

"Well, consider it," Steven told her. "You're going to have time to do plenty of thinking in the next few weeks. And while you're thinking, think about being a little nicer to that husband of yours. You're not the only one who's emotionally fragile right now. I'm sure he needs just as much TLC as you do."

After Steven left her, Amanda picked indifferently at the breakfast tray an aide brought in, and then she dozed again, until the scrape of hard-soled shoes on the tile floor startled her from her light slumber. She rolled toward the sound, expecting Mark. Instead, she saw her parents standing just inside the door.

Alden was dressed in his golf clothes, and Joan carried a spray of coral-colored roses in a crystal vase. From across the room both were regarding their daughter uncertainly, as if afraid to approach, but the instant they realized she was awake, Amanda was mused to note, they adopted nearly identical smiles of sympathetic relief and rushed to her bedside.

"Hi, dear," Alden said gruffly, leaning over the bed rail to kiss Amanda's forehead. "How are you feeling?"

"Oh, I'm okay," she replied. She tried to gesture casually, but the tubes taped to her arm restrained her, and the movement rattled the IV stand. She saw her mother quickly avert her eyes.

Setting the vase next to the telephone at Amanda's side, Joan declared in a tone a pitch higher than normal, "I was right, wasn't I, Amanda, about Tropicanas being your favorite flower? As late as it is in the season, when I went out in the garden this morning, I was worried that I wouldn't be able to find any for you, but luckily there was still one bush blooming away—"

"The roses are very beautiful, Mother," Amanda said quickly, disconcerted and moved by the uncharacteristic emotion in Joan's voice. "Thank you for bringing them."

Alden, too, seemed shaken. "You've given us quite a fright, young lady," he told her with crusty severity. "When Mark called us, we thought— Are you sure you're all right?"

Amanda nodded. "I just need some rest. My doctor says I can go home tomorrow."

Her father scowled. Picking his words, he asked, "Did he—did he say anything about the baby?"

"The baby's fine," Amanda answered with deliberate nonchalance. "None of this would have happened if I hadn't been pigheaded about continuing to work. I just have to keep reminding myself I'm not a girl anymore."

"That's the trouble," Joan blurted harshly, as if the words had been building up pressure inside her. "You're too old to be having a baby! You'll be forty-three in a couple of weeks, and every problem you've had is directly related to your age. Your health, the baby's health—none of these complications would have happened if you'd been younger. Amanda, I know you want this child, but, oh, God, you'd have been so much better off if you'd never become pregnant!''

Amanda felt slapped. Struggling to keep her voice under control, she pointed out quietly, ''When Mark and I first told you I was pregnant, you were happy.''

''I was selfish,'' Joan confessed. ''To my shame, I have to admit that all I could think about was that finally I was going to be a grandmother. I didn't stop to consider the ramifications. I didn't think about what motherhood was going to mean for you.'' She took a deep breath. ''Have *you* thought about it, Amanda? You've always been so impulsive, so easily swayed by your emotions instead of common sense. Have you really, truly considered what's in store for you and Mark, raising this child?''

''I think so,'' Amanda murmured.

Joan shook her head. ''I can't believe that. Maybe you think you know what you're doing, but you're wrong. Take my word for it, rearing a handicapped child could destroy you. By the time your baby is an adult, you're going to be almost as old as I am, and I can tell you right now I sure as hell don't feel equal to the task of—''

''Mother, please,'' Amanda cut in shakily, ''we've been through all of this before.''

''And you haven't listened,'' Joan said.

''Mother,'' Amanda cried again, trembling, but before she could say more, Alden touched her shoulder.

''Hush, Mandy,'' he crooned, his use of that long-forgotten nickname as astounding as his gentleness.

"Don't get upset. You know we only want what's best for you, but this isn't the time or place to be having this conversation." He squinted at his wife. "Don't you agree, dear?"

Joan collected herself at once. "Of course, Alden," she murmured, then she smiled contritely at Amanda. "Forgive me, darling. I didn't mean to lecture. The only thing that matters right now is you getting better. Are you sure you're going to feel well enough to go home tomorrow?"

"The doctor says she's going to be just fine," Mark announced from the doorway. With tremendous relief Amanda watched her husband stride into the room.

He must have taken Steven's admonitions to heart, she thought as she gazed hungrily at him. He looked rested and refreshed. He was wearing a dark blue blazer she particularly liked because of the way it complemented his slender build and his blondness, and as he greeted her parents and crossed to the bed, he moved alertly and with vigor. When he bent to kiss her, a gleaming lock of hair fluffed silkily over his forehead, the way it always did when newly shampooed, and on his lips Amanda could taste the minty bite of toothpaste.

"Good morning, darling," he murmured, gazing down at her intently. "How are you feeling?"

Amanda's eyes locked with his, and she grinned sheepishly. "I think mostly I feel embarrassed," she admitted. "I understand I caused quite a stir last night."

"That's putting it mildly. You scared the hell out of me, lady," Mark said deeply. He reached over the bed rail to stroke her cheek with his fingertips. In her sterile surroundings the familiar warmth of his light caress was too comforting and seductive to resist. Amanda sighed and snuggled her face against his hand. The spicy scent of his after-shave clung to his skin. Amanda inhaled luxuriously and turned her head to press her lips into his palm. Behind them Alden coughed.

Mark's lips twisted. Straightening to his full height, he handed Amanda a small gift-wrapped package. When she opened it, discovering a box of chocolate truffles and the latest Mary Higgins Clark thriller, Mark turned with a smile to her parents and noted, "It's a good thing I followed my instincts and didn't try to get flowers, because there's not a florist in town who could match your roses. Instead, I decided Amanda needed something good and gruesome to read to take her mind off being in the hospital."

Joan shuddered delicately. "I've always been partial to a nice historical romance, myself."

Alden chuckled. "Well *chacun à son goût*, as the French say—and speaking of French, Joan, did you remember to telephone l'Auberge?"

"Oh, my word, no," his wife exclaimed with a self-conscious titter. "In all the excitement, I forgot. Do you suppose it's too late to make dinner reservations for tonight?"

"There's only one way to find out," Alden said. He turned to Amanda, his expression regretful. "I'm sorry, dear. An old business acquaintance of mine will be in town tonight, a man I knew and worked with for years, and we promised to take him and his wife... Of course, we had no idea.... If it were anybody else..."

Alden's voice faded, and Amanda said with exasperation, "Oh, for heaven's sake, Father, you don't have to apologize. Nobody's expecting you to keep vigil over me. I'm not *that* sick. Go see your friends and enjoy yourselves."

"Are you certain you won't mind?" Joan asked.

Amanda said dryly, "I may have some qualms when I look at my hospital food and think of you two eating pâté and rack of lamb at l'Auberge, but other than that, no, of course, I won't mind."

Her father looked relieved. "Well, if you really mean that, then I guess we'd better be going." He patted Amanda's hand awkwardly and turned to Mark. "You take good care of her, you hear?"

"I'll call you as soon as I get her home tomorrow," Mark said. Joan hugged him, and then the two elder Smollets departed quickly. Mark's brows quirked sardonically as he watched them bustle from the room. "That had all the earmarks of a tactical retreat," he muttered. Looking at Amanda again, his smile faded and he asked seriously, "Are you all right, sweetheart?"

"I am now that you're here," she said.

He nodded. "When I walked in, I thought the conversation seemed a trifle . . . intense."

"You could say that." Amanda exhaled wearily. "I know they're only trying to help, but I really didn't feel up to another lecture just yet. Two in one morning is more than I can deal with."

"Who else has been lecturing you?"

Making a face, Amanda said, "Steven, of course. For a man whose life's work is healing people, he's damned good at ripping them to shreds. He was very pointed in his opinion of my behavior lately, what I've been doing to me and the baby, both. Without ever once raising his voice, he managed to make me feel selfish and negligent and criminally irresponsible. If I hadn't been lying in bed, I would have sunk through the floor."

Mark's eyes narrowed. "I can't say I like the idea of him browbeating you," he said darkly, "but on the other hand, if Steven was finally able to get through to you that you need to take better care of yourself, then I guess I'll forgive him this time."

"He got through to me," Amanda said glumly. For a long moment she hesitated. Then, watching her husband carefully, she said, "Steven also told me I haven't been fair to you. He said I've been neglecting you in favor of the baby, and I've hurt you as much as I've hurt myself."

Mark did not speak. He twisted his head to stare out the window, and Amanda could not see his expression, but she observed a chalky line edging his taut jaw, and the muscles in his throat suddenly looked veined and corded. Down at her eye level she noticed that his fists were clenched around the bed rail, the knuckles distended and colorless. Hesitantly she touched his hand. She could feel him shake.

"Mark," she ventured cautiously, alarmed by his anger, "is Steven right? Have I been as bitchy as he—"

Mark shook his head as if to clear it, and color returned to his face. Laying his hands over hers, he smiled down at Amanda and suggested, "Why don't we just forget all the things Steven says you've been doing wrong and concentrate on what he wants you to do to get better?"

She remained too keyed up to drop the subject. "Do you mean that? You forgive me?"

"There's nothing to forgive," Mark said soothingly. "When it comes to the problems we've been having lately, I don't suppose either one of us is altogether blameless. Still, as your parents pointed out, now isn't the time to be arguing. The only thing that matters is your health. I understand Steven ordered you to quit working, period.''

"He doesn't even want me using the computer," Amanda admitted dispiritedly. "That bothers me. Even though we always knew I wouldn't be much help by the time of the auction, I had hoped—"

"Forget about the auction. Forget the store. Considering the effort you put into the catalog, you've already done more than your share. Leave the rest of it to me." He paused. When Amanda did not respond at once, he remarked lightly, "You look as if you think we're going to get ripped off if you're not there to observe every transaction. What's the matter? Don't you trust my judgment anymore?"

His lips spread into a beguiling grin, and reluctantly Amanda smiled back. "Don't be silly," she told her husband. "You know I've always trusted your judgment."

As she stared up at him, plumbing his azure gaze, she tried not to hear the silent amendment to her words: *I've always trusted your judgment about everything—except the baby.*

"WOULD YOU CARE FOR A DRINK while you're waiting for the rest of your party to arrive?" the cocktail waitress asked, observing the vacant place settings at Mark's table.

He shook his head. "No, thank you. I'm sure they'll be here any moment." As Mark spoke, he glanced toward the front of the restaurant and saw the hostess leading two short, red-haired men into the main dining room. "In fact, here they are now." He stood up to greet his guests. "Gordon, Georgie, it's good to see you," Mark declared, shaking hands with both the

Pollard men. "Thank you for joining me on such short notice. I know you just returned from Crater Lake, Gordon. Did you have a good time?"

"Yes, thank you for asking. It was nice of you to invite us," Gordon said as he and his son took their seats. His manner was cordial but faintly reserved. "I have to admit, I was a little surprised to hear from you."

Mark nodded wryly. "I know. I haven't been the most . . . forthcoming person in the world, and I apologize. I hope things will be different in the future." He paused while the menus were handed out, scowling when he observed the waiter's momentary hesitation before giving one to Georgie. Mark stared at the man until he flushed and tried to cover his gaffe by rattling off the day's luncheon special in one long breath. "We'll think about it," Mark said in a cold, clipped tone, and the waiter retreated hastily. When Mark glanced across the table again, Gordon was smiling his approval. Georgie, admiring the gold script on the leather menu cover, seemed oblivious to the incident.

Mark said to the young man, "Do you like fish, Georgie? The seafood here is very good."

Georgie considered. "I like hamburgers better," he admitted ingenuously, "but Mom says I should eat more fish so I won't get fat."

Mark told him, "Well, there's a wide selection to choose from. I'm sure you'll find something on the menu that you like. What about you, Gordon?"

"I thought the special sounded interesting," Gordon replied. The two men waited patiently for Georgie to decide on his own meal, and then Mark summoned the waiter, who took their orders with unexceptionable efficiency and departed for the kitchen. Once he was gone, Gordon told Mark, "It was a real shock to all of us to hear that Amanda's in the hospital. I hope she's feeling better now."

"She'll get to go home tomorrow morning," Mark said. "Her doctor wanted to keep an eye on her for a couple of days, but he assures me Amanda will be fine if she'll just slow down a little."

Georgie commented, "Sandy told me she thinks Mrs. Wexler works too hard."

"She does," Mark agreed. "Amanda has always been a very hard worker, and she had trouble understanding that with the baby coming, she needs more rest."

Georgie cocked his head. "That's funny," he declared with a grin. "I thought Mrs. Wexler was really smart. Even *I* know pregnant ladies need lots of rest!"

Startled, Mark stared at the young man with amazement, moved to realize that Georgie was actually making a joke about his own condition. Swallowing thickly, Mark said, "Yeah, well, sometimes even smart people like Mrs. Wexler can do stupid things. That's why her doctor told me I have to make sure she takes things easier from now on." He hesitated. "That's why I need your help."

Georgie and his father glanced at each other before turning to Mark again. Gordon asked, "What do you mean?"

Mark explained, "One of the reasons Amanda collapsed last night was because she's been wearing herself out shopping for the baby. She wants everything to be absolutely perfect, which is normal for an expectant mother, I'm sure, but now it looks like it's going to be up to me to finish setting up the nursery. I'm not certain about a lot of the things she wants, but the one thing I do know about is the baby furniture. She has her heart set on a nursery suite she spotted out at the Gunderson place. Buying the set is no problem—in fact, I've already discussed it with the owner—but making the furniture usable is. I have some doubts about the crib, but even if I do decide it's safe to use, personally, I'm still not sure I think the set is worth the time and effort necessary to repair and refinish it. But Amanda doesn't agree with me, and right now the only thing that matters is what she wants." Mark paused, taking a deep breath. He smiled at the young man who was growing increasingly agitated as he anticipated Mark's request. Mark said, "Well, Georgie, I can see you've already guessed what I was going to ask. Do you think I could hire you to fix up the baby furniture for Mrs. Wexler? From what your sister has told me about the kind of work you were learning to do at your school, I suspect this job might seem pretty elementary to you, but if you could find the time, I'd be very grateful."

Georgie beamed. "Thank you, Mr. Wexler, I'd love to have the job! I could work in our garage, where Dad's tools are. I miss working. It's boring to watch TV all day."

"Great," Mark said. "Maybe this way we can both help each other."

A moment later the salad course was served, and Georgie excused himself to go wash his hands, leaving his father and Mark alone at the table. As Gordon picked up his fork, he looked at Mark and murmured, "Let me add my thanks to my son's. Shutting down his school was a real blow to him. Steph and I are considering getting some other parents together to hire an attorney to appeal the closure, but even if we're successful in getting the appropriation restored, it'll be months before classes start up again. Now you've given

Georgie something to keep him occupied in the interim. Thank you. I appreciate your thinking of him."

"It was Amanda's idea," Mark admitted candidly, "something she mentioned before she got sick. To be perfectly frank, I was dubious."

Gordon nodded. "I appreciate your honesty. For what it's worth, I don't think you'll be disappointed in Georgie's work. He's slow, but he's painstaking, and he has an excellent eye for detail. Under different circumstances I could see him becoming a master cabinetmaker."

"That's good to know," Mark said. "Perhaps in the future I can refer other jobs to him."

"I'm sure he'd like that," Gordon said. For several moments the two men ate in silence. Then Gordon observed, "You're a hard man to figure out, you know."

"You mean because I refuse to become involved in the support group?" Mark queried. "It's nothing personal, I promise you. I'm very impressed by the work you and your wife do, and I'll be eternally grateful for the help the two of you have given Amanda. But as for me, I've stayed away from the meetings because I know I just don't function well in a group environment. I guess you could say I've been a loner all my life. There's no way in hell I could open up to a bunch of strangers."

Gordon smiled understandingly. "Well, if you ever feel the need to open up to a friend, one-on-one, give me a call. I'll be there."

At that point Georgie returned to the table, and the three men began to make plans to transport the baby furniture to Gordon's garage....

AT THE SOUND OF MARK'S KEY in the lock, Amanda dropped her book and pushed herself laboriously from the sofa. The silky luxury of the Oriental carpet beneath her naked toes reminded her that she'd kicked off her slippers somewhere in the flat, but when she glanced around, she couldn't see them. Smoothing her short cotton sundress down over her hips, she padded across the room. By the time she waddled into the entryway, Mark was setting his briefcase on the secretary by the front door.

"You're home!" Amanda squealed with delight, flinging herself at him.

Mark staggered back slightly, absorbing the impact of her body, but when his hands reached out automatically to steady her, he held her away while he studied her face. "I've only been gone a few hours," he pointed out, "just since I brought you home from the hospital. You act as if you haven't seen me in months."

"It feels like months," Amanda said. "It's amazing how slowly the time passes when the only thing you're allowed to exercise is your finger on the TV remote control. I don't think I was cut out to be a couch potato."

Mark reassured her, "You'll get used to it. In a few days you'll be rested enough to have visitors, and that's bound to help."

Amanda made a face. "My mother did offer to come keep me company. I managed to talk her out of it."

"You mean even soap operas are preferable to Joan's well-meaning disapproval?" Mark bantered.

"You might say that." Amanda bit her lip as she gazed up at him. Despite his teasing tone, he was watching her charily. His hands rested easily on her arms, but he made no effort to pull her closer. The gap between them felt unbridgeable, and with shame Amanda admitted that the fault was her own, for keeping him at a distance. Gulping back her guilt, she laid her hands on his lapels and whispered, "I wish you'd hold me. I've missed you so much."

With a groan Mark wound his arms tightly around her, staring down with hungry eyes. Amanda stretched on tiptoe, and their mouths came together. As their tongues darted, delicious and eager, she heaved a wondering sigh, amazed to think that she could have chosen to deprive herself of his caresses even for a day, much less weeks. She needed him. Regardless of the conflicts menacing their marriage, one axiom remained, shining and constant: she needed Mark. She could not live without him.

By the time the kiss ended, Amanda was clinging dizzily to him, her arms wound beneath his sport coat, her face hidden against his shoulder as she panted for air. Mark's hands moved over her, fondling her body through the thin fabric of her dress, molding every curve as if he were a sculptor giving her shape. When his hands cupped her heavy breasts, he paused. "You're not wearing a bra," he noted in surprise.

Before her pregnancy, Amanda had frequently gone braless at home, but in recent months the changes in her body had forced her into sturdy undergarments that restricted even as they supported. She grumbled, "I know I should have put one on, but I just didn't feel like it. If all I'm allowed to do is lounge around the house, I want to be comfortable for a change, even at the risk of losing my girlish figure."

"You've kept your girlish figure a lot longer than most woman," Mark consoled, stroking her breasts appreciatively. "If you start sagging a little, it won't be the end of the world." The friction of his palms on her swollen nipples was almost too much for Amanda to bear, almost as maddening as the urgent pressure of his arousal against her belly. She wriggled provocatively, and he choked out, "My God, darling, if I'd known this was what it would be like to have you waiting at home for me in the evening, I would have started keeping you barefoot and pregnant years ago."

"Chauvinist," Amanda muttered against his chest, inhaling his tangy masculine scent with each raspy breath. She waited for him to move, to nudge her toward the sofa or the bedroom, but he did not. Lifting her head, she said teasingly, "Hey, you, are we just going to stand here, necking in the hallway?"

Mark's expression was quizzical. "You want to make love?"

Amanda blinked. "The idea had crossed my mind—and yours, too, I thought," she pointed out, sliding her hand down the front of his trousers.

He sucked in sharply when her fingers found their goal. Just for a moment he closed his eyes, his face stiff with tension, and his nostrils flared. Then he got control of himself, and when he looked at Amanda again, his smile was tender and concerned. "Sweetheart," he murmured, a rumble of laughter deep in his throat, "at the moment what I want is pretty obvious, but that's not important. Right now the only question that matters is, is it safe for you? In case you've forgotten already, you were only released from the hospital this morning."

Amanda considered. "But Steven didn't tell me we *couldn't* make love. He just doesn't want me getting worked up."

"Gee, thanks," Mark drawled.

Realizing what she'd said, Amanda giggled girlishly. "Well, maybe it wouldn't hurt to get just a little worked up.... I know I'm willing to risk it if you are."

Mark's eyes flashed. "God, I certainly hope you mean that," he growled, already urging her in the direction of the bedroom, "because I have no intention of giving you a chance to change your mind."

Moments later they lay together in the center of the wide, cool bed, naked, not touching, devouring each other with their eyes. Amanda gazed longingly at Mark's rangy body, her yearning tempered with concern. He had always been spare, rather angular in build, but now she noted that his smooth skin seemed stretched too tautly over his big bones. Despite the estrangement between them in recent weeks, she wondered how she could have been so blind—or so totally self-absorbed—to have failed to notice how haggard he looked. She laid her fingers experimentally on his chest. She could discern his ribs plainly, his heart throbbing behind them like a bird in a cage. She whispered, "You've lost weight."

"And you've gained it," Mark said, studying her ripe curves with a craving so intense it was almost palpable. The sheer womanliness of her fecund body was erotic and arousing in a way he'd never anticipated, and when he touched her swelling abdomen, tangible proof of his own potency, he felt himself harden like a teenager. Glancing ruefully at his impressive erection, he grinned and noted, "All these years and I never suspected I was attracted to Rubenesque women."

"It's the earth mother image that's getting to you," Amanda rejoined, "or else the fact that I've kept you at arm's length for over a month." Her expression sobered and she began earnestly, "Oh, Mark, I'm sorry for the way I've treated you lately. I can't believe how—how silly and selfish I've been. Sometimes I don't know what's wrong with me...."

He rolled toward her, pushing her down against the mattress while he silenced her with his kiss. With his lips pressed hard against hers, he moved his hands eagerly over her, fondling and stroking and probing, until she panted with need and her velvety skin felt dewy to his touch. Lifting his head, he stared down into her murky eyes and grated, "There's nothing wrong with you! What you're going through right now would devastate any ordinary woman, but you remain strong and brave and beautiful—not to mention stubborn and impulsive and too damned compassionate for your own good—and I love you so much I'm about to explode with wanting you."

Just for a second Amanda's passion-clouded gaze cleared. Licking her swollen lips, she whispered distractedly, "It seems so long since you said you love me."

"You haven't exactly been bubbling over with heartfelt declarations yourself," Mark shot back, an edge to his voice.

Amanda cried, "But you *know*—"

He shook his head. A hard flush painted his cheekbones as he said fiercely, "Don't talk, Amanda. Nowadays we always seem to get into trouble when we talk. So just feel. Feel my love. Let me feel yours...." The words were muffled between her breasts as he slid his arms around her and rolled onto his back, pulling her to him.

Amanda gasped dizzily, a little alarmed by his ardor, but as his hands moved over her, she realized that despite his intense tone, his driving need, Mark was exercising great restraint, making allowances for the clumsiness of her ungainly body, taking care not to hurt her by proceeding too quickly or too forcefully. When they met, faltered, then fused, Amanda's lashes fluttered and she threw back her head, shaking with recognition, amazed that the sensations pulsing through her could feel so familiar yet always tantalizingly new. Mark surged beneath her, rhythmically thrusting and withdrawing until her body felt ablaze. Conscious thought evaporated and even sensation seemed to shimmer and dissolve in his heat. Then all at once Mark shuddered and cried out, and Amanda knew he had been swept into the fire storm with her.

When, at long last, the inferno began to subside, Amanda swayed, dazzled and spent. Mark caught her and eased her onto the bed beside him. Suddenly she was too tired even to open her eyes. The crisp, fresh sheets were deliciously cool against her love-seared skin as she relaxed in his arms, and she fell asleep with the whisper of Mark's breath on her face and the sound of her name on his lips.

Moments later she awoke with a start, as if she'd been jabbed. "What—" she exclaimed groggily, but as the question formed in her mouth, her mind cleared enough for her to recognize the sensation. Swallowing her words, she collapsed back against the pillow.

Beside her Mark lay propped on one elbow. His free hand was fanned across her belly. "I think we must have really shaken up the baby," he murmured, a bemused grin on his lips, "or else he's started doing aerobics in there. He's been moving around ever since you dozed off."

"Tell me about it," Amanda griped, catching her breath at what felt like a particularly well-placed kick.

Mark felt it, too, and his smile faded. "Does that hurt you?" he demanded.

She shook her head. "It just means I have to go to the bathroom." With a grimace she pushed herself off the bed and padded out of the room.

When she returned, Mark was sprawled flat on his back, his hands behind his head, staring at the ceiling with lazy blue eyes. Amanda studied his lanky body appreciatively. From the square-cut nails on his long toes to the strands of sweat-darkened hair adhering to his broad forehead, he appeared every inch the satisfied male, at ease and just the least bit smug.

Standing next to the bed, she observed, "You're looking very pleased with yourself."

He jerked his head toward her, and she realized his repose was an illusion. With athletic grace he rolled forward into a sitting position and held out his hand to her. "I'd rather think you were pleased with me," he responded lightly, but his wary undertone made it clear the words were meant as a question.

Quickly Amanda slipped her fingers into Mark's and allowed him to tug her back onto the mattress beside him. "You know you always please me," she told him, snuggling close. "You're a wonderful lover."

He draped his arm over her shoulder, his fingertips just brushing the slope of her breast. "I'd prefer to be a wonderful husband," he said.

Amanda stiffened. "I'm not sure I understand exactly what you mean by that."

Mark took a deep breath that sounded frayed around the edges. "I keep thinking," he began painfully, "that if I were the kind of husband I've always told myself I was, I'd be better equipped to protect you against the future. I see you blindly rushing headlong toward disaster, almost like a teenager playing chicken in a hot rod—or like my mother—and I don't know how to stop you.''

Horrified, Amanda tried to pull away from him, but his arm tightened, clamping her to his side. "My God, Mark," she said, gasping, "surely you aren't still thinking about abortion at this late date?''

"Of course not," he dismissed impatiently. "I know as well as you do that we lost that option months ago."

Amanda felt her eyes sting. "But you still think I should have had one.''

Mark shook his head. "What I think—or thought—doesn't matter. The choice was always yours, and you made it." He hesitated before continuing sadly, "No, my darling, the thing that worries me most isn't the fact that you've ignored your family's advice and chosen to have this baby. What I find truly terrifying is that you don't have any doubts about your decision."

In a very small voice, Amanda said, "I have doubts. I have lots of them.''

"None that show," Mark persisted. "As far as I can tell, you're deluding yourself that the future is going to be perfectly normal. That appalls me. I know you think you're prepared to raise a handicapped child. You've met Georgie and you've talked to his parents and you're convinced you can cope as well as they have. I hope and pray you're right. But what you're obviously *not* prepared for is the possibility that despite hopes and prayers and determination, you may yet find yourself in a situation that can't be coped with."

Amanda grew very still. "For instance?''

Railing silently at the gods, Mark said drearily, "Oh, Amanda, do you really want me to hurt you by spelling it out? Do I have to remind you that not all Down's syndrome people are lucky enough to be as healthy and persevering and—damn it—*intelligent* as Georgie Pollard? Do I have to remind you that we'll have no way of knowing how severely our own child is afflicted until well after his birth? Hateful as the prospect is, there's always a possibility that the baby's handicaps will prove so profound that some sort of hospital, some institution, may be the only place where he can be given the care he requires in order to survive."

Amanda took a deep breath and asked, "So what is it you want me to do, Mark? Am I supposed to pretend I'm not pregnant? Should I delay making any preparations at all for the baby until after he's born and we know whether or not he's going to be a 'keeper'?"

Her flippant words broke Mark's heart. In anguish he declared, "It's too late for what I really want, which is for you to find some way to avoid bonding with the baby just yet, to protect yourself by insulating your emotions—"

"The way you have?" Amanda cut in sharply.

Mark lifted his bony shoulders. "I guess so."

She smiled with mirthless irony. "You're right, Mark—it is too late. It was too late for me the day I found out I was pregnant."

Again they lapsed into silence. Finally Mark shook himself and muttered, "You mentioned something about getting ready for the baby."

Puzzled by the abrupt change of subject, Amanda glanced at him. "At the hospital Steven told me I was supposed to leave the shopping and preparations up to you."

"I know. He told me the same thing. I suppose you'd better start making lists of things you want me to buy. What do we need?"

Amanda relaxed fractionally. "That's easy—every-thing. Or maybe not quite everything. Since Cheryl is determined to give me a shower, we'll probably get clothes and some of the small stuff as gifts. But there's still the issue of baby furniture."

"I've already taken care of it," Mark said.

"You what?" Amanda gasped, flabbergasted.

Gratified by the effect of his offhand announce-ment, Mark remarked, "Don't you remember? You told me you wanted the nursery suite from the Gunder-son house, so I've already mailed a check to Susan Hendrix, and next Saturday, Georgie and Gordon and I are going to drive out there and pick it all up—includ-ing the crib, although I might as well warn you I may trash that once I've inspected it. I really think we're best off going with a new, safe one. Georgie's going to re-finish the other pieces in his dad's garage workshop. I don't know why you look so surprised," he added in-genuously. "We discussed all this the other night, right before you went to the hospital."

Amanda frowned suspiciously at his innocent tone. Her memory of the events immediately preceding her collapse was patchy—bits and pieces returned to her at odd moments—but she felt very certain that their dis-cussion about the baby furniture, if "discussion" was the appropriate word, had been neither innocent nor casual. From what little she could recall, she'd screamed like a harpy and generally behaved badly enough to alienate Mother Teresa. And here was Mark calmly telling her that he was investing time and money in a set of furniture he neither liked nor valued, all because of a whim of hers....

She gazed up at him with dark, liquid eyes. "Why are you doing this?" she whispered awefully. "Consider-

ing your doubts about the nursery set—and the baby—
why are you going to all this trouble?''

Mark smiled tenderly. Shaping the delicate oval of her
face with his hands, he rubbed his thumb lightly across
her lips, urging them to part. "I'm doing this because
it's important to you," he murmured, lowering his head
with delicious slowness. "Anything that's important to
you is important to me. Besides," he added, his breath
sweet and warm on her skin, "after ten years it's kind
of nice to still be able to surprise my wife once in a
while." Their mouths met, and for the moment
Amanda forgot all her questions.

CHAPTER ELEVEN

"Happy birthday to yo-ou," Cheryl warbled, deliberately off-key, as she stood on the wet doorstep at the rear of the condominium, an umbrella in one hand and a big beribboned box in the other. With a flourish she presented the gift to Amanda.

"After a performance like that, I don't know if I dare let you in," Amanda said teasingly, opening the door for her friend. "And to think we once sang together in the church choir."

"Just consider yourself lucky I didn't go with my first impulse," Cheryl said, grinning. "I wanted to hire a male stripper for you, but Jim reminded me that it probably wouldn't be good for your blood pressure."

Amanda countered, "I don't know about that. I'm beginning to think my system could use a little shaking up. After doing nothing but sitting all this time, I sometimes wonder if I even have blood pressure anymore."

In the kitchen Cheryl folded her rain-spattered umbrella. "I'm glad I was able to find a parking space out back under the overhang," she muttered as she removed the scarf covering her blond curls. "Otherwise I'd be dripping all over your pretty front entryway."

"During the day most of the parking lot is empty, except for my Chrysler," Amanda noted, hanging up Cheryl's raincoat. "Sometimes I feel as if I'm marooned on a desert island—except Robinson Crusoe's life was a lot more exciting than mine has been lately.''

The two women hugged warmly. ''Be patient, dear,'' Cheryl urged her. ''I know the last couple of months seem to drag on forever, but believe me, the big day will arrive sooner than you think.'' She stepped sideways to study Amanda's figure in profile. ''Nope,'' she judged critically, ''it shouldn't be much longer now.''

Amanda regarded her askance. ''You remind me of a farmer checking out her prize cow.''

''Sorry, hon,'' Cheryl said, patting Amanda's tummy. ''It's one of the occupational hazards of motherhood. Every pregnant woman has to put up with it. But you do look as if you're getting close to term, you know. Do you think you're going to make it to the baby shower?''

Because of the auction, Cheryl had put off the party she was hosting for Amanda and a number of their old school chums until the last week of September. Amanda considered her question. ''Well, the baby isn't due officially for another six weeks yet, but even if the date is kind of iffy, I'm probably safe till after the first of October. So, yes, I think I should make it to the shower.''

''That's a relief,'' Cheryl said. ''Events like this are always a lot more fun if the guest of honor is in attendance.''

''I'll try my best to be there,'' Amanda promised. She waved Cheryl toward the living room. ''Why don't you make yourself comfortable while I get us some tea?''

''Should you be doing that?'' Cheryl asked anxiously.

Amanda smiled. ''Don't worry, I'm allowed to boil water. I may send out for pizza for dinner tonight, but in the meantime I can manage tea. So go find a place and I'll be with you in a minute." She rummaged in the cupboard for the teakettle, pausing to call after Cheryl, "Just watch out for my knitting!"

A few moments later, when Amanda carried a tray and Cheryl's gift into the living room, she found her friend on the sofa, examining a tiny, half-finished baby jacket. Cheryl laughed. "It's a good thing you warned me—I nearly speared myself when I sat down!" Setting the yarn and needles onto the cocktail table next to where Amanda had put the birthday present, she remarked, "That's a pretty shade of blue wool. I didn't realize you know how to knit."

"One of Mom's maids taught me when I was eight," Amanda said as she poured two cups of tea, "but the last time I made anything was back in college, when I knitted matching ski sweaters for my fiancé and me— which is probably why I haven't made anything since. However, it took about two days of enforced rest to make it clear that I was going to become a raving madwoman if I didn't find something to do with my hands. The very next evening, when Mark came home from work, I discovered that on his lunch hour he'd trotted off to a yarn shop on Hawthorne and bought me knitting supplies and books and even an instructional videotape to refresh my skills."

"That husband of yours is a real sweetheart," Cheryl noted with approval. "How's it going, him running the store without you?"

"He's managing too damn well for my peace of mind," Amanda admitted ruefully. "After all these years of supposedly doing half the work, it's rather daunting to discover how easily I can be replaced. Against all expectation, our clerk, Sandra, has turned out to be a real gem, and now as things gear up for the auction, Ted, one of the pickers who supplies a lot of our stock, has agreed to work part-time in the store on the condition that Mark will train him to open his own place. Mark says that one of these days Ted will probably be our biggest competitor, but in the meantime, business is booming—''

"While you sit at home and feel left out," Cheryl finished sympathetically.

Amanda nodded. "I try to keep my spirits up, but sometimes it's hard not to get depressed." She glanced out the window, where the view of Portland was obscured by a gray veil of mist. "Today, for instance. The weather's lousy, and all of a sudden I'm forty-three years old, which seems hard to take, even if Mark did give me ruby earrings this morning, and . . ." Her voice trailed off as she thought gloomily, *And I have no idea what the future is going to bring for me or my child or my marriage.*

Obviously trying to cheer her friend, Cheryl said brightly, "That reminds me—you haven't opened your birthday present from me yet." She pushed the package across the table to Amanda. "Here, dear. After I ventured out into the thunderstorm to bring this to you, you might at least show some enthusiasm."

"There's no storm, just a little drizzle," Amanda murmured, but her lips curved with genuine pleasure when she opened the box and discovered a slim, ravishing negligee of heavy, cream-colored silk. "Oh, Cheryl, it's beautiful," she whispered, reverently stroking the cool, shimmering fabric.

Cheryl said, "You won't be able to fit into it till after the baby's born, of course, but at times like this, when everything in your life seems to be geared toward motherhood, it's nice to have something to remind you that you're still a desirable woman." She grinned. "Who knows? Let Mark see you in that nightgown, and maybe in a year or so we'll have to start planning another shower!"

Amanda's smile evaporated. "No, Cheryl," she whispered, slowly shaking her head, "there won't be any chance of that. This is the only baby I'll ever have."

Her somber tone seemed to catch her friend off guard. For several moments both women were silent. Then Cheryl ventured diffidently, "You know, Amanda, I've always rather envied you being able to work alongside your husband. If must be nice to have so much in common. One of the peculiar aspects of being married to an attorney is that no matter how close the two of you are, there are certain subjects you can't discuss—like the problems of his clients. Anything revealed to Jim in his professional capacity remains absolutely confidential, even from me."

She eyed Amanda warily, waiting for her to reply. Amanda said nothing. After a moment, Cheryl continued, "I'm explaining this so you won't think Jim has been blabbing your secrets to me, but you might as well know that I'm aware you've consulted him recently. A couple of weeks ago he came home from the office really upset—which surprised me, since most of the time he's able to keep his cool no matter what happens at work—and all I could get him to say was that you'd seen him and he was worried about you."

With a dispirited sigh, Amanda broke her silence. "I'm sorry. I should have gone to some other law firm. It was wrong of me to involve a personal friend in a situation like this."

Leaning forward in her chair, Cheryl pressed, "A situation like what? Amanda, you and I have known each other for close to forty years, and even though there were periods when we drifted apart for a while, you matter more to me than just about any other person on this planet—except for my husband and children, of course. So if something's wrong, I want to help.''

''But there's nothing you can do to help!'' Amanda cried, suddenly exasperated by the futility of it all. ''There's nothing anyone can do. My life is falling apart and my marriage is falling apart, and there's not a goddamned thing anybody can do about it, because there's no cure for Down's syndrome!''

Visibly staggered by the news, Cheryl stared at Amanda with dismay. ''You're sure about this?'' she asked, her voice reedy. Amanda nodded. Cheryl took a deep breath to steady herself. She cursed succinctly.

''My thoughts exactly,'' Amanda replied, moved to mordant wit by the other woman's disgruntled tone.

''How long have you known?'' Cheryl asked.

''Since May. It showed up in the amnio.''

Cheryl's eyes widened, then narrowed. ''And after all these months, all the times we've been together since you found out, you still weren't going to tell me?''

Amanda gestured helplessly. ''I knew you'd feel hurt when you finally learned I'd kept the news from you, but I never could work up the nerve to say anything. Don't you realize how jealous I am of you? You have healthy children and a happy, placid marriage. Every time I see you, you're bubbling over with the sheer joy of life. How am I supposed to tell you that my baby's going to be born handicapped and my husband doesn't want him?''

Cheryl said quietly, "You tell me the way you just did. You tell me any way you bloody well please. But tell me."

Folding her hands together over her stomach, Amanda began toying with her wedding and engagement rings, watching the rainbow-hued light that reflected off the facets of the square-cut diamond solitaire in the old-fashioned setting. She'd always loved her engagement ring. When Mark gave it to her, she had asked him if it was an heirloom. "Not yet," he'd said.

She asked Cheryl, "Do you remember any of the stories we used to read in school, the myths where mortals were supposed to be afraid to say a child was beautiful or that life was good, for fear of tempting the gods? When I was a kid, I thought that was a really stupid superstition, but I'm not sure anymore. Last January when Mark and I took that cruise for our anniversary, we were so happy. Life *was* good. But since I became pregnant, everything's gone wrong."

Cheryl's expression was unreadable. "Are you saying you think this baby is a curse from God?"

Amanda shook her head emphatically. "No, no, no! I will never believe that—even though a lot of people seem to think I should."

"Mark, you mean?"

Biting her lip, Amanda admitted, "I don't know exactly what I mean. When it comes right down to it, I'm not really sure how Mark feels. He seems so ambivalent. On the one hand, he can be very tender and caring. He's done everything I've asked him, and more, as far as setting up the nursery. He tracked down a new crib that will go with the furniture we're having refinished, he found me a beautiful old Boston rocker, and he even hung the wallpaper himself! On the other hand,

I get the distinct impression that he regards the baby as a dreadful inconvenience he'd rather not have to put up with."

"It's different for men," Cheryl mused. "Biology, I guess. No matter how much they want children, they just don't relate to pregnancy the same way we do." She paused. "Have I told you about the time I had a miscarriage?"

Amanda frowned. "No, I didn't realize you'd ever lost a baby. What I have heard about—courtesy of your husband—is the time you threw a chocolate pie at him."

Cheryl grimaced. "Isn't that just like a man? He probably remembers that lousy pie more often than he does the child we lost...." Her voice faded. Picking up Amanda's knitting, Cheryl toyed with the half-completed infant sweater as she said poignantly, "This was right after we got married. You were back in Pennsylvania, which is probably why you never heard about it, and by the time you returned home for summer vacation, it was all over. Apparently I became pregnant on our honeymoon, or maybe shortly before then—I never could remember to take those blasted pills—but within two months of the wedding, I got confirmation. You can imagine what the news did to Jim and me. There we were, newlyweds, both still in college, him with years more to go. Unless we moved in with our parents, the only way we'd be able to afford a baby would be for Jim to give up law school. Neither option was very appealing. Jim insisted that the logical thing for me to do was have an abortion, but as soon as he suggested it, I realized I wanted to keep the baby. I told him there had to be alternatives. We had terrible fights. But before I had to make my final decision, the question became academic. I miscarried."

"I'm sorry," Amanda murmured.

Cheryl nodded. "Yeah, so am I. And, to be fair, in my heart I'm sure that Jim grieved the loss as much as I did, but it was ages before I could forgive him for the flash of relief I saw in his eyes when the doctor told him the baby was gone." She set down the knitting once more and picked up her teacup. Stirring the brew with agitated strokes, she reflected, "It's funny, but even after more than twenty years, even though we have four lovely children who mean the world to me, I still miss that first one. For the rest of my life I'm going to keep wondering what he would have been like."

Placing her spoon on the saucer, Cheryl peered at Amanda over the rim of her cup. "I'm glad you're having your baby," she said.

Amanda stared at her friend. "Do you know that in all these months, you're the very first person to tell me that?" she whispered plaintively. Then she burst into tears.

WHEN THE DAY of the Gunderson estate auction finally arrived, Steven reluctantly gave Amanda permission to attend, but only on the condition that she remain within reach of a telephone. At the slightest suspicion that she was about to go into labor, she was to head immediately for the hospital, where, he emphasized, there was a very real possibility that the baby would have to be delivered by cesarean section. The most recent ultrasounds showed him in position and apparently thriving, and Steven was still hoping for a normal delivery, but because of the possibility of congenital heart defects, if monitors disclosed even a hint of fetal distress during labor, he intended to remove the baby surgically. Amanda reminded Steven of the cellular telephone in her Chrysler and the overnight bag she kept packed and ready, and she promised not to become overstimulated.

Ironically, obtaining her obstetrician's permission to attend the auction proved easier than getting Mark to agree. "What if something happens while I'm right in the middle of conducting the sale?" he demanded. "You know I won't be able to stop what I'm doing to help you. Who's going to take you to the hospital—Sandra?"

"Nothing will happen yet," Amanda responded imperturbably, "and anyway, if it does, would you rather have me in labor while you're miles out of town and I'm home alone?"

In the end Mark acceded grudgingly to Amanda's wishes, but she knew he remained unconvinced. Early on the day of the auction, when the two of them arrived at the Gunderson house, they discovered not only Sandra but her parents and brother as well, waiting for them. "Sandra's been so excited, we just had to come and see what all the fuss was about," Gordon explained lightly, but the look that Amanda intercepted between Mark and Stephanie convinced her that he had asked their clerk's family to attend specifically to keep an eye on her.

Amanda's annoyance at being assigned a sitter was forgotten when she took a closer look at Otto's old home. After long-distance consultations with the Hendrixes—who had opted to remain in Delaware rather than attend the auction, since their presence would be required in Oregon yet again when the property was finally disposed of—Mark had arranged for gardeners to spruce up the grounds, mow and rake the first autumn leaves that had fallen, while the interior had been aired and polished by a janitorial service. Their efforts had paid off. Washed clean by recent rains, the old white house looked impressive, radiating Victorian splendor despite the unfortunate "updating" of its decoration. People attending the sale would recognize immediately that the items that had once furnished this home were real treasures, worthy of respect—and high bids.

If Mark and Amanda had ever had any doubts about the value of the Gunderson estate, the interest generated by the auction catalog would have reassured them. Dealers and collectors from all over the Northwest had replied to the announcement of the sale, two East Coast museums had submitted sealed bids for the Herter Brothers parlor suite, and a wealthy and renowned Los Angeles enthusiast was dispatching the curator of his private gallery in person. At times the magnitude of the response had seemed almost overwhelming, but gradually Amanda and Mark had recognized that what was happening to their business was a natural progression, the result of their years of hard work. Wexlers' was no longer a one-man stall in the antique mart or even a two-person shop on the mall. Almost without their realizing it, their cozy little establishment had evolved into a dealership of regional importance—and today was the culmination of all they'd strived for together.

"Oh, Mark," Amanda whispered with elation, surveying the rows of folding chairs arranged in the living room, the auctioneer's podium and the display area discreetly flanked by security guards, "did you ever think we'd come this far?"

Her husband slipped his arm around her thick waist and squeezed affectionately. His blue eyes were warm as he said with a laugh, "I have to admit, I'm pretty impressed with us, too. If we keep this up, maybe someday we'll give Sotheby's a run for their money." He glanced across the room, where a cluster of young people were donning badges that identified them as part of the auction staff. "Amanda, as much as I hate to leave you, I need to talk to those college kids Ted brought in to help us, to make sure they all know what they're supposed to do."

"You mean it's time to get to work, and I'm in your way," Amanda interpreted, suddenly miffed.

At her glum tone, Mark paused. "Darling, I did ask you to stay home," he reminded her gently.

Amanda's mouth twisted. "I know. Don't worry. I promise I won't be a pest. In fact, I think I'll go upstairs for a while."

Mark frowned. "If you're hunting for a place to lie down, there's nothing left up there. Everything's on display on this floor."

"I just want to look around," Amanda said. "I love this place, and who knows if I'll ever get a chance to be inside it again?" She turned and trudged toward the stairs, with Mark's worried gaze trained on her back.

Amanda wandered around the upper reaches of the house for more than an hour. With the rooms empty of furniture, she realized that whoever had blighted the downstairs with latex paint and wall-to-wall carpeting had not touched the second story. Upstairs the spacious, high-ceilinged bedrooms still had hardwood floors and wallpaper, faded but charming, and wonderful bay windows overlooking the grounds, where a person could sit and read or just daydream. One of the things that had always bothered her about her mother and father's home was that there was no good spot for daydreaming or licking one's wounds—no snug hidey-hole secure from the ferreting gaze of servants or parents. When she was a very little girl, for a brief period she'd created a haven for herself in a hollow spot under the evergreen hedge in the backyard. There she had played—and cried—in blissful privacy, but her little den had vanished along with the hedge when her mother decided to expand the rose garden.

Curling with difficulty on the floor, Amanda rested her chin on a sill and gazed out over the lawn. From her vantage point she could see a steady stream of cars turning off the highway onto the long driveway, where a parking attendant directed them to a roped-off area at the side of the house. Squinting, Amanda could make out vehicles with license plates from as far away as Idaho and British Columbia. She wondered if there was going to be space enough for all the potential buyers.

As people crowded into the rooms downstairs, she could hear chairs scrape and doors bang, and the murmur of voices rose to a dull roar. Suddenly the sharp rap of a gavel ricocheted through the house. The noise of the crowd subsided instantly. Amanda froze. She heard a squeal of feedback, followed by Mark's voice booming up the stairwell, hollow and almost unrecognizable over the public address system. "Ladies and gentlemen, the staff of Wexlers' Antiques and Collectibles of Portland would like to take this opportunity to welcome you here today and thank you for coming. We hope you've had time to look over your catalogs and the items on display. We're sure you'll agree that there are some rare prizes among them...."

Amanda started to push herself up from her cramped position, then she sank back onto the floor again. There was no reason for her to watch the auction. The packed, airless rooms would only make her uncomfortable, and if the bidding proved spirited, the excitement might elevate her blood pressure. It wasn't as if her presence were necessary anymore. Her part in the proceedings had been completed months ago. Now Mark and Sandra and that crew of able-bodied students Ted had recruited appeared to have the situation well under control. They didn't need her. Nobody seemed to need her.

The baby moved inside her, and Amanda grinned wistfully. Here, at least, was somebody who needed her, would always need her.... She rubbed her belly, shaping the bony protuberance that seemed to move just beneath her skin, making breathing difficult. She shifted awkwardly, fascinated despite the discomfort. How amazing it was to know that in a few short weeks she'd actually be able to see that foot or elbow or whatever that was jabbing her in the diaphragm, how impossible to believe that finally, after forty-three barren years, she was actually going to be a *mother*—

"Mrs. Wexler, are you okay?"

Amanda glanced up to discover Georgie shambling toward her, his eyes wide with worry. Looming over her, he asked again, "Are you okay? Why are you sitting on the floor?"

"I'm fine, dear," Amanda replied, smiling reassuringly. "I just wanted to look out the window for a while, and I'm sitting on the floor because there aren't any chairs."

"They're all downstairs," Georgie agreed. "I can go get you one if you want me to."

Amanda shook her head. "No, that won't be necessary. But thank you for offering."

"You're welcome," Georgie answered politely. He paused. "Can I sit here, too? Mr. Wexler asked me to keep an eye on you."

"Help yourself," Amanda murmured. The young man knelt beside her in the bay, and together they gazed out over the grounds. The roped-off parking area appeared to be completely packed with cars and vans, and Amanda could see even more vehicles lined along the shoulder of the highway. She declared, "I can't get over how many people have driven all the way out here for this auction. The turnout is unbelievable."

"I guess they all like old stuff," Georgie commented. "Sandy told me the things downstairs are worth lots of money."

"Some of them are," Amanda responded. Noting Georgie's dubious expression, she asked, "Don't you like what we're selling?"

He considered her question a moment. "I like the china animal statues, and a few of the pictures are pretty. Some of the furniture is nice, and some isn't. Before Mr. Wexler started selling things, I saw a lady looking at a little walnut desk that was kind of beat-up, and I told her not to spend too much on it because the dovetail joints in one of the drawers are broken."

Amanda knew the "desk" Georgie was referring to—a girl's dressing table in the aesthetic style, with the damage duly noted in the catalog description—but she wondered which of their customers he'd approached and how the woman had reacted to him and his well-meaning interference. "What did the lady say when you pointed out the broken drawer?"

"She thanked me for the warning and asked if I work for you and Mr. Wexler. When I told her I was fixing up some baby furniture for you, she seemed real interested. We talked for a while, and I told her about the school I used to go to before they took the money away.

Then Mr. Wexler banged that little hammer, and the lady went and sat down.''

"Well, I'm glad you were able to help her out," Amanda said, grateful that the client, whoever she was, had responded to the young man with tact and sensitivity. She paused. Downstairs the rap of the gavel and a brief round of applause signaled the disposal of yet another item. Amanda asked, "Speaking of the nursery furniture, how's the job going?"

Georgie beamed. "I think the set's going to be real pretty. When I took off all that old brown varnish, the wood was nice white pine underneath. I bleached out the stains and reglued the joints so nothing squeaks anymore. I've been working extra carefully, and I'm almost finished."

"It sounds wonderful," Amanda said sincerely. "I can't wait to see it." She closed her eyes and envisioned the set in place in the newly decorated nursery, a downy head peaking out from beneath a calico-print patchwork quilt. Amanda smiled, hugging herself. Soon, so very soon....

When she raised her lashes again, Georgie was gazing at her with a troubled expression. "Mrs. Wexler..." he began uneasily, his voice trailing off in confusion.

"Yes, Georgie?" Amanda prompted, surprised by his hesitation. One of the qualities she'd always found most appealing about the youth was his simple forthrightness, his utter lack of evasion.

He bit his lip. "Mrs. Wexler," he tried again, "my mother says that when your baby is born, he's going to be like me. Is she right?"

Amanda ached with compassion. She wondered why it had never occurred to her that Georgie was bright enough to recognize that in some critical ways he was different from other people. How had awareness come—gradually, when he was a teenager, already tormented with the usual adolescent doubts about his self-image? Or had some insensitive lout spelled out his deficiencies for him all at once, like those uncaring boys she and Mark had encountered in the park the day of the Rose Festival? Amanda began to appreciate even more what a remarkable job the Pollards had done raising their son into the contented, confident adult that he was. She prayed she would prove even half as good a parent for her own child.

"Yes, Georgie," Amanda said quietly, "your mother is right. My baby is going to have Down's syndrome, just like you."

He nodded thoughtfully. Then he asked, "Do you mind?"

Amanda gazed at the attractive, red-haired young man seated cross-legged beside her, one elbow on his knee, his chin in his hand. He was staring back at her with gentle candor, trusting and completely unaware of the consternation his guileless question would arouse in most people. With a flash of insight Amanda realized that although Georgie was to some extent conscious of his own limitations, he remained innocent of malice or deceit or cynicism. In a skeptical world, he had been blessed with the rare and beautiful gift of simple honesty.

Reaching out to pat his cheek affectionately, Amanda smiled and repeated, "Do I mind if my son turns out to be like you? No, Georgie, I don't mind at all."

A great sense of peace and consolation welled up in her as she spoke the words, because she knew at last that they were true.

MARK PRODDED AMANDA'S shoulder and said, "Wake up, sleepyhead, it's almost noon."

Amanda lifted her head from the pillow and glared blearily at her husband. "Have a little mercy, will you? You kept me up half the night talking about the auction." She tried to pull the covers over her head, but Mark tugged them out of her grasp and began kissing her face and shoulders, teasing her bare skin above the top of her nightgown until finally she wriggled in reaction.

When he could see that she was fully awake, he rolled over onto his back to gaze at the bedroom ceiling. Stretching luxuriously, he crowed, "I can't believe how well it all went yesterday!"

Amanda propped herself on one elbow and flashed a drowsy smile at her husband. "You keep saying that," she murmured, swallowing a yawn. "Don't you know any other topics of conversation?"

"Who wants to talk about anything else?" Mark shot back. "We were always sure the Gunderson job would be a plum, but, my God, never in my wildest dreams..."

The auction had proved an unqualified success. After the noise and the hubbub were over, after the parking area had emptied and Mark had dismissed the temporary staff, he had sat down with Sandra and Ted and begun tallying the receipts. Amanda had watched from the sidelines, rather chagrined that Steven had vetoed her participation even in this portion of the proceedings, but as the total mounted, her annoyance had turned to amazement. The amount of money raised by the auction far surpassed even the most optimistic estimates she and Mark had given Susan Hendrix. Otto's granddaughter was going to find herself a wealthy woman, especially considering that the house itself had yet to be sold. By the same token, the commission earned by Wexlers' Antiques and Collectibles for its role in the liquidation of the estate would place the company at an entirely new level in the business community.

Snuggling into the crook of Mark's arm, Amanda pressed as close as her ponderous body would permit, but he remained so exultant that he scarcely seemed aware of her. "You work hard all your life," he declared with breathless incredulity, "and regardless of how badly the deck is stacked against you, you always know that someday you're going to make it—make it big—but then when it really happens, when you finally prove to the world and yourself that you're somebody, that you *matter*, it seems too fantastic to believe...."

As she listened to her husband ramble, his deep, usually serious voice boyishly exuberant, almost giddy, Amanda felt her eyes grow wet with tears of joy. He sounded so happy. She'd never guessed before just how much their business meant to him, how much he identified with it. Far more than Amanda ever had, Mark regarded the store's success as his own, an affirmation of his own personal worth, a vindication for his miserable, tortured childhood. With dawning comprehension Amanda began to realize that what she had misinterpreted in recent months as indifference or ambivalence toward her pregnancy on Mark's part might have been simple preoccupation with work—work that meant as much to him as the baby did to her.

Amanda pressed her lips against Mark's smooth, slumber-cool skin, inhaling his musky fragrance. "I love you," she murmured. Her hands began to wander. He laughed and kicked back the sheets. When

Amanda observed his arousal, she giggled. "I never realized you could be so turned on by mere money."

"It's not just the money," Mark corrected, rolling toward her. "It's publicity and professional status and connections, too. Did you happen to meet that woman from Los Angeles, the one who works for the oilman with the private museum? When I think of the possibilities—"

"Hey, you," Amanda growled erotically, "how about forgetting business for a few minutes and thinking of some possibilities for the two of us?" She kissed Mark hard, and neither of them spoke again until their feverish explorations were interrupted by the jangling of the telephone.

Reluctantly Mark lifted his head from Amanda's breast. His eyes looked slightly glazed. "Should I answer that?" he asked throatily.

Crestfallen, Amanda shrugged. "You might as well. The mood's already been broken."

He stretched a long arm to the nightstand and picked up the receiver on the third ring. "Hello?" he grumbled. When the party on the other line replied, Mark sat up in bed and cleared his throat. "Oh, hello, Alden. How are you this morning—this afternoon?" He listened, grimacing, and said, "Well, actually we're still resting up from all the excitement of yesterday. What about getting together tonight, instead? . . . You can't? All right, we'll see you in a little while."

Mark hung up the telephone and regarded Amanda quizzically. "I don't know what's up, but your father insists that he and Joan have to talk to us right away. They're heading over here now."

"Damn," Amanda muttered. "That sounds ominous." Sighing, she climbed out of bed. She jumped into the shower for a minute, and by the time she jerked on stretch slacks and a voluminous smock top, her parents were knocking at the front door.

"You look tired, Amanda," Joan said in greeting.

Her daughter clenched her teeth. "I haven't been awake very long, Mother. We were sleeping in."

"Smart girl," Alden declared. "You're wise to enjoy your rest while you can, because I guarantee, once the baby's born—"

Aware of Amanda's growing tension, Mark cut in quickly, "We haven't had a chance to eat yet today. I was just about to fix Amanda a sandwich. May I get you two something, as well?"

"Some coffee, perhaps?" Joan suggested with an arch smile. She seated herself next to Alden on the couch, and after Mark brought out refreshments, for a quarter of an hour the two couples observed ritual pleasantries, while the atmosphere in the living room grew electric with anxiety. Finally Joan placed her cup on the cocktail table and announced flatly, "Your father and I have found the perfect solution to your problem."

In the armchair across the room, Amanda stiffened. "What problem?" she asked tonelessly, dropping her half-eaten sandwich onto her plate.

Joan's smile was tolerant. "There's no purpose served by being deliberately obtuse, dear. You know perfectly well what we're talking about—the problem of how a woman of your age and temperament is going to raise a handicapped baby."

Mark, seated on the arm of Amanda's chair, said quietly, "With all due respect, Joan, how we choose to raise our child is none of your business."

Alden scowled. "Are you saying grandparents have no rights at all where their grandchildren are concerned?"

"You have a right to your opinions," Mark told him firmly, "but the final decisions are ours."

"But all we want to do is help you make those decisions," Joan insisted. "I know you both think you're prepared for what's to come, but the fact is, for months now, everything that's happened has been colored by the fact of Amanda's pregnancy. Having a baby—any baby—is a very moving, emotional experience, and it's virtually impossible to think objectively while you're right in the middle of it." She paused. "So what we've done is found a way to give you two a break from the responsibility of parenthood while you assess the future and decide what's best for you and the baby."

Amanda's eyes narrowed. "What on earth are you talking about?"

Alden explained, "Through some business connections of mine, I've just learned about a woman in the Salem area who provides foster care for Down's syndrome children."

Indignantly Amanda gasped, "Damn it, I've told you a dozen times that there is no way in hell I'll ever let my child be institutionalized!"

"But this isn't an institution," Joan corrected hastily. "This woman cares for these children in the privacy of her own home. I believe she had a Down's syndrome baby herself some years ago, and since then she's taken in others from all over the country. That's why we needed to talk to you right away, because her services are always in demand, and with your baby due at any moment, we'll have to make arrangements immediately—''

"There aren't going to be any arrangements," Amanda declared tightly, but her mother ignored her.

"Naturally we've investigated this woman, and from every source the reports are glowing. She gives the infants excellent, loving care while their mothers recover from childbirth, and she takes the pressure off the parents so they can think clearly about their options. She isn't cheap, but your father and I would be more than happy to pay her fees, if that's what you two need to make up your minds. In the meantime, Salem is near enough that you'd be able to visit your baby any time you wanted and—" Joan paused to stare piercingly at her daughter "—if you and Mark should finally decide that raising him is simply more than you can handle, this woman can even find adoptive parents for him, *young* adoptive parents with the strength to cope with a difficult child."

The plate shook in Amanda's fingers. "I can't believe I'm hearing this," she croaked, her face pinched and ashen with outrage. "No matter how much you two have tried to meddle in my life in the past, I can't believe even you would have the sheer gall—"

"But we're not trying to meddle—we only want to *help*," Alden asserted, offended. He appealed to his son-in-law. "Mark, she's your wife—you talk some sense into her. Make her understand that there's nothing shameful about seeking outside assistance in a difficult situation."

Amanda sat hunched in her chair, trembling, as she closed her eyes and waited anxiously for Mark's explosion. With equal portions of dread and anticipation, she listened for his blistering denunciation of her parents' unjustifiable interference in their personal life—but the attack did not come.

Silence boomed in her ears. Gulping back the acid taste in her throat, Amanda slowly opened her eyes again and peeked up at her husband, looming over her, his expression unreadable. "M-Mark?" she stammered dreadfully. She put her hand on his knee. She could feel his muscles vibrate with tension. "Mark, please," she repeated, her voice thready with foreboding, "you don't think they're right, do you? You don't think we should give our son away, even for a little while?"

Mark took a deep, ragged breath. Laying his big hand on her glossy hair, he began to stroke her soothingly as he admitted, "I'm sorry, Amanda, but if you want me to state categorically that your parents are wrong, I can't do it. I know you want to raise this child yourself, but somehow it doesn't seem prudent or reasonable to reject the option of foster care outright before we even know the extent of his disabilities. Besides, what if you have to have a cesarean? You may need an extended period of recuperation yourself, and to be perfectly honest, I'm not sure I'm capable of caring for you and the business *and* the baby, all at the same time. I'm not Superman. You know I still have a lot of doubts that have to be worked out. If this woman in Salem could take the baby for a few weeks or whatever, the break might be exactly the opportunity I need to get my head straight."

Amanda blinked. Carefully removing her hand from her husband's knee, she stated with painful precision, "If this woman takes our baby, we will never get him back again."

Mark's heart wrenched at her anguish. "Darling, nobody is going to take your baby away from you," he promised. "I swear nothing will ever be done for him without your complete permission and approval."

"I don't believe you," Amanda said in dull, defeated tones so low they were almost inaudible. She glanced down at the half-empty plate in her hands and discovered that while they had talked, without realizing what she was doing, she had toyed with the sandwich until the crusts were reduced to crumbs, now littering her lap and the rug around her feet. "God, what a disgusting mess," she muttered, struggling to push herself into a standing position. "I'd better go get something to clean it with."

"I'll take care of it later," Mark offered quickly, but Amanda shook her head.

"Don't bother. I can manage without you." She headed for the kitchen.

Mark remained seated on the arm of the chair. As he gazed mutely across the room at Amanda's parents, who were regarding him with equal blankness, it occurred to him that he'd known the other couple for eleven years and still had nothing to say to them. He shifted restlessly and stifled a yawn while he waited for Amanda.

She did not return.

Suddenly in charged silence Mark could hear the ticking of his wristwatch—or was it the panicky pounding of his heart? He jumped up and lunged for the kitchen. Amanda was not there.

The back door hung open, swinging easily on its hinges.

Her car was gone.

CHAPTER TWELVE

"OH, MY GOD," Mark croaked as he stared at the empty space in the carport where Amanda's Chrysler had been parked. On the pavement four identical piles of dust and crushed leaves marked the spots where the tires had rested undisturbed for two months, since Amanda had last driven. One part of Mark's mind expressed surprise that she'd been able to squeeze herself behind the steering wheel at all, while the rest angrily demanded to know why he had not paid more attention to her parting words as she headed for the kitchen—and flight. What was it she'd murmured as she passed him, plate in hand? *I can manage without you.* A peculiar, coppery taste bloomed in Mark's mouth: the taste of fear. With absolute certainty he knew that when Amanda had walked out of the living room, she had been walking out of his life.

With equal certainty he also knew that he would not let her go.

He ran out onto the sidewalk, but there was no sign of Amanda's sedan on the quiet residential street. Mark swore with frustration. She could not yet have traveled very far, but he realized in dismay that he had no idea whatsoever of where she was headed. He wondered if she knew herself. The thought of Amanda, distraught and on the run, trying to maneuver through Portland's heavy traffic in her condition was terrifying. "Oh, my

God," he whispered again, but this time the words were a prayer.

Mark sprinted back to the house. Amanda's parents were standing inside the kitchen door, watching in bewilderment. "What on earth has happened?" Alden demanded.

"She's gone," Mark said brusquely, elbowing between them. He grabbed the telephone and started punching in the codes for Amanda's car phone. "C'mon, darling, don't be stubborn," he pleaded under his breath as he waited restlessly for her ring. Suddenly Alden reached past him and pressed the plunger, breaking the connection. Mark gaped at him. "What the hell—"

"You're going about this all wrong," Alden declared calmly. Mark stared at the older man, too flabbergasted to speak. Alden commented, "One would think that after living with Amanda all these years, you'd know her well enough to recognize when she's grandstanding. Taking off in a huff like this is just her way of trying to get attention, and if you humor her, you'll only encourage more histrionics."

Joan added, "She used to do the same thing when she was a little girl. No matter how much we loved Amanda, she could be very tiresome and demanding at times. She was always oversensitive as a child, always wanting us to play with her when it was totally inconvenient. If we ignored her, she'd go hide in a hole under the hedge in the backyard, hoping somebody would come looking for her."

"We finally cured that little habit by digging up the hedge," Alden noted, "or, at least, we thought we'd cured her. Actually I'm rather surprised and disappointed to see her behaving so immaturely, but I suppose the strain of her condition has made her revert to childhood temporarily." He grinned at his wife and squeezed her shoulders. "Pregnant women can be emotional, can't they, dear?"

"I never was," Joan said. She smiled sympathetically at her son-in-law. "Amanda's going to be all right, Mark. If you're wise, you won't try to contact her or track her down. That's what she wants you to do, but I guarantee that if you just go about your business today as if nothing's wrong, sooner or later she'll drag herself home with her tail between her legs."

Throughout the bantering exchange between Amanda's parents, Mark remained silent, appalled by their casual revelations of emotional abuse, abuse that must have been as crippling as the childhood traumas he himself had suffered. Finally he asked in genuine bewilderment, "Didn't it ever occur to either of you that the reason Amanda was always trying to get your attention was because she *needed* more attention?"

Offended, Joan asserted, "Our daughter has always had everything she needed."

"The best of everything," Alden added with dignity.

Exasperated, Mark declared, "You two don't even know what you've done to her, do you? You're completely oblivious to your own faults."

"I don't think we've done such a bad job of raising Amanda," Alden said. "She's temperamental and headstrong, yes, but I think you'll agree that basically she's a good, bright, loving woman."

"Oh, I do agree," Mark said coldly. "That's what's so remarkable about her. After the way you two have treated Amanda, the miracle is not that she still loves you—which, amazingly, she does. No, the real miracle is that she's capable of love at all!"

Bristling, Joan glanced at her husband. "I think it's time for us to leave."

"I quite agree," he muttered. They turned to march out of the kitchen. Alden paused, regarding his son-in-law sternly. "Mark, I'm not going to demand an apology, because I realize that right now you're upset about Amanda. But later, after she's wandered home safe and sound and you've calmed down, I think you're going to feel very ashamed of yourself for speaking to us the way you have. You know perfectly well that we've never wanted anything except what's best for our daughter and you."

Squelching a scathing retort, Mark watched them go.

As soon as he heard the front door close behind Amanda's parents, Mark picked up the receiver again and dialed her number. She did not answer. He tried again, but if Amanda was still in her car, she was ignoring the buzz of the cellular phone at her side. Sweat beaded on his forehead. Thinking quickly, he called Cheryl and Jim Bishop's home. Their teenage son informed Mark that his parents were in Seattle for the weekend, but if Mrs. Wexler dropped by the house, he'd be sure to let her know her husband was looking for her. Next Mark contacted the highway patrol. The officer he spoke with sounded sympathetic as he took down Amanda's license number and description, but something about his tone gave Mark the feeling he was being humored, dismissed as a typical panicky expectant father, like a character in a comedy sketch. Mark hung up.

He was still gripping the handset when the phone rang, its electronic warble as jarring as the scrape of nails on a chalkboard. He snatched up the receiver and barked, "For heaven's sake, Amanda, is that you?"

"No, Mr. Wexler, it's me, Georgie," the voice on the other end of the line explained carefully, startled and obviously confused. "You scared me, yelling like that. Isn't Mrs. Wexler there?"

Forcing himself to be patient, Mark replied, "I'm sorry I shouted, Georgie, and no, Mrs. Wexler isn't here right now."

"Oh, that's too bad," Georgie said, "because I need to talk to her. I want to tell her—"

"Could you please call back later?" Mark requested urgently, desperate to keep the line open yet certain that Amanda would never forgive him if he hurt her young friend's feelings. Quickly he improvised, "I was just about to make an important call, but I promise that when I see Mrs. Wexler, I'll tell her you phoned."

"Tell her the lady who was looking at the desk yesterday called my mom last night," Georgie persisted doggedly. "Tell her the lady asked Mom about the school I used to go to. She says she knows somebody who maybe can help me finish my training and get a real job."

Mark paused, baffled. "The lady told you that?" he murmured, not certain what Georgie was talking about but willing to go along with anything if it would get him off the telephone. "That is good news, Georgie. I know Mrs. Wexler will be delighted. I'll be sure to tell her the moment I see her."

"Will you please tell her I promise I'll finish fixing the baby furniture first, even if I do get a chance to go back to school?" Georgie pressed. "I don't want her to think I might forget."

"Amanda would never think that. She has confidence in you," Mark reassured him, but as soon as he spoke his wife's name, his agitation returned. "Look,

Georgie,'' Mark said roughly, wondering if he sounded as frantic as he felt, ''I'll be glad to talk about this some more later, but right now I'm going to have to hang up. I'm trying to find Mrs. Wexler. She drove off in her car, and I don't know where she was going. I'm worried about her.''

Georgie suggested, ''Maybe she went to the old house. She really likes it there. She told me she was sorry she wasn't going to get to see it anymore.''

Mark froze. *My God, of course,* he thought, mortified that he had tried to dismiss the youth so brusquely. He ought to have guessed himself. He recalled Amanda's fascination with the Gunderson place and her repeated references to the ''love'' she felt there. Through the months, for whatever reason, the rambling Queen Anne cottage had begun to signify warmth and security to Amanda. Now, in flight like a wounded doe, instinctively she'd head for the sanctuary the big, empty house offered.

Struggling to keep his voice steady, Mark said, ''You're right, Georgie. Amanda probably did drive out to the old house for a last look this afternoon. Thank you for reminding me. I think I'll go hunt for her there.'' Hastily bidding him goodbye, Mark grabbed his keys and bolted for his own car.

The half-hour trip west into Washington County seemed interminable. Mark raced all the way at speeds that might have astounded the manufacturers of his sedate Swedish station wagon, swerving around slower vehicles, gunning his engine through every yellow light. He felt surprised and almost disappointed that his erratic driving did not attract police attention. If a traffic officer pulled him over, he reasoned, at least he might be able to arrange an escort. But nobody tried to flag him down, nobody appeared even to notice him, and when he skidded his Volvo to a halt behind Amanda's Chrysler at the foot of the stone steps to the Gunderson house, he was alone and unobserved.

Glancing inside Amanda's car, Mark spotted the cellular phone lying disconnected on the passenger seat amid a heap of wadded, tear-stained tissues. He shook his head and loped up the steps.

"Amanda, where are you?" he shouted as he burst through the front door, slamming it so hard the stained glass fanlight rattled. His voice echoed mockingly down the long hallway. Mark dashed through the big rooms, empty now except for the rented folding chairs and tables that were stacked neatly in a corner of the parlor, awaiting pickup. Almost every item offered for sale had been carried away by its purchaser at the conclusion of the auction. The few pieces remaining—primarily the Herter parlor suite, which had to be crated for shipment to a museum in the East, plus a piano and one or two other bulky articles of furniture that would require professional movers—were stored in a single room Mark had outfitted with security locks. Unbolting the door, Mark looked inside. Amanda was not there. She was nowhere on the ground floor.

He mounted the steep staircase two steps at a time, braying her name breathlessly. He reached the landing, finally, and as he gasped for air beneath the ornate light fixture dangling from the high, bordered ceiling, he heard a faint, thready moan, like a kitten mewling in distress, coming from the direction of the nursery. Mark ran.

He found her huddled in the alcove where the crib had been. She was slumped against the wall, her arms wrapped around her belly. Her face was gray with pain.

When Mark galloped into the room, she looked up in disbelief. "You found me," she whispered.

Mark fell on his knees beside her. Despite her obvious relief, he could still see wariness in her stricken expression. Gently he touched her cheek. "Don't you know I'll always find you, wherever you go?" he murmured, aching for her. "After ten years, haven't you figured out that you're a beacon to me? I could be blind and deaf and lame and still I'd home in on you, because you're the one thing in my life that's precious to me...." He laid his hand over hers. He could feel his child move within her. Swallowing thickly, he corrected himself. "The two precious things in my life."

Amanda stared at him with glistening eyes. "Do you really mean that?"

"Would I lie?" Mark quipped, then wished he hadn't. He held his breath, waiting for Amanda to remind him of the past he'd kept secret from her, the single sin of omission she'd never forgiven.

After an endless silence, Amanda frowned pensively and said, "No, Mark, you've always been honest with me. You've never lied—not about anything that mattered."

Mark exhaled in a long, shuddering sigh. "Thank God you understand that now." He stood and reached down to pull her to her feet. "Come on, darling, let's go home. This house is no place for you right now."

Amanda shook her head fiercely. "I can't walk," she whimpered. "My water broke."

Mark blanched, noticing for the first time the telltale signs. "You're in labor?"

"If having a boa constrictor wrapped around your belly is what being in labor feels like, then yes, I am,"

Amanda said with grisly humor. "It looks like I'm going to miss Cheryl's baby shower, after all."

"I think Cheryl will understand," Mark responded grimly. "When did the contractions start? How far apart are they?"

Amanda held up the naked wrist where she usually wore her watch. "Ten, fifteen minutes apart, maybe a little longer—I'm not sure. I'm not sure when it started, either. It must have been while I was driving. I felt sick, but I thought that was because I was so upset. I was clear up here in the nursery before it finally dawned on me what was happening." She tried to flash a sickly smile. "It was pretty stupid of me, wasn't it, running off that way without my overnight bag or even..." The words faded in a gurgle. As Mark watched helplessly, her eyes grew glazed and she doubled over.

An eternity later, when the spasm passed, Mark stripped off his own wristwatch and handed it to Amanda. "Here, darling," he said, his voice cracked and raw, "I'll be back in a minute. You hang on to this while I—"

The watch slipped through her limp fingers, and she stared at him in disbelief. "You're leaving me?" she asked, gasping.

"I'm just running down to your car," Mark promised. "I have to use the telephone to call the para—"

"Don't leave me!" Amanda cried hysterically, clutching at his arm. He could feel her nails gouging his skin.

"But, darling—"

"No!"

He gazed into her eyes and knew he could not leave her alone, even for a moment. What little control she'd still possessed when he first discovered her was gone now, wiped out by pain and panic and fear. He scooped her into his arms and started to carry her downstairs.

"How the hell were you able to climb these steps in your condition?" he groused as he picked his way carefully down the steep staircase.

Amanda's face was buried against his shoulder. "I told myself if I could get to the nursery, the baby would be safe," she explained in a tiny voice, the words muffled in the front of his shirt. "I know it doesn't make sense...."

"Don't worry about it. The baby's safe now," Mark vowed intensely.

Recognizing Amanda's dread of being left alone, he settled her on the carpet in the entryway by the open front door, where she could watch while he bounded down the stone steps to her car. When, after what seemed an interminable delay but was probably only a matter of seconds, he was able to make contact with her doctor, Mark flashed a reassuring thumbs-up signal to Amanda—but he was extremely grateful that she could not hear the obstetrician's reaction to Mark's news.

"Goddamn it, I knew I should have kept her in the hospital!" Steven swore, startling Mark with a stream of eloquent profanity that made Mark wonder whether the younger man had received part of his medical training in the marines. Then, with equal abruptness, Steven resumed his professional facade and promised to dispatch an ambulance at once. "Under no circumstances are you to try to bring her in yourself. All you have to do is keep her calm till the paramedics arrive," he said firmly. "If her contractions are ten minutes apart, then there's plenty of time to get her to the hospital, even from out there in the boondocks. I promise you Amanda's going to be all right."

"But what about the baby?" Mark asked, his heart in his throat as he recalled his own promise to his wife.

Steven said, "We'll know more about that after you get here."

"Then for heaven's sake, hurry!" Mark blurted out.

Before returning to Amanda, he opened the tailgate of his station wagon and pulled out two thick, quilted furniture pads he always carried with him in case he picked up any fragile antiques for the store. In the entryway he spread one of the pads at the foot of the staircase and rolled the other into a soft pillow. "Here, love," he said soothingly, "this will be more comfortable than sitting on the floor, and you'll be able to relax. Steven says all you have to do is keep calm, and the ambulance will be here before you know it."

As Amanda lay down, she pursed her lips, mildly interested. "I've never ridden in an ambulance before."

"Yes, you have," Mark reminded her, hunching on the bottom tread beside her. "An ambulance took you to the hospital the night you collapsed in our office."

She nodded. "Oh, right, of course. Well, at least this time maybe I'll remember the trip." Her feathery brows ruffled whimsically. "I guess today's going to be pretty memorable for a lot of reasons."

"It's not a day I'm likely to forget in a hurry," Mark drawled, a faint edge to his voice. "I've never been so terrified in my life as I was when I realized you'd run off and I didn't have a clue where you were headed."

"How did you find me?"

"Georgie told me where to look," Mark explained. "He called to tell you some news he was excited about, and when I said I didn't know where you were, he immediately suggested looking for you here."

"Wise kid," Amanda commented.

Mark nodded. "Yes, he is. Georgie is wise in a lot of ways that I'm only now beginning to appreciate."

"Did he say what the news was the he was so anxious to tell me?"

Mark shrugged. "That part of the conversation I didn't understand. It was something about a lady who was looking at a desk and might know how to help him finish his job training. Do you have any idea what he's talking about?"

"Possibly," Amanda said. "Apparently yesterday at the auction Georgie carried on a long conversation with a woman who was interested in that girl's vanity table, the walnut one with the damaged drawer. He kept referring to it as a desk."

Scowling, Mark recalled, "That item was sold to the woman who works for that millionaire collector in L.A. I remember being surprised she'd want it, since similar pieces in mint condition are relatively easy to find, but later when she was paying for her purchases, she told me the little dressing table wasn't for the museum, it was for her daughter." He paused, considering. "I do know her boss is reputed to be quite a philanthropist. You don't suppose she's going to try to talk him into giving Georgie a scholarship or sponsoring his school or something, do you?"

"Who knows?" Amanda responded happily. "More miraculous things have occurred. I guess we can only..." Once again her words were swallowed as she was silenced by another contraction.

Mark glanced at his watch. Nine and a half minutes had passed since the previous contraction. The labor pains were closer together and, to gauge by the strain on Amanda's sallow, sweat-dewed face, stronger. He held her hand and wondered when the paramedics were going to arrive.

When she was able to relax, Mark patted Amanda's face dry with his handkerchief and flicked damp tendrils of dark hair away from her eyes. He kissed her tenderly. "I'm sorry," he told her, aching with love and guilt. "I wish there was something I could do for you."

"It's not your fault," Amanda murmured.

Mark's lips twisted in a wry smile. "Oh, yeah? Whose fault is it, then?"

Amanda chuckled tiredly at the feeble joke. "Okay, so it is your fault I'm pregnant," she conceded, "but it's my own damned fault I'm not in a nice, cozy hospital right now, with nice, cozy nurses offering me something for the pain." She grimaced. "I can't believe I was actually stupid enough to drive off the way I did. I don't even know why I did it. I was sitting there listening to you and my folks, and suddenly I just couldn't take it anymore."

"I think you had justification," Mark acknowledged darkly. He hesitated. "I owe you an apology, Amanda. Ever since I first met them, I've always known your parents could be remarkably insensitive where you're concerned, but until today I never truly realized how very repressive your upbringing must have been. Your mother and father have a lot to answer for."

Amanda sighed. "Whatever they did, they thought they were doing for my own good."

Mark said, "When my mother killed my sister, she claimed she was doing it for Marilyn's own good, too."

Abruptly he jumped to his feet, his fists jammed in the pockets of his slacks, his jaw clenched. He gazed up the length of the tall staircase as if he were looking into the past. "Have you ever wondered why I don't like this house?" he asked.

Grateful for any topic of conversation that would distract her from her current predicament, Amanda admitted, "Yes, I have wondered about that. Considering its history and your taste, this place has always struck me as exactly the sort of house that ought to appeal to you. It certainly appeals to me. I've even had a pipe dream that we might buy it from Susan Hendrix."

"Oh, really?" Mark muttered in surprise. "That's a thought. How come you never said anything?"

"Because I've known from the first time we stepped inside that something here bugs you, and I don't think it's the rotten redecoration."

Mark nodded. "It's the staircase," he declared unexpectedly. "The rest of the house is fine, but this blasted staircase with the hand-carved balusters reminds me of the one in the house in Spokane where my mother worked as a maid after Dad left. From what I can recall, that house must have been much larger than this one, and probably of a later period, but I've never forgotten that staircase. I broke my nose on one of those damned balusters."

Amanda scowled. "I thought you told me you got into a fight with the owner's son and he broke your nose."

Mark lifted his shoulders stiffly. "I did. After the kid called Marilyn a dummy, I tore into him. He was bigger than I was, but I was so enraged that at first I actually had the advantage. Then he ran into the house. I followed right after him. I'd chased him halfway up the staircase when suddenly he turned around and pushed me. I tumbled all the way down, fracturing my nose as I fell. I lay there stunned for several moments. My face was a bloody mess, and my mother was sobbing and cradling me in her arms, but when my head cleared and I opened my eyes, all I could see was the owner's wife standing at the top of the stairs, staring down at us like a disapproving goddess, while her sniveling hellion of a son hid behind her skirts. She told my mother to pack up and get herself and her ungrateful brats off the property by nightfall—and my poor mother never knew another day's happiness in her life."

Mark turned and squatted beside Amanda once more. Clearing his throat, he added dully, "Whenever I remember that incident, I feel ashamed."

Amanda touched his arm. "You have nothing to be ashamed of, Mark. It's not your fault your mother got fired. You were a child, trying to protect your family."

"But I wasn't strong enough," he said. "I loved Mom and Marilyn with all my heart, but I lost them because my love wasn't strong enough to protect them or stop their pain." He sighed. "I've loved you from the first moment I saw you, and it hasn't been enough to keep you from suffering, either."

As another contraction began, Amanda countered with difficulty, "The only time you've ever made me suffer was when I thought you didn't love our baby as much as I do."

"How could I not love him, when he's part of you?" Mark murmured reassuringly, but Amanda did not seem to hear him.

He watched uneasily as her agony increased. Regardless of Steven's promise that Amanda would come through the birth all right, Mark was beginning to have doubts. He tried to coach her through breathing exercises, but Amanda was growing too tired to concentrate. Fatigue bruised and clouded her bright eyes, and her skin looked sickly pale. The constant tension and worry of the past months had robbed her of her usual vitality, and now, when she needed it most, she lacked stamina for the ordeal yet to come. Mark listened anxiously for approaching sirens. He wondered if it was time to countermand Steven's instructions and try to carry his wife to a hospital himself.

Amanda sensed his apprehension. "What's wrong?" she panted.

"Nothing's wrong," he lied. "I just want you to promise you won't ever try to run off again."

Rallying slightly, she tried to jest. "Run off in this condition?"

"In any condition," Mark said roughly. "I couldn't bear for you to leave me."

The banked fear in his eyes made her realize he was thinking about a separation more final than divorce. Pushing herself up on her elbows, Amanda cried, "Damn it, Mark Wexler, I'm not going to leave you! I'm not going to die. *I'm stronger than your mother!*"

Suddenly he knew it was true. "You're the strongest woman I've ever known," Mark told her huskily. "We're going to need your strength—"

"And yours," Amanda said. "I can't do it without you. It's your love that makes me strong."

"You and the baby are never going to be without me or my love," he vowed. Gathering her in his arms, he prayed silently until at last the distant screech of a siren announced the approach of the paramedics.

DAVID MARK WEXLER was born in the evening of the first day of autumn, a day as soft and golden as the downy ringlets covering his pink scalp. He was delivered by cesarean section, and when his mother awoke from the anesthesia, she looked up blearily to discover her husband standing beside her bed, almost unrecognizable in green hospital scrubs, with a surgical mask dangling comically from one ear by a long string. In his arms he was gingerly holding a small blue bundle. When he stepped closer and Amanda's vision cleared, she spotted a small, wrinkled face still flushed with newness beneath a doll-size knit cap.

"Is that our baby?" she whispered awefully, afraid to awaken the sleeping miracle. Mark beamed. Carefully, so very carefully, Amanda raised her hand. When she touched a silken cheek, two big eyes blinked, revealing irises of indeterminate dark blue that she knew instinctively would someday be as brown as her own. Amanda held her breath. Delicately she stroked his skin, teasing his lashes, shaping a tiny, shell-like ear. The baby opened his eyes again and focused uncertainly on his mother. Amanda gazed back. It was love at first sight.

Although he apparently suffered from none of the gross health defects that sometimes afflicted Down's syndrome infants, he did suckle weakly, a common problem. However, both the pediatrician who took over the baby's care as soon as he was born and the private-duty nurse engaged to look after Amanda and the baby while Mark was working claimed to be encouraged by David's efforts. They predicted that as the infant grew stronger, the need for supplemental bottles would decrease.

Mark tried to arrive at the hospital each evening in time to watch Amanda feed the baby—an experience both of them were finding astonishingly erotic—and he heartened her by volunteering to handle the baby's night feedings so that she could get the rest she needed to regain her own strength. But when a hospital volunteer scurried into Amanda's room with a sheaf of white roses in a Wedgwood urn and announced that the donors of those glorious flowers were on their way up, Amanda wondered if she'd ever gain enough strength to face her parents. Amanda had just finished nursing David, and he lay asleep in a clear plastic crib alongside Amanda's bed.

Mark set Joan's roses on the bedside stand next to a potted chrysanthemum in a cheerfully tacky plaster vase shaped like a lamb. A painstakingly lettered card read "Love, Georgie." There was no question in Amanda's mind which flowers she preferred, but when her parents appeared at the door, none of her reservations showed on her face.

"How are you feeling, dear?" Joan murmured, pecking Amanda's cheek. "You're looking better than you did a few days ago."

"Except for my incision being sore, I feel a lot better," Amanda admitted. "I'm still rather wobbly on my feet, but it's nice to have the rough part behind me. Thank you for the roses. They're lovely, as always."

Across the room Alden regarded Mark warily. Although Mark stood up politely when his in-laws entered the room, something about the older man's stance gave Amanda the impression he was uncertain of his welcome. She wondered exactly what had transpired between them on that traumatic day when she ran out of the condominium. Stiffly Alden extended his hand. "Congratulations, Mark," he intoned. "You must be very proud."

"I am," Mark said. He nodded toward the bassinet. "Don't you want to see him?"

The mixture of apprehension and curiosity on her parents' faces was painful for Amanda to behold. "Please," she urged them, and reluctantly Joan and Alden approached the sleeping infant.

Faced with the reality of their grandchild, Amanda's parents seemed strangely moved and a little bewildered. She understood the reason for their consternation when her father confessed gruffly, "He's beautiful, Amanda. I thought he'd be...different."

"He *is* different—he's ours," she reminded her father. "There's never been anyone exactly like him before."

Mark stood between the crib and Amanda's bed, figuratively sheltering his wife and son. "David is unique," he told his in-laws. "With our love and support he'll grow and develop in his own unique way."

Joan gazed thoughtfully at her daughter's family. "I guess your father and I have a lot to learn," she admitted.

"We all do, all three of us—all *five* of us, if you two want to be part of your grandson's life," Amanda said.

Mark added, "Nobody pretends the future is going to be smooth sailing, least of all me. There are bound to be problems, serious ones, but they'll be a lot easier to cope with if we all work together."

Alden and Joan did not reply. They were both peering down at the baby, and in silvery rivulets on Joan's powdered cheeks Amanda saw the first tears she'd ever known her mother to shed. Observing them, Amanda realized that her parents were torn, drawn instinctively to their grandchild yet not ready to abandon their prejudices. She glanced questioningly at Mark, but he shook his head faintly. Amanda relaxed and returned her gaze to her parents. Mark was right; there was no need to press the issue. For the moment it was enough that Alden and Joan did not reject the overture out-right.

Amanda felt Mark's hand on her shoulder. She looked up at him. He was smiling at her with an expression of such blinding tenderness that her breath caught in her throat. As she watched, he silently mouthed the words, "I love you."

Amanda nodded, her face glowing. "I love you, too," she whispered back, brushing her lips against his hand.

Secure in their love at last, Amanda and her husband began to tell her parents of their plans for the future.

Harlequin
Superromance ®

**A June title
not to be missed....**

Superromance author Judith Duncan has created her
most powerfully emotional novel yet, a book about
love too strong to forget and hate too painful to
remember....

Risen from the ashes of her past like a phoenix,
Sydney Foster knew too well the price of wisdom,
especially that gained in the underbelly of the city.
She'd sworn she'd never go back, but in order to
embrace a future with the man she loved, she had to
return to the streets...and settle an old score.

Once in a long while, you read a book that affects you
so strongly, you're never the same again. Harlequin is
proud to present such a book, STREETS OF FIRE by
Judith Duncan (Superromance #407). Her book merits
Harlequin's AWARD OF EXCELLENCE for June 1990,
conferred each month to one specially selected title.

S407-1

Have You Ever Wondered If You Could Write A Harlequin Novel?

Here's great news—Harlequin is offering a series of cassette tapes to help you do just that. Written by Harlequin editors, these tapes give practical advice on how to make your characters—and your story— come alive. There's a tape for each contemporary romance series Harlequin publishes.

Mail order only

All sales final

Indulge a Little
Give a Lot

A LITTLE SELF-INDULGENCE CAN DO A WORLD OF GOOD!

Last fall readers indulged themselves with fine romance and free gifts during the Harlequin®/Silhouette® "Indulge A Little—Give A Lot" promotion. For every specially marked book purchased, 5¢ was donated by Harlequin/Silhouette to Big Brothers/Big Sisters Programs and Services in the United States and Canada. We are pleased to announce that your participation in this unique promotion resulted in a total contribution of $100,000.

*

Watch for details on Harlequin® and Silhouette®'s next exciting promotion in September.